Too damned quiet . . .

The clever makers of 21st-century firearms back on Earth had cut down the shout of a .30 caliber to a trivial snap—how could Vestoia's savage army be panicked by a silly pop and a spark? Paul could kill them one by one, but not rout the conquest-crazed queen's legions.

The war canoes swarmed across the lake, growing larger with each paddle stroke. Then the lifeboat appeared. It curved grandly over the lake, hovering in the air, tilting. The jet spoke for one second, blasting the near canoes into nothing, sending up the further ones in yellow fire.

Paul relaxed for an instant—then the sound of firing came from behind him. The invaders had broken through to the camp!

THE BEST IN SCIENCE FICTION FROM DELL BOOKS

CLANS OF THE ALPHANE MOON
Philip K. Dick

STARDANCE   Spider & Jeanne Robinson

THE PENULTIMATE TRUTH   Philip K. Dick

*BINARY STAR #4:   LEGACY   Joan D. Vinge
                    THE JANUS EQUATION
                    Steven G. Spruill

ZELDE M'TANA   F. M. Busby

MEDUSA'S CHILDREN   Bob Shaw

PANGLOR   Jeffrey A. Carver

EARTHBLOOD
Keith Laumer & Rosel George Brown

THE GOLDEN HELIX   Theodore Sturgeon

BEYOND HEAVEN'S RIVER   Greg Bear

ALSO IN DELL EDITION BY EDGAR PANGBORN:

STILL I PERSIST IN WONDERING

A MIRROR FOR OBSERVERS (forthcoming)

* denotes an illustrated book

WEST

A DELL BOOK

OF THE SUN

EDGAR PANGBORN

To Mary C. Pangborn

Published by
Dell Publishing Co., Inc.
1 Dag Hammarskjold Plaza
New York, New York 10017

ISBN: 0-440-19366-4

Reprinted by arrangement with Doubleday & Company, Inc.
Printed in the United States of America
Previous Dell edition—#9366
New Dell edition
First printing—July 1980

Contents

Part One

A.D. 2056

1 MORNING WAS FLOWING OVER THE RED-GREEN PLANET. "What do we know?" The delicate brown face of Dorothy Leeds kindled with questions. "Summarize it."

Edmund Spearman achieved casualness. "Diameter and mass a trifle more than Earth's, larger orbit around a larger sun. A year of 458 days, twenty-six hours each. Moderate seasonal changes, axial tilt less than Earth's, orbit less elliptical. See the smallness of the north polar ice cap? The equatorial region—much too hot; the rest is subtropical to temperate. We should go down (if we do) near the 50th parallel—north, I'd say. Too much desert in the southern hemisphere. Might be hot winds, sandstorms."

"The red-green *is* vegetation?" Dr. Christopher Wright teetered on long legs before the screen, a classroom mannerism unchanged by eleven years in the wilderness of space. He pinched and pulled the skin on his Adam's apple, his hawk's beak, small-chinned head jutting forward with an awkwardness not aggressive but intent. Paul Mason thought: *You love him or hate him. In either case he's never quite grotesque.* Wright's too-soft voice insisted: "It *is*, of course?"

"It has to be, Doc," Spearman said, and rubbed his bluish cheeks, looking older than his thirty-two years. Already he showed frontal baldness, deeply bracketed mouth corners. On Spearman's big shoulders was the burden of the ship. Watching him now, Paul Mason was troubled by a familiar thought: *Captain Jensen should not have died.* . . . "It has to be. The instruments show oxygen in Earth proportion, or somewhat richer, plus nitrogen and carbon dioxide. The camera gives us tree shadows in these latest photographs with the stronger lens.

The air may make us oxygen-happy—if we go down.
. . . Well, Dorothy—two continents, two oceans, both
smaller than the Atlantic, connected narrowly at north
and south polar regions. Dozens of lakes bigger than the
Caspian. The proportion of land to water surface works
out nearly the same as on Earth. No mountains to match
the Himalayas, but some pretty high ranges. Unlimited
forest, prairie, desert." He closed bloodshot eyes, pressing
the lids. Paul Mason thought: *I should never try to paint
Ed. The portrait would always come out as Hercules
Frustrated, and he wouldn't care for it.* . . . Spearman
said, "Even most of the tallest mountains look smooth—
old. If there were glaciers it was a long time ago."

"Geologically a quiet phase," Sears Oliphant remarked.
"As Earth looked in the Jurassic and may look again."
Born fifty years ago in Tel Aviv, brought up in London,
Rio, and New York because his parents were medical
trouble shooters for the Federation, and possessed of a
doctorate in biology (more exactly, taxonomy) from
Johns Hopkins, Sears Oliphant claimed that his original
Polish name could not have been spelled with the aid of
two dictionaries and a crowbar. His fat face blinked at
Dorothy with little kind eyes. "I forget, sugar—you
weren't around in the Jurassic, were you?"

"Maybe." Her slow smile was for Paul. "As a very early
mammal."

Wright said, "No artifacts. . . . At first it looked like
Venus." His crinkled asymmetrical face probed at them
with a wistful half smile like a child's. "May we call this
planet Lucifer, son of the morning? And if we land and
found a city (or am I being ridiculous?)—let it be Jensen
City, in honor of a more-than-solar myth."

Shading closed lids, Spearman said with harshness,
"Myth?"

"Why, Ed, yes—like all remembered heroes who continue in the love of others, a love that magnifies. How else
would you have it?"

"But"—Ann Bryan was high-voiced, troubled—"Lucifer
——"

"My dear, Lucifer was an angel. Devils and angels

have a way of turning out to be the same organism. I noticed that first when I was a damned interne. I noticed it again when I switched to anthropology. I even noticed it on a space ship with the five persons I love best. . . . No artifacts, huh?"

Dorothy said, "You haven't seen these latest pictures, Doc."

"Something?" Wright hurried over, gray eyes wide and sparkling. "I'd quit hoping." Ann joined him, quick-motioned in her slimness, too taut. Wright slipped an elderly arm around her. "Parallel lines, in jungle? Ah. . . . Now, why none in the open ground?"

Spearman suggested: "We could take more shots. But . . ."

Paul Mason broke the darkening silence. "But what, Ed?"

"We're falling, some. I could move us out into a self-sustaining orbit by using more of the reaction mass. We have none to waste. Jensen's death eleven years ago——" Spearman shook his gaunt but heavy head. "Thirty pre-calculated accelerations—and the rest periods they allowed us were insufficient, I think. You remember what wrecks we were when it was finished; that's why I tried to allow more time in deceleration." His brassy voice slowed, fetching out words with care: "The last acceleration, as you know, was not precalculated. Jensen was already dead (must have been heart) when his hand took us out of automatic, made another acceleration that damn near flattened us——"

"Still here though." Sears Oliphant chuckled and patted his middle. "We made it, didn't we, boy?" It sounded a little forced.

"In deceleration I had to allow for the big step Jensen never meant; more of the mass was used to correct a deflection. Same allowance must be made in returning, not to mention the biggest drain of all—getting out of gravity here, a problem not present at the spaceport. Oh, it's planned for—she's built to do it, even from a heavier planet than this. But after she's done it the margin for return will be—narrower than I care to think."

Dorothy, small and soft, leaned back in Paul's arms. Her even voice was for everyone in the control room: "Nevertheless we'll go down."

Spearman gazed across at her without apparent comprehension. He went on, deliberate, harassed: "Here's a thing I never told you. In that accidental acceleration the ship did not respond normally: the deflection happened then, and it may have been due to a defect in the building of *Argo,* a fault in the tail jets. At the time, it was all I could do to reach Jensen before I blacked out—I still don't know how I ever managed it. Later I tried to think there could be no defect. The forward jets took care of us nicely in deceleration. Until we start braking, we can't know. Indicators *say* everything's all right down there. Instruments can lie. Lord, they've sweated out atomic motors since before 1960, almost a century now —and we're still kids playing with grown-up toys."

Sears smiled into plump hands. "So I must be sure to pack my microscope in one of the lifeboats—hey?"

"You're for landing, then."

Sears nodded. Ann Bryan thrust thin ivory fingers into her loose black hair. "*I* couldn't take another eleven years." She attempted a smile. "Tell me, somebody—tell me there'll be music on Lucifer—a way to make new strings for my violin before I forget everything. . . ."

Dorothy said, "Land." Gently, as one might say time for lunch. And she added: "We'll find strings, Nan."

"Land, of course," said Christopher Wright, preoccupied; his long finger tapped on the photograph; his lips went on moving silently, carrying through some private meditation. "Land. Give protoplasm a chance."

"Land," Paul Mason said. *Did anyone suppose the First Interstellar would just turn around and go home? We're here, aren't we . . . ?*

Through hours when spoken words were few, inner words riotous, Lucifer turned an evening face. A morning descent might have been pleasanter in human terms, but the calculator, churning its mathematical brew, said the time was now.

Paul Mason squirmed into his pilot's seat. It was good, he thought, that they could at least meet the challenge of the unexplored with adequate bodies. Wright was dryly indestructible; Ed Spearman a gaunt monolith; the plumpness of Sears Oliphant had nothing flabby. The women were in the warm vigor of a youth that had never known illness. As for his own body, Paul felt for it now a twinge of amused admiration, as if he were seeing an animated statue by an artist better than himself: slender, tough, nothing too much, built for endurance and speed— it would serve. Spearman was already talking in the earphones: "Close lock. Retract shield." Paul responded from ingrained training. Beyond the window that would give him forward vision in the (impossible) event he had to fly the lifeboat, the heavens opened. Withdrawal of the shield into the belly of the mother ship *Argo* was a dream motion within a wider dream. Dorothy and Wright were strapped in the two seats behind him: half of *Argo's* human treasure was here. "Go over what you do if you have to drive off. Over."

"Lever for release. No action till wing-lock indicator is green. No jet unless to correct position. In atmosphere handle as glider, jet only in emergency. Over." After all, Paul considered, he had had a thousand hours of atmospheric flying, and two years' drill on these boats. Ed could worry less and save wind. Beautiful mechanisms in their own right, Model L-46, lying eleven years secret but alert in the streamlined blisters, powered by charlesite to avoid the ponderous shielding still necessary for atomic motors —and charlesite, perfected only thirty years ago in 2026, was obedient stuff. In space, the boats were small rocket ships; in atmosphere, gliders or low-speed jet planes. While *Argo* had been in the long ordeal of building, Paul had been shot from gleaming tubes like this into the atmosphere of Earth, the blind depth at the spaceport, the desolate thin air of Mars. Spearman said, "Turning in five minutes."

In the port lifeboat Ann and Sears would be waiting, but that lock would be open, for Ed must be in the control room. If they had to abandon ship (ridiculous!) Ed's boat would be many moments behind.

The stars moved. "Paul—check straps. Over."

Paul glanced behind him. "All set. Over."

The forward jets spoke once, and softly. Spearman said, "Out of orbit. We start braking sooner than you think. Then we'll know . . ."

The depth of quiet was a depth of eternity. Time to reflect—to marvel, if you wished. One hundred and eleven years since Hiroshima, which the inveterate insanity of history textbooks sometimes referred to as a great experiment. Eighty-five years since the first-manned spaceport; seventy since the founding of stations on Luna and Mars. But to Paul Mason a greater marvel was the responding warmth of the woman, the brooding charity of the old man, whose lives were upheld with him in this silent nothing, dependent on the magic bundle of muscle and nerve that was himself. *What is love?*

The greater spaceport had been twelve years in building. Then *Argo*. More than a century from early rocket experiments to the mile-long factories turning out charlesite. In that century man had even added to his morsels of self-knowledge a trifle more than he possessed in the days of flint ax and reeking cave. "We are in atmosphere," said the earphones. . . . *Time: a cerebral invention? How long is a May fly's life to a May fly . . . ?* "Braking starts in forty-five seconds. Warn the others."

Paul shoved down the mouthpiece, echoing the message. Wright said, "Six pushed-around people. The arrogance of man! Doing fine, Paul."

Pressure—not too bad. A long roaring. But then the stars . . .

The stars went mad. A glare—a cruel second of the light of the star that was now the sun and a flicker of red-green, not real. The roaring paused. Stopped.

The earphones screamed: "Release! *Drive off!*"

"Releasing." The amused voice was Paul's own. "Good luck, Ed."

No answer. There was still such a thing as time. *Now, look: the Federation was a grand thing, potentially, if only, as Doc insists, it weren't for the damned cultural lag of the humanistic sciences, but there is unfortunately no TIME to turn around and see if that little brown cowlick is over her forehead the way it——* Meantime he said aloud, "Doc, Dorothy, get ready for a big one." And his hand pulled for release—nicely, as you might steer a road car for a turn. The pressure torment . . .

Finished. He looked at a friendly green eye. So the retractile wings were as good as eleven years ago—you hoped. Atmosphere—thin, said the gauge. Never mind, thicker soon. *And down you go——*

Too steep. Level off, if there's stuff to bite on. There is. . . . Thank you, Machine Age Man, for a sweet boat. That thing gibbering in the autonomic and voluntary nervous systems—merely fear. Overlook it. . . .

The ship was alien, far away. Turning, bright and deliberate, like a mirror dropped in a well. The other lifeboat? But Ed would have to reach it, close lock, strap in, open shield, while the ship went . . .

"Down"—lately an artificiality, now the plainest word in the language. A gleaming disturbance in the air "down" yonder—something streaking away from the dot that was a dying ship? "Ed, can you hear me? Over."

"Yes," said the voice in the earphones.

Paul noticed himself weeping. "They made it! They made it!"

The voice said coldly, "Quiet. Your altitude? Over."

"Forty-six thousand. All under control. Over, jerk."

"I'm going to head for——*Ah!* Can you see the ship?"

It was possible to find the silver dot of *Argo* above an S-shaped expanse of blue. The blue, Paul understood, was not becoming larger, simply nearer. The dot changed to a white flower, which swelled and hung tranquilly over the blue, a brief memorial. The radio carried a groan, and then: "Better maybe. The lake may be shallow enough for salvage. If it'd hit ground there'd be nothing at all. Get nearer, Paul. Keep me in sight—not too damn' near."

Time . . . Delicately Paul asked the boat for a steeper glide. The response was even. Was it? Some peevish sound. He flattened the glide a thousand feet above Ed's boat. The red-green below—anything real about it? Yes, if time was real, but one had to think that over. . . .

Mild hills of dark red-green, in the—west? Yes, because now there was a birth of sunset beyond them. Lighter green below, alongside the lake: that would be meadow. Not one of the great lakes—no larger than

Lake Champlain, its outlet in the south blurred by marsh; only a portion of its northwest shore adjoined the meadow—except in that region the lake was a blue S written on red-green dark of jungle. A winged brown thing slipped by, teasing the edge of vision. "Bird or something. . . ."

In the earphones was a dazed note, like shame. "Power was out of control, Paul—port motor. Had to be a defect in the building—something that couldn't take the strain of what happened eleven years ago. All the way—God!—and then to be loused up by a builder's error!" To Spearman, Paul knew, a mechanical defect was the gravest of indecencies, beyond any forgiveness.

True sunset here. A world. And you don't climb out of gravity on charlesite. Paul said, "Doc—parallel lines—I think."

But the speed of the glide allowed no certainty, only a glimpse of three dark bars, perhaps half a mile long in the jungle area northwest of the meadow, and a hint of other groups further north. They *should* be there, according to a map Spearman had made in orbit from the final photographs. And some fifty miles south of here was a great network of them thirty miles long. The glide brought them out over meadow once more.

A thing was riding with them. A grumbling moan. Paul told himself: *With Model L-46 it cannot happen—it cannot—Dorothy—Doc——*

Dorothy cried, "Specks—in the open ground. Moving, hundreds of 'em. Oh, look! *Smoke,* Paul—campfires. How high are we?"

"Under seven thousand. Check your compass by the sunset, Doc. See if we have a magnetic north."

"We do. . . ."

Spearman's far-off voice said, "Life all right. I can't make out——"

Paul cut in with hurried precision: "Ed—vibration, port wing, bad. I'm going to make one more circle over the woods if I can and try for the north end of this meadow."

A startled croak: "I'll jet off—give you room." Paul saw the squirt of green flame. Ed's boat darted westward like a squeezed apple seed. Paul dipped and leveled off as much as he dared. "We're—all right."

He lived with it a timeless time. Knowing it would happen. They were circling over jungle, pointed into sunset. The jet would only make matters worse—rip the heart out. Soon the meadow would come around again. . . .

But the moment was now. An end of the moaning vibration. A lurch. Paul's hand leaped stupidly for the charlesite ignition and checked itself.

Calm, but for the reeling of sunset. *I must tell Dorothy not to fight the straps: L-46 is solid—is solid——*

Then the smash, the tearing and grinding. Somehow no death. Sky in the window changed to a gloom of purple and green. No death. Elastic branches? Metal whimpered and shrieked. *Is that us?* They built them solid. . . .

There was settling into silence. The pressure on Paul's cheek, he knew, was the wonderfully living pressure of Dorothy's hand, because it moved, it pinched his ear, it groped for his mouth. A hiss. Through the wrenched seams the old air of Earth yielded to the stronger weight of Lucifer's. The starboard wing parted with a squeal like amusement, letting the boat's body rest evenly on the ground, and Christopher Wright said, "Amen."

2   THE EARPHONES WERE SQUAWKING: "SPEAK UP! CAN
you hear me? Can you——"

"Not hurt. Seams open, and there goes Sears' thirty-six-hour test for air-borne bacteria. Down and safe, Ed."

"Listen." In relief, Ed Spearman was heavily didactic again. "You are three quarters of a mile inside the jungle. I will land near the woods. It will be dark in about an hour. Wait there until we——"

"One minute," Paul said in sudden exhaustion. "We can find you, easier. Sears' test is important. We're already exposed to the air, but——"

"What? Can't hear—damn it——" The voice dimmed and crackled.

"Stay sealed up!" Nothing. "Can you hear?" Nothing. "Oh, well, good," said Paul, discarding the headset, adding foolishly: "I'm tired."

Dorothy unfastened his straps; her kiss was warm and quick.

"Radio kaput, huh?" Wright flexed lean cautious legs. "Pity. I did want to tell Sears one I just remembered after eleven years, about poor lackadaisical Lou, who painted her torso bright blue, not for love, not for money, not because it looked funny, but simply for something to do."

"You're not hurt, Doc," Dorothy said. "Not where it counts."

"Can't kill an anthropologist. Ask my student Paul Mason. Leather hides, pickled in a solution ten parts curiosity to one of statistics. Doctors are mighty viable too. Ask my student Dorothy Leeds."

Paul's forehead was wet. "Dark in an hour, he reminded me."

"How close are we to the nearest of those parallel lines?"

"Three or four miles, Doc, at a loose guess."

"Remember that great mess of 'em fifty or sixty miles south of here? Shows on Ed's map. We must be—mm—seventy miles from the smallest of the two oceans—oh, let's call it the Atlantic, huh? And the other one the East Atlantic? Anyway the ocean's beyond that range of hills we saw on the way down."

"I saw campfires in the meadow," Dorothy said. "Things running."

"I thought so too. . . . Paul, I wonder if Sears can do any testing of the air from the lifeboat? Some of the equipment couldn't be transferred from *Argo*. And—how could they communicate with us? They'll have to breathe it soon in any case."

Paul checked a shuddering yawn. "I must have been thinking in terms of *Argo,* which is—history. . . . You know, I believe the artificial gravity was stronger than we thought? I feel light, not heavy."

"High oxygen?" Dorothy suggested. "Hot, too."

"Eighty-plus. Crash suits can't do us any more good." They struggled out of them in the cramped space, down to faded jackets and shorts.

Wright brooded on it, pinching his throat. "Only advantage in the others' staying sealed up a while is that if we get sick, they'll get sick a bit later. Could be some advantage. Paul—think we should try to reach them this evening?"

"Three quarters of a mile, dark coming on—no. But so far as I'm concerned, Doc, you're boss of this expedition. In the ship, Ed had to be—matter of engineering knowledge. No longer applies. I wanted to say that."

Wright turned away. "Dorothy?"

She said warmly, "Yes. You."

"I—oh, my dear, I don't know that it's—best." Fretfully he added: "Shouldn't need a leader. Only six of us—agreement——"

Dorothy held her voice to lightness: "I can even disagree with myself. Sears will want you to take over. Ann too, probably."

His gray head sank in his hands. "As for that," he said, "inside of me I'm apt to be a committee of fifteen." Paul thought: *But he's not old! Fifty-two. When did he turn gray, and we never noticing it . . . ?* "For now," Wright said, "let's not be official about it, huh? What if my dreams for Lucifer are—not shared?"

"Dreams are never quite shared," Dorothy said. "I want you to lead us."

Wright whispered with difficulty, "I will try."

Dorothy continued: "Ed may want things black and white. Not Ann, I think—she hates discussions, being obliged to make up her mind. You're elected, soldier. . . . Can you open the door, Paul?"

It jammed in the spoiled frame after opening enough for a tight exit. Wright stared into evening. "Not the leader kind. Academic." His white hands moved in doubtful protest. "Hate snap decisions—we'll be forced to make a lot of them."

Paul said, "They're best made by one who hates making them."

The lean face became gentle. "Taught you that myself, didn't I, son . . . ? Well—inventory. What've we got, right here?"

"Thirty days' rations for three, packed eleven years ago. Two automatic rifles, one shotgun, three automatic pistols, three hundred rounds for each weapon. Should have transferred more from the ship, but—we didn't. Three four-inch hunting knives, very good——"

"They at least won't give out. With care."

"Right. Two sealed cases of garden seeds—anybody's guess about them. Six sets of overalls, shorts, and jackets. Three pairs of shoes apiece—the Federation allowed that you and Ann might grow a little, Dot—plasta soles and uppers, should last several years. Carpentry tools. Ed's boat has the garden tools instead. Sears did pack his microscope, didn't he?"

"Oh my, yes," said Dorothy, in affectionate mimicry of the fat man's turn of speech.

"Each crash suit has first-aid kit, radion flashlight (good for two years maybe), compass, field glasses, plus whatever else we had sense enough to stuff in. Set of technical manuals, mostly useless without the ship, but I think there's one on woodcraft, primitive tools and weapons—survival stuff——"

"Oh, the books!" Wright clutched his hair, groaning. "The books——"

"Just that woodcraft——"

"No, no, no—the books on *Argo!* Everything—the library—I've only just understood that it's gone. The whole flowering of human thought—man's best, uncorrupted—*Odyssey*—Ann's music, the art volumes you selected, Paul, and your own sketches and paintings——"

"No loss there——"

"Don't talk like a damn fool! Shakespeare—*Divina commedia*——"

Dorothy twisted in the narrowness to put both arms around him. "Doc—quiet, dear—please——"

"I can remember pages of *Huck Finn—a few pages!*"

Dorothy was wiping his face with a loose corner of her jacket. "Doc—subside! Please now—make it stop hurting inside yourself. Oh, quiet. . . ."

After a time he said lifelessly, "Go on with the inventory, Paul."

"Well—there's a duplicate of that map Ed made yesterday from orbit photographs of this area, about a hundred miles square. We're near the eastern edge of that square. There's the other map he made of the whole globe. We didn't duplicate that one. I guess that's about it."

"Knives," Wright muttered. "Knives and a few tools."

"The firearms may make a difference while they last."

"Yes, perhaps. But thirty years from now——"

"Thirty years from now," said Dorothy, still sheltering his head, "thirty years from now our children will be grown."

"Oh." Wright groped for her fingers. "You almost wanted it like this, didn't you? I mean, to land and not return?"

"I don't know, Doc. Maybe. I'm not sure I ever quite believed in the possibility of return. State Orphanage children like Ann and me, growing up in a tiny world within a big one, we weren't quite human ever, were we? Not that the big world didn't seep in plenty." She smiled off at private shadows of memory. "We did learn things not in the directors' curriculum. When they started grooming Ann and me for this—Youth Volunteers! Stuffing our little heads with the best they had—oh, it was fun too. By that time I think I had a fair idea of the big world. The Orphanage was pleasant, you know—clean, humanitarian, good teachers, all of them kind and more than a bit hurried. They did try so hard never to let me hear the word 'nigger'! Ignorance is poor insulating material, don't you think? And why, Doc, after all that's been known and thought and argued for the last hundred years, couldn't they select at least one Oriental for our little trip? Wouldn't have had to come from Jenga's empire—our own states in the Federation had plenty of 'em—scholars, technicians, anything you care to name."

Wright had calmed. He said, "I argued for it and got told. They even said that the spaceport rights and privileges recently given to Jenga's empire would allow the Asiatics to build their own ship—tacitly implying that humanity should stay in two camps world without end. Ach! You can shove the political mind just so far, then it stalls in its own dirt. Even Jensen wasn't able to budge them."

"It's history," said Dorothy, and Paul wondered: *How does she do it? Speaking hands and voice, enough to shove away the black sorrow even before it fairly had hold of him—and she'd try to do it for anyone, loved or not. She was the first (and only one) who said to me there are some things more important than love—and she herself would be bothered to explain that in words.* "Well," Dorothy reflected, "I believe the Orphanage slapped too much destiny of Man on the backs of our little necks—they're just necks. Paul, why don't you sleep awhile? You too, Doc. Let me keep watch. I'll wake you both if anything stirs out there. Doze off, boys."

Paul tried to, his mind restless in weary flesh. No permissible margin of error, said the twenty-first century. But *Argo* lay at the bottom of a lake because of an error. Not an error like the gross errors twenty-first century man still made in dealing with his own kind and still noisily disregarded, but an engineering error—something

twenty-first-century man viewed with a horror once re-
served, in not so ancient times, for moral evil. The
cardinal sin was to drop a decimal. If, like Wright, or
Paul himself, you were concerned with the agony and
growing pains of human nature, disturbed by the paralytic
sterility of state socialism and the worse paralysis of open
tyranny, you kept your mouth shut—or even yielded, almost unknowingly, to the pressures that reduced ethical
realities to a piddling checker game perverting the uses of
semantics. They said, "There won't be· any war. If there
is, look what we've got!" If you were like the majority of
Earth's three billion, you hoped to get by with as much as
the traffic would bear and never stuck your neck out. They
celebrated the turn of the third millennium with a jolly new
song: "Snuggle up, Baby—Uncle pays the bill . . ."
But for all that, you mustn't use the wrong bolt.

Unreasonably quiet here. A jungle evening on Earth
would have been riotous with bird and insect noises.
. . . He slept.

It was dark when Wright's finger prodded him. "A
visitor."

The darkness was rose-tinged, not with sunset. There
were two moons, Paul remembered, one white and large
and far away, one red and near. Should the red moon be
shining now? He gazed through the half-open doorway,
wondering why he was not afraid, seeing something pale
and vast, washed in—yes, surely in reddish moon-light. A
thing swaying on the pillars of its legs, perhaps listening,
tasting the air for strangeness. And scattered through the
night, sapphires on black velvet, were tiny dots of blue,
moving, vanishing, reappearing. "Blue fireflies," Dorothy
whispered, "blue fireflies, that's all they are." He felt her
controlled breathing, forced down a foolish laugh. *We
could have done without a white elephant.*

Nine or ten feet tall at the shoulder, a tapir-like snout,
black tusks bending more nearly downward than an elephant's, from milk-white flesh. The ears were mobile,
waving to study the night. There was an oval hump near
the base of the neck. The beast had been facing them; it
turned to pull down a branch, munch the leaves, casually

drop the stalk. In silence it drifted away, pausing to meditate, grumbling juicily, but with no alarm.

Wright whispered, "The planet Lucifer did not ask for us."

"Paul—I stepped out for a minute, while you were both asleep. Firm ground. A smell—flowers, I think—made me remember frangipani."

"I'll try it."

"Oh, but not with that thing——"

"He didn't seem to mind us. I'll stay near the door." He knew Dorothy would come with him. Feeling earth under legs that had nearly forgotten it, he turned to help her down; her dark eyes played diamond games with the moonlight.

It could have been a night anywhere in the Galaxy, up there beyond torn branches, stars, and red moon in a vagueness of cloud. Blue fireflies . . .

But there was a child wailing somewhere. Far-off and weak, a dim rise and fall of sound, grief and remoteness. A waterfall? Wind in upper branches? But they were still, and the sound carried the timbre of animal life. Dorothy murmured, "It's been crying that way ever since moonrise." She came closely into his arms.

"I can read one thing inside of you—you're not scared."

"I'm not, Paul?"

"No."

"But don't ever leave me—Adam."

3 THIS WAS DAWN: VISION OUT OF THE DARK: RIPPLES of music coalescent in one forest voice moving toward a crescendo of daytime.

Paul watched a spreading of color in the leaves, a shift from black to gray to a loveliness more green than red; the trees were massively old, with varied bark of green or purple-brown. Phantoms in the more distant shadows could be understood now that light was advancing: they were thick trees with a white bark like that of the never-forgotten birches of New Hampshire. Underfoot Paul felt a humus that might have been a thousand years in growing; he prodded it with his knife—a white worm curled in mimic death.

Everywhere purple-leaved vines, vastly proliferating, climbed in a riot of greed for the sunlight of the forest ceiling. Paul sensed a mute cruelty in them, a shoving lust of growth. It might have been these, elastically yielding, that had saved the lifeboat from total ruin.

Overnight the gravity of Lucifer had become natural. His closeknit body accepted and relished it, finding a new pleasure in strength: thirty-seven years old and very young.

One tiny voice was near, persistent. Paul walked around the boat, where Dorothy and Wright still slept. The starboard wing, parting from the lifeboat, had gashed a tree trunk, littering the ground with branches. The source of the voice was a brown lump, twenty feet up, clinging head downward, a body small as a sparrow's, wings folded like a bat's. As he watched they spread, quivered, and relaxed. Head and ears were mousy, the neck long, with a hump at its base. The throat pulsed at each cry. Near Paul's foot lay a fabric like an oriole's nest, fastened to a twig that had been torn from the tree. Three young had tumbled out. One was not mangled but all were dead, hairless, poignantly ugly. "Sorry, baby—our first act on Lucifer." The parent creature made another abortive motion as Paul took up the young.

Its high lament was not what he and Dorothy had heard in the night. That had been continuing when he slipped out to watch for dawn, and it had ended at some unnoticed moment—profoundly different, surely far off. . . .

He tried to study the dead things as Sears Oliphant would want to do. Two were hopelessly torn; he dug a hole in the humus and dropped those in, smoothing the surface, wondering at his need for an act which could mean nothing to the unhappy morsel of perception on the tree trunk. The third, and the nest, he carried around the boat where the light was better.

All seven digits of the forelimb spread into a membranous wing; the hind leg divided at the ankle, three toes anchoring the wing, the other four fused into a slim foot which had suction pads. He cradled the bit of mortality in his palm, recalling a thing Wright had said when they entered the lifeboat. Captain Jensen, waiting for take-off at the spaceport, trying, as he drank sherry with Christopher Wright, to look at the venture under the aspect of eternity, had said he liked the philosophical implications of *Argo's* converter, into which his own body was strangely soon to pass. What was Wright's comment eleven years later? "All life is cannibalism, benign or not: we are still eating the dinosaurs." There had been more, which Paul could not remember. So, man drove eleven years through space and killed three babies. *But there was no element of malevolence. . . .*

Perhaps there was none in most of man's actions over the millennia.

Wright crawled out, stiff-limbed and unrested.

" 'Morning, Doc. Let me introduce *Enigma Luciferensis*."

" 'Luciferensis' won't do." Wright peered down. "Everything is 'Luciferensis,' including the posterity Dot mentioned. Well now, what——"

"A nestling. Our crash broke the nest and killed the young."

Wright fingered the fabric. "Beautiful. Leaves gummed together with some secretion." With a doctor's intentness he added: "How d'you feel?"

"Good."

A shadow circled Paul, settled on his arm, hobbling toward his palm and what it held. He felt the suction cups; with a careful mouth the creature took up its dead and flew away. "I've been remembering something you said: life eating life—without too much concern for the second law of thermodynamics. Forgive us our trespasses . . . Good morning, lady."

"What did I miss?" Dorothy had glimpsed the departure.

"Lucifer's idea of a bat. I think that big flying thing I saw from the lifeboat was shaped like this midget. Haven't seen any birds."

Dorothy hugged his arm. "Not even one measly robin?"

"Sorry, Whifflepuff—fresh out of robins."

Wright blinked at his compass. "Meadow that way." Paul was inattentive, needing the warm quiet of the woman beside him. Wright added: "First, breakfast." He broke the seal of a ration package and snarled. "Thirty days, I b'lieve you said. Antique garbage—dehydrated hay."

Dorothy said, "You're nicest when you're mad, Doc. We'll soon have to try the local stuff, I suppose."

"Uh-huh. But no guinea-pig work for you or Ann."

She was startled. "Why not? I can digest boilerplate."

"Two women on Lucifer: valuable livestock." Wright smiled with his mouth full. "I'm boss, remember? For guinea-pig work, the men draw lots."

She was grave. "I won't argue. It so happens——" She peeked into the nest. "Poor little fuzzies lined it with fur. Their own, I'll bet."

"It so happens what, dear?"

"Ah . . . This eleven-year-old gookum claims to be coffee. Can we make a fire? Looks like dead wood over there."

The branches burned aromatically; the morning was growing into deep warmth, but still with freshness. Wright said, "Coffee my shirt."

Dorothy tasted it. "Brr . . . ! I was about to say when I interrupted myself, it so happens I'm six or seven weeks pregnant, I think."

"Six——" Wright set his aluminum cup carefully upside down. Paul mumbled, "That's what's been on your mind."

Behind her eyes he glimpsed the primitive thing, deeper than thought, not like a part of her but a force that sustained her, himself, all others: the three billion of Earth, the small grieving spirit now flown away into the trees. "Yes, Adam. I would have told you sooner, but we all had a lot on our minds."

"Even before we got in orbit, you saw us settling—staying——"

Dorothy grinned then. "No-o, Paul. I just wanted the baby. Could have been born on the ship. The Federation said no, but . . ."

Gradually Paul began to realize it. "But you said yes."

She leaned to him, no longer smiling. "I said yes. . . ."

The forest floor hushed footsteps; some coolness lingered. Paul walked in front, then Dorothy, and Wright marked blazes on the tree trunks. Paul glanced backward often, to capture the receding patterns. At the third such pause the lifeboat was no longer visible—only a sameness of trees and sparse young life groping through shadow for the food of the sun. In this depth of forest there was no brush; the going was easy except for the nuisance of purple vines that sometimes looped from tree to tree. Paul searched for any change of light ahead.

The boat held all but what they wore, the two rifles, the three pistols holstered at their hips, the three knives, three sealed ration packages. Damage had prevented locking the door of the boat: to rob, an inhabitant of Lucifer would need only intelligence enough to solve the sliding mechanism. They had seen no life but that huge nocturnal leaf eater, the small fliers, a white worm, and now a few timid ten-legged scuttlers on the warm ground and midge-like specks dancing in shafts of sunlight. Too quietly, Wright said, "Stop."

Paul raised his rifle as he turned. Only untroubled forest. Wright's warning hand lowered. "Almost saw it. Heard nothing, just felt a—watching. Might be in my head. Let's go on. And don't hurry."

It would have been possible to hurry, even with an eye on the compass. It would have been possible, Paul thought, to run in panic, fall whimpering and waiting. But you wouldn't do it. . . .

No shape in this dim region could be right or wrong; the trees themselves were no sweetly familiar beech or pine. They halted at sight of a new sprawling type of vine, uprooted where a break in the forest ceiling admitted more sunshine. The earth displayed hoofprints like a pig's. Some scattered tuberous roots were marked by teeth; Dorothy sniffed one. "Spud with garlic for a papa." Paul pocketed a sample. She said, "Not that Lucifer cares, Doc, but what time is it?"

"My watch says we've been walking fifteen minutes. Take it slow." Wright presently added: "I've had another glimpse. Not a good one. Furry, gray and white—white face, splashes of white on a gray body seven or eight feet tall. Human shape. We may be all right if we don't bother him."

"Or blunder into territory where he doesn't want us."

"There is that, Paul."

"Human shape," said Dorothy evenly. "How human?"

"Very. Upright. Good-sized head . . . Ah—hear that?" It was Ann's voice, calling, from someplace where there should be sunlight. "Don't answer just yet—no sudden noises."

Close to Paul, Dorothy whispered, "The baby—I don't want to tell the others quite yet."

That made it real—so real that in spite of a patch of beckoning blue Paul had to turn to her.

Behind Wright, he saw it, among the pillars of the trees, retreating in fluid slowness till it was only a black ear, part of a white-furred cheek, an iridescent green eye showing, like a cat's, no white. But the blue was also real. . . .

The edge of the forest was a mass of young growth fighting for the gold coin of sunlight. "Shield your faces" —Wright was panting—"could be poisonous leaves." They broke through to a red-green field, the slim silver of the undamaged boat, the certainty of friends, an expanse of lake no longer blue but sickly white. The boat's nose was thrust under an overhang of branches. Ann Bryan was unsteady and wan, but there was welcome in her gray eyes for Dorothy, who joined her at once and whispered with her. Sears' fat affectionate face carried a determined smile. Ed Spearman came forward, alert and commanding. Wright asked, "How long have you been out in the air?"

"An hour." Ed was impatient. "Sealed overnight. Nothing in the boat for a test of the air, no point in waiting. You——"

"Okay." Wright watched brown wings over the lake. "What are those?"

"Birds or some damn thing. The white on the lake is dead fish. I suppose the ship blew under water or the impact killed them. Our Geiger says the water isn't radioactive. We haven't gone into the meadow—been waiting for you."

In the south the meadow reached the horizon—twenty miles of it, Paul remembered from the air view, before jungle again took over. Near by, threads of smoke were rising straight from the grass. "Abandoned fires? We scared off——"

"Maybe," Spearman said. "Seen no life except those birds."

"Bat wings," Sears Oliphant remarked. "Mammalian, I think—oh my, yes. Can't have furry birds, you know, with a taxonomist in the family, hey?"

Spearman shrugged. "Must get organized. How much damage, Paul?"

"The boat itself. Both wings off, radio dead. Couldn't lock the door. . . ." It was like an Earth landscape. Tall grass carried oatlike ruddy seed clusters on green stems. The lake was bordered by white sand except close by, where jungle reached into water. There was casual buzzing traffic above the grass, reminiscent of bees, wasps, flies. Far up, something drifted on motionless wings, circling. And ten or fifteen miles to the west there was the calm of hills—rounded, old, more green than blue in a sleepy haze, but to paint them, Paul thought, you would shade off into the purple. Paul went on, absently: "We'll have the charlesite of the wrecked boat of course. That gives this one a theoretical twenty hours of jet. We have ammunition for long enough to learn how to use bow and arrow, I think."

Ann muttered, "Paul, don't———"

"What?" Spearman was disgusted. "Oh, you could be right at that, Paul. Hard to realize . . . Well, we must make some kind of camp."

Wright began: "Some knowledge of the life around us———"

"Oh my, yes———"

"We'll have to make a camp before we can do any exploring, Doc. Here, out in the open. See anything in the woods?"

"Something followed. More or less human———"

"So we know the camp has to be in the open."

"Do we, Ed?" Wright watched the distant bat wings. Spearman stared. "Can't chance a forest we don't know."

"Still, I mean to look things over a bit. Feel not so good, Ann?"

"All right," she said, glancing from Wright to Spearman, silently begging to know: *Who is leader?* "Slightly slap-happy, Doc."

"Mm, sure." Wright hitched his rifle. "Going to look at that nearest smoke. You come, Paul—or you, Ed. One of you should stay here."

Spearman leaned against the lifeboat, still-faced. "Paul can go if he wants to. I think it's a risk and a waste of time."

Paul watched him a moment, frightened not by a man whom he had never quite been able to like, but by the withdrawal itself, the sense of a barrier to communication. *We start with a division on this first morning of the world . . . ?* Paul hugged his own rifle and followed Wright into the long whisper of the grass.

4 MOIST HEAT PRESSED DOWN, BUT THE AIR OF THE
meadow was sweet. There were marks of trampling as
well as the swath the boat had cut—trails, places where
something might have crouched. Under his breath Wright
asked, "Feel all right, Paul?"

Truth was more needed than a show of courage. "Not
perfect, Doc. Am I flushed? You are, a little."

"Yes. Trace of fever; may wear off. Here's something——"

They had not come far. Two red bodies barely three
feet tall sprawled near each other face down in the
grass. Paul noticed oval bulges between shoulder blades
modified to accommodate them, the pathos of fingers—
seven-fingered hands—holding earth in a final grasp. The
male wore a loincloth of black fabric and a quiver almost
full of arrows; the female had a grass skirt, and her hand
was tight on a stone-headed spear longer than herself. A
bow of carved wood lay some distance away; one could
see how the little man had crawled in his agony after the
bow was lost. Wright turned them over gently—bald
skulls, no trace of body hair on skin of a rich copper
color exciting to a painter's vision, green eyes with no
visible whites in human faces heavily tattooed, wide-open
eyes, accusing no one. The bodies were in rigor, a shaft in
the man's neck, the woman pierced by an arrow in the
side. Blood colored the grass, dry but eloquent.

"War too," said Wright, and pulled out the arrows, showing Paul the stone heads, the intricate carving of the
wood, thin-whittled wooden vanes taking the place of
feathers. "Stone Age war . . ."

The male pygmy was the smaller of the two, and softer,

his shape not feminine but rounded and smooth. Both seemed mature, so far as age could be guessed at all. The woman was rugged, with a coarser skin and the scar tissue of old wounds; her two pairs of breasts were scarcely more prominent than the ridged muscles of her midget chest.

Wright mulled it over, kneading his wrinkled throat. "Physical refinements of evolution as far along as our own. Straight thigh and neck, perfect upright posture; there was no slouch or belly sag when they were on their feet. Human jaw, big brain case. That furry giant I saw in the woods had complete upright posture too. Oh, it's natural, Paul. You stick fins on an ocean vertebrate, turn him into a four-legged land animal, give him a few hundred million years. Almost bound to free his front limbs if they've stayed unspecialized." In the gaunt face, sadness and pity struggled with a bitter sort of mirth. "The brain gets large, boy, and away you go, to—ach—to the Federation versus the Asian Empire—Lincoln, Rembrandt, the state papers of Abraham Brown. And to you and Dorothy and the baby." Wright stood erect, brushing bony knees, calm again. "I'm almost pleased to find it this primitive. I don't think it can have gone further anywhere on the planet, or we'd have seen cities, farms, roads, in the photographs. Unless——"

"Unless what, Doctor?"

"Oh   unless there might be forms with no Earth parallel. In the forests perhaps—even underground. Thought of that? But that's speculations, and our little soldiers here are fact. They have a civilization—arrows say so, tattooing, garments. Rigid, tradition-bound—or maybe not, depending on how much language they've developed to tie 'emselves in knots with."

"Bow and arrow—why, suh, almost as advanced as not being afraid to end a sentence with a preposition."

"Hell with you. Twenty thousand years ago, or whenever it was we reached our present physique, if there'd been anything external to teach men how to behave like grownups——. Well, we had to sweat it out—tribal wars, bigger wars, venerated fears, errors, and stupidities. But maybe here——"

"Are *we* big enough?"

Wright shut his eyes. His thin cheeks were too bright; there was a tremor in the rifle tip. "Wish I knew, Paul. We have to try."

Ed Spearman yelled, "Look out!" A rifle banged, and a pistol.

A brown darkness had come swooping from the lake. Others followed—mud-brown, squealing. They had banked at the noise of the shots to circle overhead. Paul fired; a near one tumbled, screeching, thrashing a narrow wolfish head on a long neck, black teeth snapping in the death throes—but even now it was trying to hobble forward and get at them. The others wheeled lower until Wright's rifle spoke, and Spearman's; there was the dry slap of Dorothy's automatic pistol. "Back to the trees!" The wounded thing on the ground set up a bubbling howl.

More were coming, with weaving of pointed red-eyed heads on mobile necks. Paul ran, Wright loping beside him, hearing the crash of their friends' weapons. Something slammed Paul's shoulder, flopped against his leg, tripping him. He tumbled over a shape furry and violent that smelled of fish and carrion. He fought clear of it, sobbing in animal wrath, and reached the shelter of the trees and Dorothy's embrace. Sweat blinded him.

Wright was clutching him too, getting his jacket off. "Flesh wound. The hind foot got you——"

"I saw it." Ann Bryan choked. "Saw it happen. Filthy claws——"

Wright had a bottle of antiseptic. "Son, you ain't going to like this. Hang on to the lady." But the pain was a welcome flare. Paul's eyes cleared as Wright made him a bandage of gauze, with Dorothy's help. He could look from the shelter of overhanging branches at a confusion of wings. The creatures had not followed as far as the lifeboat; perhaps its shining mass disturbed them.

Spearman groaned: "You *would* go out."

Wright snapped at him. "Camp in the open—some disadvantages——"

"Granted. But you sure learned it the hard way."

"Eating"—Ann pointed, nauseated—"their own wounded—"

Wright stepped between her and the loud orgy in the

meadow. "Wing spread, fifteen feet. Well—sky's bad, woods maybe. What do you suggest?"

"Clear underbrush," Spearman said, "so we can see into the woods. Pile it just beyond this overhang of branches for a barrier, leave a space so we can reach the lifeboat. We can get to the lake for water without going much in the open."

"Good," said Wright. A peace offering. Spearman smiled neutrally.

"If the water's safe," said Sears Oliphant.

Wright grinned at the fat man. "Pal, it better be."

"Miracles?" Sears' shoulders shot up amiably. "We can hope it is, with boiling. Gotta have it. Canteens won't last the day, in this heat."

Paul helped Ed unpack tools from the lifeboat. "One sickle," Spearman noted. "No scythe. Garden gadgets. Pruning shears. One ax, one damned hatchet. No scythe, no scythe——. There were two or three on the ship."

"Maybe the lake's not so deep."

"Maybe we'll play hell trying to find out too. Those things weren't much scared by the shooting. . . ."

Hot, tedious work created a circle of clear shaded ground which must be called home. A fire was boiling lake water in the few aluminum vessels. It had a fishy, mud-bottom taste and could not be cooled, but it eased thirst. Paul had glimpsed Ann in the lifeboat, opening her violin case, closing it, sick-faced. He had marveled again at the mystery of a Federation governing two-thirds of a world, which had genially allowed a fourteen-year-old musician to carry her violin on man's greatest venture—with enough strings to last two or three years and no means of restringing the bow. Later Ann threw herself into the labor of clearing brush but tired quickly from her own violence. Sears' microscope occupied a camp table; Paul and Dorothy joined him in a pause for rest. "Got anything for the local newspaper?"

"Unboiled lake water–assorted wrigglers." Sears mopped his cheeks. " 'Twas never meant my name should be Linnaeus. Have a look." The world on the slide seemed not unlike what Sears had once shown him in water from the hydroponics room of *Argo:* protoplasmic abundance no mind could grasp. "So far, nothing basically different from what you'd find in lake water on Earth—except for the trifle that every species is unknown, hey? I suppose that's why they heaved a taxonomist into space, to see what the poor cluck would do, hey? Now, those red dots are something like algae. Notice a big ciliated schlemihl blundering around? He could almost be old man paramecium, oh my, yes. Gi'me your sickle, muscle man."

"Hot work, Jocko. Take it slow and easy."

"Believe me, Mistuh Mason, I will. What——"

In undergrowth beyond the clearing there was deep-throated fury, a crashing of branches. A gray and white man shape staggered out of concealment, wrenching at what looked like swollen black rope. But the rope had a head, gripping the giant's forearm; a black loop circled the giant's loins and his free arm, tearing and pounding, could not loosen it. A saurian hind leg groped, hooking for purchase into gray fur.

Paul's hunting knife was out; there was time only for recognition. The gray and white being was everything human caught in a coil. Paul forced himself through a barrier of fear, hearing Wright yell, "Don't shoot, Ed! Put that away." There was no shot. Paul knew he was between Spearman and the confusion of combat; someone was blundering behind him. A black reptilian tail stretched into bushes, grasping something for anchorage. Paul slashed at that. The mass of heaving life rolled on the ground as the giant lost his footing, serpent teeth still buried in his forearm. Green eyes were pleading in a universal language.

Wright was clutching a black neck, with no strength to move it, and Paul stabbed at scaled hide behind a triangular head, but the skin was like metal. The forelimbs were degenerate vestiges, the hind legs cruelly functional. At last the steel penetrated; Paul twisted it, probing for a brain. The giant had ceased struggling; the furred face was close. Paul could feel the difficult breath, sense a rigid waiting. . . . The teeth let go. The giant leaped free, returning at once with a stone the size of Paul's chest, to fling it down on the slow-dying body, repeating the action till his enemy was a smear of black and red.

Now in returning quiet a furred man eight feet tall

watched them openly. Wright said, "Ed, put away that gun. This man is a friend."

"Man!" Spearman holstered his automatic, ready for a draw. "Your daydreams will kill us all yet."

"Smile, all of you—maybe his mouth does the same thing." Wright stepped to the trembling monster, hands open. Ann was sobbing in reaction, smothering the sound. Wright pointed at himself. "Man." He touched the gray fur. "Man. . . ."

The giant drew back, not with violence. Paul felt Dorothy's small fingers shivering on his arm. The giant sucked his wound and spat, turning his head away from Wright to do it. "Man—man. . . ." Wright's hand, small and pale as an oyster shell, spread beside the huge palm, six fingers, long four-jointed thumb. "Paul—your first-aid kit. I want just the gauze."

Spearman said, "Are you crazy?"

"It's a chance," Sears Oliphant said in a level, careful voice. "Doc knows what he's doing. Ed, you should know you can't stop him."

Wright was pointing to Paul's bandaged shoulder and to the giant's wound. The high furred forehead puckered in obvious effort. Dorothy was choking on a word or two: "Doc—must you—"

"He knows we're friends. He's been watching a long time. He saw Paul get hurt and then bandaged." The giant's trembling was only a spasmodic shuddering. "Man—man. . . ." Wright snipped off gauze. "And he knows that thing is a weapon, Ed. Will you put it away?"

"He could break you in two. You know that, don't you?"

"But he won't. Give protoplasm a chance." Now Wright was winding gauze lightly, firmly, hiding the already clotting blood, and the giant made no move of rejection. "Man—man."

"Man." The giant murmured it cautiously, prolonging the vowel; he touched his chest. *"Essa kana."* A finger ran exploringly over the gauze.

"Essa kana—man," said Wright, and swayed on his feet.

The giant pointed at the bloody mess on the ground and rumbled: *"Kawan."* He shuddered, and his arm swept in a loose gesture that appeared to indicate the curving quarter mile where lake and jungle met each other in a black-water marsh. Then he was staring out, muttering, at the wings in the meadow, and presently he touched Paul's bandage with fantastic lightness. *"Omasha,"* he said, pointing at the flying beasts. He indicated the rifle wobbling in Sears' arm and held up two fingers. "Omasha."

"Yes, we killed two omasha. Sears-man. Paul-man. Wright-man."

The giant rumpled his chest fur. "Mijok."

"Mijok-man. . . . Mijok, why didn't I have you in Anthropology IA fifteen years ago? We'd've cleaned up the joint." Mijok knew laughter; his booming in response to Wright's tone and smile could mean nothing else. But Wright staggered and was breathing hard. Dorothy whispered, "Paul—"

It could not be pushed aside any more—the pain separate from the smart of his shoulder, tightness in the eyeballs, chill, nausea. "The air—"

Wright's knees buckled. Sears had dropped the rifle and was helping him to the lifeboat, Paul watching the action in a daze of stupidity. Wright's eyes had gone empty. . . . Paul was uncertain how he himself came to be sitting on the ground. Dorothy's face was somewhere; he touched it. Her brown cheek was fire-hot, and she was trying to speak. "Paul—take care of you—always—"

The face of Mijok was there too—red vapor turning black.

5 PAUL MASON STARED INTO BLUE CALM: AIRY MOtion of branches against the sky, a mystery remembered from long ago, in a place called New Hampshire. Those years were not dead: secretly the mind had brought them here. *What a small journey! Less than five light-years: on a star map you could hardly represent it with the shortest of lines.* . . . . . . He was without pain, and cool. Time? Why, that amiable thud of a heart in a firm, familiar body (his own, surely?), that was indicating time. The boy in New Hampshire, after sprawling on his lazy back and discovering the miracle of sky—hadn't he tried to paint it, even then? Messed about with his uncle's palette, creating a daub that had—oh, something, a little something. *Very well. Once upon a time there was a painter named Paul Mason . . . Dorothy . . .*

"You're back—oh, darling! No, Paul, don't sit up fast or your head'll hurt. Mine did." Now she was curling into the hollow of his arm, laughing and weeping. "You're back. . . ."

A thin old man sat cross-legged on gray moss. Paul asked him, "How long?"

Christopher Wright smiled, twisting and teasing the skin of his gaunt throat, gray with a thick beard stubble. "A day and a night, the nurse says. You know—the nurse? You were kissing her a moment ago. It's early morning again, Paul. She was never quite unconscious, she claims. I recovered an hour ago. No ill effects. It knocked out the others at nightfall—predictable. They were exposed to Lucifer's air thirteen hours later than we were." Paul saw them now, lying on beds of the gray—moss? And where he and Dorothy clung to each other was the same pleasant stuff—dry, spongy, with an odor like clover hay.

"Beds by courtesy of Mijok." Wright nodded toward the gray giant, who had also brought moss for himself and now sprawled belly down, breathing silently, the bulge between his shoulder blades lightly rising and falling. Mijok's face was on his arm, turned away toward the purple shadow of forest.

Dorothy whispered, "He watched over us all night."

"So you were conscious all the time? Tell me."

Dorothy kept her voice low. Paul noticed the towering slimness of the lifeboat beyond the barrier of branches, reversed—Ed Spearman's work, he supposed. It pointed toward the west. Turned so, the jet would blast toward the lake, harming nothing. Its shadow held away the heat of the sun, a gleaming artifact of twenty-first century man, the one alien thing in this wilderness morning. The sickness, Dorothy said, had taken her with a sudden paralysis: she could see, hear, be aware of boiling fever, but could not move. Then even the sense of heat left her —she was only observing eyes, ears, and a brain. She had had a fantasy that she was dead, no longer breathing. "But I breathed." Her small brown face crinkled with a laughter rich in more than amusement. "It's a habit I don't mean to abandon."

"Neurotoxin," said Wright, "and a damn funny one. Back on Earth, when I believed myself to be a doctor, I never heard of anything like it."

The condition had lasted all day, she said; at nightfall her sense of touch had gradually returned. She could move her hands, later her feet and head. At length she had sat up, briefly blinded by pain in the forehead, then she had given way to an overwhelming need for sleep. "I got a glimpse of you, Paul, and tumbled off into a set of dreams that were—not so bad, not so bad. I woke before sunrise. Different. Don't ask me how. Never felt healthier. Not even weak, as you should be after a fever. But Doc—what if the illness—"

Wright looked away from the terror that had crossed her face. "If you go on feeling all right, we can assume nothing's wrong with the baby. Don't borrow trouble, sugarpuss—we've got enough."

"Maybe," Paul suggested, "the illness was just—oh, some of our Earth metabolism getting burned out of us.

A stiff acclimation course." Wright grunted, pinching his long nose. Paul said, "Wish it had burned out the yen for a cigarette that I've had for eleven years."

Sears Oliphant, the only other with some medical knowledge, had taken charge immediately after their collapse. "He is—scared, Paul," Dorothy murmured. "Of Lucifer, I mean. I could feel it when I was just a pair of eyes and ears. More physical shrinking in him than in the rest of us, and he's fighting it back with all he's got. He's a very big man, Paul. . . ." Sears looked peaceful enough now, in the dark sleep of the sickness, his moon face bristling with black beard growth but relaxed and bland. On another couch of moss, Spearman was more restless, powerful arms twitching as if he needed to fight the disaster even in sleep. Ann Bryan was deeply flushed and moaned a little now and then. "Ed was all right too. Considerate. Took all Sears' orders without any fuss or question; I don't think he's much scared. He feels he can bull his way through anything, and maybe he's right." Dorothy's helpless eyes had also seen Mijok bringing moss in great armfuls. This, she thought, had helped Ed Spearman to accept the giant as a man and perhaps as a friend. She remembered Mijok raising Paul and herself in one careful swing of his arms to set them down beside each other on the moss. Later she had watched him turning the lifeboat under direction of Spearman's blunt gestures. Its length was thirty-four feet, its weight over three tons Earth gravity—more here. One gray-white arm had lifted the tail and swung the boat on its landing gear as a man might push a light automobile. "I wasn't afraid. After dark, when I knew the sickness had got the others, I still wasn't afraid. Believe me? I could see Mijok moving around. Once I heard him growl—I think he was driving something off. And then while the red moon was coming up, he sat by us—his eyes are red in the dark, Paul, not green. He smells musky at close range, but clean. I wasn't afraid. Now and then he'd look us over and smile with his funny black lips and touch the furry back of his finger to our foreheads. . . . I could see the blue fireflies, Paul. Someday you'll make up stories about them for the baby. . . . I heard that crying again—much nearer than when we heard it that first night by the other lifeboat. Like a group of children crying, if you can imagine that synchronized, almost musical. Mijok growled and fretted when it began,. but it came no nearer. It had stopped when I woke."

"Some of Earth's critters sounded human—panthers, owls, frogs—"

"Ye-es. Just possibly something like tree frogs. . . ."

Wright said, "Mijok brought us raw meat this morning before he went to sleep, something like a deer haunch. The fire bothers him—he evidently didn't go near it last night after the others collapsed."

"Ed tried to show him about fire," Dorothy said. "I remember. Mijok was scared, and Sears told Ed to let it wait."

"Meat was good too." Wright smirked. "We got the fire going, and Mijok did try some cooked and liked it. You and Dorothy can have some tomorrow if I don't turn purple."

"Not guinea-pig," said Dorothy. "Just pig."

"Hungry?" Wright tossed Paul a ration package.

"Gah!" But he opened it. "Learned any more of Mijok's words?"

"No. He won't have many. Nouns, simple descriptives. Must have some continuing association with his own breed, or he'd have no words at all. A hunter—with only nature's weapons, I think. That haunch was torn, not cut—some hoofed animal smaller than a pony, fresh-killed and well bled. He must have got it while Dorothy slept. It may have strayed into the camp during the night. I think Mijok lives in the woods, maybe not even a shelter or a permanent mate. Anthropology IA," said Wright, and bowed in mimic apology to the sleeping giant. "Those pygmies will be something else again—Neolithic. Wish I understood that bulge between the shoulder blades. All the creatures we've seen have it—even that damn black reptile, I believe, though things were too mixed up to be sure."

Mijok woke—all at once, like a cat. He stretched, extending his arms twelve feet from wrist to wrist. He smiled down at Paul. He studied the helpless ones, peering longest at Ann Bryan; the black-haired girl was breathing harshly, fidgeting. Now and then her eyes flickered open and perhaps they saw. Softly as smoke Mijok stepped into the shadow of the trees and listened. Wright remarked,

"Speaking of that reptile, we should set up a monument to it. Nothing luckier could have happened than that chance to lend Mijok a hand." His gray eyes fixed on Paul, lids lowered in a speculative smile. "I'm not the only one who remembers, Paul, that you were the first to go to his help. He hasn't forgotten. . . . Dot, you're sure Ed understood that we have a friend there?"

"He seemed to, Doc. I watched them. They got along—practically buddies."

Paul saw the bandage was still on Mijok's arm, earth-stained and with fragments of gray moss, but not disarranged; the bandage on his own shoulder had been removed. The flying beast's attack had left only a heavy scratch, which looked clean; there was no pain, only an itching. The meadow was empty of brown wings. The dead fish were gone from the lake. Perhaps other scavengers had been busy in the thirteen-hour night. The water was an innocent blue, a luminous stillness under the sun.

Mijok stole out into the grass, gazing westward along the line where meadow met jungle. Returning, he squatted by Wright and muttered, *"Migan."* He spread a hand three feet above the ground; two fingers drooped and indicated the motion of walking legs. Paul suggested: "Pygmies?"

"Could be." Mijok stared eloquently at Wright's rifle then crouched at the barrier of branches, complaining in his throat. Taking up his own rifle, Paul joined him. Dorothy hurried to the lifeboat and came back with field glasses for him and Wright and herself. In spite of the great planet's heavy pull, her body moved with even more light easiness than it had shown in the unreal years of *Argo*. With the glasses, vague motion a quarter mile away in the meadow leaped shockingly into precision.

The pygmies were not approaching but heading out from the edge of the forest, a group of nine, barely taller than the grass, bald red heads and shoulders in single file. The rearmost had a burden: seven others carried bows, with quivers on the right hip. "Left-handed," Paul observed aloud. The leader was the tallest—a woman, with a long spear. All were sending anxious glances at the sky and toward the human shelter; their motions suggested a fear so deep it must be pain, yet something drew them out there in spite of it. The pygmy with the burden, a rolled-up hide, was also a woman. The leader was bald as the others, slender, muscular, her head round, with prominent forehead and thin nose, tattooed cheeks. The bowmen had only simple loincloths, and belts for their arrow quivers. The women's knee-length grass skirts were like the Melanesian, but the leader's was dyed a brilliant blue. Her two little pairs of breasts were youthfully firm and pointed. Dorothy murmured, "American civilization would have gone mad about those people."

"What a girl!" Wright sighed. "I mean Dorothy—the Dope."

"Even a dope can be jealous. Do you s'pose Mrs. Mijok has—Oh! Oh, poor darling! Not funny after all, gentlemen—"

The pygmy leader had turned full face, as the nine paused at trampled grass. She wore a necklace of shell. These had no glitter, but their yellow and blue made handsome splashes against the red of her skin. Reason told Paul that she could see at most only dazzling spots where sunlight might be touching the glasses he had thrust through wilted leaves. It made no difference: she was staring directly into him, making her grief a part of his life. A still-faced grief, too profound for any tears, if she knew of tears. The green cat eyes lowered; she stabbed her spear into the ground and lifted her arms, a giving, yielding motion. Her lips moved—in prayer, surely, since all but one of the men were bowed, performing ritual gestures toward whatever lay on the ground. The one who did not bow never ceased to watch the sky. The prayer was brief. The woman's left hand dropped meaningly, the hide was unrolled, and its bearer raised what the grass had hidden—no more than a skull and a few bones, a broken spear, a muddy scrap that might have been a grass skirt. The hide was folded gently over these; the group went on.

"Dorothy—those things you saw running when we were circling down—I missed 'em," Wright said. "Poor eyesight, and seems to me the air was still misty from *Argo's* crash in the lake. They were going south, away from here? And they could have been—people like these?"

"Yes. Hundreds or thousands of them. I suppose the crash of *Argo* must have seemed like the heavens falling. The lifeboats too."

"I think we interrupted a war."

"These would be survivors? Live in this part of the jungle maybe? Looking for what's left after those—those flying beasts—"

"It makes sense," Wright said. "They're more afraid of the sky than of our setup over here. Maybe we're gods who came down to help them. If we did help them. Look: they've found another. . . . Yes, now the prayer. . . . Wish Mijok wasn't so afraid of them. Inevitable. To them I suppose he's an ugly wild animal. Different species, similar enough to be shocked at the similarity. 'Tain't good."

"Do we try for a foot in both camps?"

"Paul, I think I'll take a rain check on answering that. . . . Ach—if I could go out there now—communicate—"

"No!" Dorothy gasped. "Not while the others are still sick."

"You're right of course." Wright fretted at his beard stubble. "I get sillier all the time. As Ed would tell me if he were up and around. It's the high oxygen. . . ."

There were brown splashes in the sky. The pygmies saw the peril first and darted for the woods—an orderly flight however—the woman with the hide in front, the blue-skirted woman next, then the bowmen. Three of the latter turned bravely and shot arrows that glittered and whined. The brown beasts wheeled and flapped angrily upward, though the buzzing arrows dropped far short of them. The pygmies gained the trees; the omasha scouted the edge of the woods, squawking, three of them drifting toward the lifeboat, weaving heads surveying the ground. Paul gave way to unfamiliar savage enjoyment. "Do we, Doc?"

"Yes," said Wright, and took aim himself.

All three were brought down, at a cost of four irreplaceable rifle bullets and two shots from Dorothy's automatic. Mijok bellowed with satisfaction but recoiled as Wright dragged a dirty brown carcass into the clearing. "A dissection is in order." Mijok grumbled and fidgeted. "Don't fret, Mijok." Wright pegged down the wings of the dead animal with sharp sticks and drew an incision on the leathery belly with his hunting knife. "Good head shot, Paul—this one's yours. We'll do a brain job from

one of the others, but I think we'll let that wait for Sears
—oh my, yes . . . ! Doesn't weigh over thirty pounds.
Hollow bones like a bird's, very likely. Hope they'll keep."

"You hope," Dorothy sniffed. "What do you do when I
turn housewife and instruct you to get that awful mess
the hell off my nice clean floor?"

"Dope! And you my best and only medical student." He
worked at the cutting dubiously, inexpertly. "Conven-
tional mammalian setup, more or less. Small lungs, big
stomach. Hah—two pairs of kidneys?" He spread the vis-
cera out on the wing. "Short intestine, also like a bird.
And she was preparing a blessed event multiplied by—
count 'em—six."

"Too many," said Paul. "Altogether too industrious."

"What I really want to know—Oh . . . ?" With the
lungs removed, it could be seen that the hump on the
back was caused by a great enlargement of four thoracic
vertebrae, which swelled into the chest cavity as well as
outward. Wright cut away spinal cartilage. "Damn, I *wish*
Sears was doing this. Well, it's neural tissue, nothing else—
a big swelling of the spinal cord." He sliced at the ugly
head, but the hermorrhage from a .30-caliber bullet confused the picture. "The brain looks too simple. Could that
lump in the cord be the hind brain? I hereby leave the
theories to Sears. But, son, you might slit the stomach
and see what the old lady had for breakfast."

Paul's clumsy cut on the slippery stomach bag made
it plain what the omasha had eaten—among other things,
an almost complete seven-fingered hand. Dorothy choked
and walked away, saying, "I am going to be—"

"Cheer up." Paul held her forehead. "Never mind the
clean floor—"

"Go away. I mean stay very close. Sorry to be so physiological. Me a medic student! Even blood bothers me."

"Never mind, sugar—"

"Sugar yourself, and wash your paws. We smell."

Mijok was muttering in alarm. Wright had abandoned
the dissection and gone out in the meadow, cautious but
swift, to the spot where yesterday they had found the
pygmy soldiers. He took up a small skull and arm bone,
pathetically clean—perhaps there were insect scavengers
that followed after the omasha—and the discarded bow.

But instead of bringing back these relics, Wright held them high over his head, facing westward. Tall and gray in the heavy sun, he stepped twenty paces further toward the region where the pgymies had entered the jungle; then he set the bones down in the grass and strode back to the shelter, fingers twitching, lips moving in his old habit of talking half to himself, half to the world. "The omasha," he said, "cracked the enlarged vertebrae—favorite morsel maybe."

Mijok moaned, blinking and sighing. He stared long at the silent grace of the lifeboat, then at Christopher Wright. He too was talking to himself. Abruptly, something gave way in him. He was kneeling before Wright, bending forward, taking Wright's hands and pressing them against the gray-white fur of his face and his closed eyes. "Oh, now," Wright said, "now, friend—"

Paul remarked, "You're elected."

"I will not be a god."

6 MIJOK RELEASED THE HANDS OF HIS DEITY AND SAT back on his haunches, foggy-eyed. Wright stroked the great furry head, troubled and amazed. "It won't do," Wright said. "We'll have no gods on this planet. Unless human nature can make itself a little godlike. And no final Armageddon—for that's within too, and always was. Well, he'll learn language fast. As he does, the first thing he must discover is that we're all one flesh." But Mijok was gazing up in adoration at the sound of the voice, trembling, not in fear, smiling when he saw Wright smile. "I believe he never had a god before—hadn't reached the stage of personalizing the forces of nature. They're just forces, and himself a bundle of perception, not even realizing that he's more knowing and sensitive than other animals. Not arrogant yet, not sophisticated enough to be cruel, or mean, or even ambitious. . . ."

Dorothy pushed her fists into her cheeks, brown eyes upturned to study the old man: a way she had, carrying Paul back eleven years to the day he had come aboard the ship and seen her for the first time and loved the woman who was, even then, manifest in the leggy, awkward child. "Doc, why did you do that, out there in the meadow?"

"Why, Dorothy, we must make contact with those pygmies too. They are—advanced. It'll be more difficult. They'll have traditions—maybe some very ancient ones. But we must make contact."

"Mijok hates them though. If they come here—"

Wright grinned. "Temporary advantage of being little tin deities. I think Mijok will do whatever we indicate —until we're able to teach him independence."

Paul said, "Don't think for a minute I'm not with you.

But Doc, with the others helpless we're only three—"

"Four."

"Yes, four. There's our own survival to think of. It's a big planet. Seems to me you're taking it on all at once."

Wright slouched, loose-limbed, at the barrier, where he could watch the meadow, and Mijok stayed close to him. "I think we must, Paul. If we start right perhaps we can go on right. A mistake at this point could go on burning for a thousand years. . . . Why do you think he broke out into worship when he did? Our superior achievements —lifeboat, guns, the rescue from that reptile? The fact that I wasn't afraid of a poor pygmy's bones? All that, sure, but something else. Ed would say I was daydreaming —but I think Mijok's heart knows what his brain can't yet interpret. Sears would agree, I think—his own heart's bigger than Lucifer. Mijok hasn't the least conscious idea why I invited those pygmies to come and get their dead. Down deeper, in the part of him that made him bring the moss and the meat and take care of us, I think he knows very well."

"You're proposing," Dorothy said, "to take a chance on love?"

Wright was tranquil, watching the meadow. "Whenever men put their chips on the other thing they always lost, didn't they? Repeatedly, for twenty or thirty thousand years? Did they ever create anything good except in a milieu of co operation, friendship, forbearance? One of the oldest of commonplaces—the teachers all knew it. Lao-tse—Buddha—or stated negatively: 'He who lives by the sword . . .' And so on. Good is not the mere absence of evil, but the most positive of human forces. The instruments of good are charity, patience, courage, effort and self-knowledge, each unavailing without the others; remember that. And that's all the basic ethics I know. The rest is detail, solution of immediate problems as they arise. Even on Earth the good tended to win out in the long run: at least it did until the mechanical toys got out of hand. Then there was a century of living under a question mark. There was also the Collectivist Party. Yes, as a prime example of a part of my own philosophy totally perverted, I give you the Collectivist Party." Wright was talking to himself again, the bitterness of Earth's history goading him into soft-spoken monotone, drawling and dark, on a planet nearly five light-years distant from the ancient confusions. "The Collectivist Party, which turns 'co-operation' into the same sort of word fetish that 'democracy' was less than a hundred years ago—co-operation *without* charity, without patience, without courage and always, always, without self-knowledge."

Dorothy still watched him with sober upturned eyes. "Ed told me once his father was a pilot in the Collectivist Army during the Civil War."

"I know." Wright smiled at her in bashful half apology. "Some of the old wounds still bleed too, I guess. I generally manage to keep my political mouth shut when he's listening, if I can. Not that Ed could be accused of still fighting the war that ended before he was born . . . Relax: I think they're coming."

Paul joined Wright and the giant at the barrier, but Dorothy stayed a moment with the sick, feeling their wrists, murmuring something close to Ann's ear, although the girl could not respond. "Past the fever stage, I believe," she said. "They're all breathing well. No chance they'll be out of it before night, I suppose. . . ."

The pygmies were still some distance away, slipping along the edge of the woods in plain sight. There were only three—the two women and one bowman; perhaps the others were paralleling their course inside the forest —perhaps a hundred others were. Wright whispered, "Have we anything that would make a respectable gift?"

Mijok was rumbling in misery and fright. Dorothy came over holding a locket. "This—you remember, Doc—a matron at the Orphanage gave it to me. I used to imagine it could be a portrait of my mother—"

"But my dear—"

The brown girl shook her head. "This ship-metal wedding ring Paul hammered out for me—that's the only Earth jewelry I want to keep. This face that might be like my mother's—Oh, Doc, I'm getting to be a big girl now. Besides, Lucifer will have plenty of pretties for us later on. And Doc—let me do this, will you? They've got a woman leading 'em, so—wouldn't she be less afraid of another woman? I'll uncover, so she—" Dorothy shrugged out of her jacket. "Please, Doc? I'm scared, but—"

Wright glanced helplessly at Paul. "We—"

Dorothy said quickly, "*My* decision." Holding the locket up for the sun to gleam on it, she walked into the meadow and waited in the brightness. Paul's hand sweated on the rifle stock. He saw Wright patting Mijok's arm, heard his restraining murmur: "Quiet, Mijok—keep your shirt on, Mijok, old man—man. . . ." Mijok searched the face of his god with a mute desperation and remained as he was.

The pygmy woman halted fifty feet away in still-faced musing. As Paul had seen through the binoculars, she was elaborately tattooed and young. The pause was long. Dorothy stepped nearer to the place where Wright had left the bones, displaying the locket, her open left hand waving down at her body to demonstrate that she carried no weapons. For the first time Paul realized she had left her holster belt behind.

The blue-skirted woman shrilled a word; her two followers fell back. She thrust the blunt end of her spear in the ground and came forward steadily until she was only a few feet from the woman of the twenty-first century; mask-faced, she met Dorothy's smile with a long scrutiny. Now and then the green eyes shifted to study the clearing, the lifeboat, the quiet shapes of Paul and Wright. And Mijok. Perhaps she stared longest at Mijok, but by some heavy discipline her face refused to tell of anything but dignity and caution.

She spoke at last. It was complex, in a tone like the piping of a tree frog. There were pauses, studied inflections, no gestures: her seven-fingered hands hung limp against the blue grass skirt. The closing words seemed to have a note of questioning and of sternness; she waited.

Dorothy's contralto was startlingly deep in contrast: "Darling, I would like to know where you picked up that perfectly adorable wrap-around, only I don't think it would suit me. I'm, to put it frankly, a shade too hippy for such. In case you're wondering, I'm a female sample of man"—she touched herself and pointed to the pygmy lady—"man—"

"Oh!" Wright whispered. "Good girl, good—"

"—and it does seem to me us girls ought to stick together, because"—she held out the locket—"well, just because. And anyway look: I have only ten toes, fastened on to the ends of my feet, and if I had more, Heaven knows (just count 'em and *see* how each grows!) I'd have trouble in keeping them neat. Pome. There now, sweetie pie, please take it, huh?" And she opened the locket—Paul remembering in lessening panic how much the unknown portrait did resemble her—and held it face out to the woman of Lucifer. A tiny palm came up dubiously; Dorothy placed the locket in it. "It won't bite, baby." The pygmy woman turned it about, puzzling at the hinge. Dorothy stooped to demonstrate the mechanism a few times. "I'm Dorothy, by the way, more widely known as the Dope, which is a title of uncommon distinction among my people, achieved only after long study of the art of saying the right thing at the wrong time, burning the bacon, and preserving at all times an air of sweet and addled dignity—Dorothy. . . ." She indicated herself plainly and pointed, with questioning eyebrows.

The tree-frog voice, with no sternness, but a hint of friendliness: "Tor-o-thee . . . ?" She imitated Dorothy's motions. "Abro Pakriaa—"

"Pakriaa."

"Abro Pakriaa." There was sternness again in that correction.

"Abro Pakriaa. . . ."

Wright muttered, "Royalty, I believe. Don't dare do any coaching. Trust Dot's instinct. Ah, here we go—"

The pygmy woman had taken off her shell necklace. She crushed the dainty blue and yellow against her upper right breast; she set it for a moment on her shining hairless skull, and then offered it. Wright sighed, shaken, "It *had* to work—exchange of gifts—a universal—"

When Dorothy dropped on one knee to take it, the mask relaxed for the first time in a wintry smile. Over the proud bald head went the chain of the locket, and Abro Pakriaa watched Dorothy put the necklace on—fortunately it was long, even drooping a little below Dorothy's throat. A flutter of red hands seemed to mean that Dorothy was to stand back; another motion brought forward the woman who carried the hide, her face a chip of red stone. The hide was unrolled, and the bones placed on it. There was more intricate speech, with touching of the locket and graceful, apparently kindly waving of thin arms. Dorothy responded: "Four score and seven years ago . . ." She went on to the end without mirth or hesitation, fondling the shell necklace, giving the words the power of music that belongs to them even apart from knowledge of their meaning. When she was silent, Abro Pakriaa motioned the woman with the hide to go and held up her two hands clasped together, the Chinese salutation. She waited till Dorothy had done the same and strode away, recovering her spear without a backward look, vanishing under the trees.

Dorothy collapsed in the shadow of the barrier. Tentatively she groaned: "How'm I doing?"

Wright snarled; "Suppose you know that damn bowman had an arrow trained on you the whole time?"

She glanced at him, lips quivering. "I was kind of aware of it."

"Can I," said Paul, "touch the hand that touched the hand—"

"Oh no. I ain' gonna 'sociate with no common scum no mo'."

Mijok stared in wonder at their sudden paroxysms of hysterical laughter. He rumbled in doubt. Then the contagion caught him. Whatever his own interpretation might be, he was bellowing, hammering his chest, rolling over on the moss and scattering handfuls of it while he roared.

He did not sober until he saw Wright drawing pictures on the earth—three stylized but obvious human figures, one small, one medium-sized, one large. Only the middle one had five fingers. Wright gouged a circle around all three. He said, "C'm'on, Mijok—language lesson."

7 THE TRAIL WAS OBVIOUS ONLY TO THE PYGMIES, through a border region of meadow and forest that was full of dappled light, a warm hurry of life feeding, struggling, wandering. Aware of his own power and readiness, able now to enjoy the shifting scents and noises of this new trail, Paul watched Ann's quick slenderness and the swing of Spearman's solid shoulders. They, and Sears Oliphant, had emerged unharmed from the illness. During a week unmeasurably long in retrospect, all six of the party had found the ease and sureness of physical acclimation. Their bodies rejoiced in the hot clean air of day and the moist moderate nights; the only rebel was the Earthborn brain—grudging, frightened, trailing, making endless reservations and timid of shadows. In Sears Oliphant it was an almost open battle between a brave and curious mind and flesh that could not hide its wincing from pain and danger. His "Oh my, yes" had a tremor which angered himself and oppressed his natural garrulity.

When Ann Bryan had drifted out of the sleep of illness, Ed Spearman was petting her hands, sponging her forehead. Paul had seen something happen in Ann at that moment, like an innocent putting forth of leaves when winter is not surely gone. Ann had never taken a lover. On the ship, not so much unawakened as unwilling, she had rejected all that; Spearman, making no secret of wanting her, had not been insistent. Now had he seemed outwardly much distressed, but (at a time when Earthharbored youth of his nature would have been in their liveliest and most demanding prime) he had buried himself in *Argo's* technical library to the point of red-eyed exhaustion, a desperation of unceasing study in the technologies that Captain Jensen would have helped him explore if

Jensen had lived. Ann had read other matters after the
violin strings were gone, read and daydreamed. If she'd
wept (and Paul thought she had) she had done it alone,
in that pocket of a room sacred to herself. To the others,
she was a passionately silent adolescent turning into a
tiredly silent woman, who made too much point of doing
her own work and asking for nothing.

Yes, Ann was different now. The thin beauty of her face,
vivid white under heavy black hair, was still too quiet,
but with a troubled radiance. During this long week
she had talked much with Dorothy—talk superficially in-
consequential, but Paul assumed it had a meaning below
words, as if Ann had only just realized, probably without
envy, that the brown girl was a thousand years older in
heart and mind.

Beyond Ann and Spearman were the six bowmen of the
escort, bodies bright with a sour-smelling oil, grouped
around Abro Pakriaa at a deferential distance. The princess wore Dorothy's locket. "Abro," Paul had learned,
was best translated as "princess" or "queen." A flame-red
flower behind her ear caught sunlight from the early afternoon. Five others were following Paul—women, with
skirts of every tint but Pakriaa's blue, taller than the men,
carrying spears with blades of a white stone resembling
quartz. The men were unvaryingly soft, rounded in contour,
lacking the women's tough sinewed vigor. It was plain,
merely from the manner of Abro Pakriaa and her spear
bearers, that among this people to be a woman was to
be a leader and soldier, no doubt a hunter and head of
the household by virtue of size and strength. In muscular
power, a male pygmy was to a female as the weakest of
Earth's women was to the toughest male athlete. These of
the bodyguard were soldiers of a sort: the bows were
small, the arrows only big darts. The bowmen never
spoke except meekly in response to some patronizing
word of the princess. Pakriaa's height topped forty inches;
none of the bowmen was quite three feet tall. Paul's fingers itched for brush and palette. They were available in
the lifeboat. The fact that he had not even unpacked
them he blamed on a preoccupation with the daily work
needed for mere survival, but there was a deeper reason:
perhaps a fear of finding his moderate ability vanished if

he should once try to hint with oil at the welling profusion of color and line that was Lucifer. Now he found himself trying to measure the quality of Pakriaa's rich copper against the softness of leaves that were burnt umber, malachite green, saffron, purple, and he thought: *I must be recovering. Wake up, ego, and look around.*

Spearman was carrying rifle and automatic; Paul had preferred to leave his rifle behind; Ann, hating firearms, had only her knife.

Abro Pakriaa had entered the camp at noon, her fourth visit in the week. Her gloomy majesty unchanging, she had indicated that she wished them to come to her village. But Dorothy had turned her ankle the evening before and it still pained her. Wright, no doubt hungering more than any of the others for a sight of Pakriaa's way of living, had fretted and humbled and elected to remain with Dorothy and Sears, urging Paul needlessly to remember his anthropology. Sears, sweating out a microsection of a water insect from Lake Argo, had flapped a fat hand and boomed: "You be sure 'n' telephone, damn it, if you're staying for dinner, hey?"

Remaining uneasily close to Wright, as he did whenever the pygmies appeared, Mijok had said carefully, "Telephone?"

"Word without meaning," said Wright gently, patting the huge arm. "Noise word for fun."

The attitude of Pakriaa's people to Mijok suggested the studious ignoring of an indecency. They would not harm the ugly animal, their manner said, so long as he was the property of the important sky people. . . .

Life was generously abundant in this thinner forest. Things buzzed and flew; Paul noticed a few webs cunningly extended before burrows in the humus. Ann's ocean-gray eyes glanced back, brave and uncertain. "Those girls are too quiet. Paul, how much *do* they know of our language?"

"Not much." He moved up to walk on her other side. "Doc and I have made only those two efforts to swap languages. A lot of that time had to be wasted on theirs, a dead end for us."

Spearman grunted, "Why? They've got a civilization, as Doc says."

"Our voices are wrong. Pitch effects meaning for them. You've noticed there's no pitch difference between their male and female voices. Their language is tied to one section of the scale; a full octave of it is above the range of even Ann's voice. They can shape our words though, if they're willing. Basic English may appeal to the princess when she condescends to take it seriously."

"They could have picked up more than we suspect. They could have been eavesdropping outside the camp."

"No, Ed. Mijok would have known and told us."

"Yeah—Fido. Can hardly speak freely in front of him now."

"Don't think anything you wouldn't want him to hear."

"Paul, I swear, sometimes you're worse than Doc." But Spearman wanted to cancel the ill temper of the remark, and added: "You know, I thought *I* knew something about Basic English—we all had drill enough in it. Beats me, the things Doc can do with it—the man's a wizard."

Paul was silent with unappeased annoyance. It was true: Mijok appeared to be a natural student too, already far beyond Basic English in a week of keen listening. "Nan," Paul said, "how did you like Mijok's humming when you were singing for us yesterday evening?"

"Good." She flashed him an almost cheerful smile. But when Ann spoke of her singing—and in the singing itself —there was, in spite of her, an aching wordless reminder of the violin gone silent. Her voice was sweet but without strength or resonance, and she took no ardent pleasure in using it. Her love was the violin—covered as well as might be in the comparative safety of the lifeboat, waiting for a distant day. If the day ever came (Sears had already dissected out, dried, and oiled some long leg-tendon fibers of a deerlike animal in a humble experiment aimed chiefly at Ann's morale)—if the day came, there would still be no piano, no answering of other strings, no splendid cry of brass. Crude wood winds, perhaps, sometime. . . . "Yes, he was good," said Ann, smiling. "Organ point in the tonic, and right in our own scale. Once he even upped to the dominant. Instinct, huh? Sounded good, Paul, even with you trying to fill in the middle."

"Hell, I didn't think you heard me," Spearman snorted.

"You kind of stood out," she said, "because Mijok was much better on pitch, my good man. It did sound hollow without something to fill in. He was on A-flat below the bass clef and no fooling. . . . *Why* haven't we seen other giants?"

"We got something on that this morning. I guess it was while you were in swimming. Each giant male has an inviolate hunting territory, and they don't trespass. Definite breeding season: the month before the rains. That was five or maybe six red-moon changes ago. Mijok wasn't too clear on the count—doesn't like mathematics much better than I do. The women go where they please, in small groups, with the children who still need care, but I gather the males are expected to stay in their own private grounds until the Red-Moon-before-the-Rains."

Spearman wondered: "Will the pygmies have a season too?"

"Doubt it. Probably like us—except that women are the bosses. The clothes suggest a continuing sex consciousness."

The pygmy leaders halted. A murmuring explained itself as the music of a stream. Paul consulted his memory of the map made from orbit photographs and of his one solo exploration flight in the lifeboat. There could be few such flights: the charlesite, even with the surplus salvaged from the wrecked boat, must be hoarded. Ann and Ed had flown over the lake on the day after their recovery, searching for any sign of *Argo*. Returning, Ed's face had been a leather mask of grief, and neither had wanted to talk of it. Later they explained: the lake was a profundity of secret blue; a shelf of sand or possibly white stone ran out some yards offshore, under water marvelously clear, and ended abruptly. Beyond it, where *Argo* must have fallen, no bottom could even be guessed at; the lifeboat's camera confirmed the presence of an abyss that would have thwarted the most complex twenty-first-century machinery.

This stream, Paul knew, came from the western hills, flowing east and slightly north until it entered the lake northeast of the clearing called home. Another creek joined it east of the spot where they now stood, and Pakriaa's village—if the parallel lines did represent its location—was not far upstream from that junction.

Worn boulders rose above noisy water. The stream was twenty yards wide, sluggish even here in the shallows. A steppingstone crossing.

Nearly all the rivers on the map passed through jungle for most of their length; numberless smaller streams would be hidden from the sky. There was grassland for fifteen to twenty miles on the eastern side of every range of hills. The prevailing winds were from the west; perhaps a dryness in the lee of the hills favored the grass. The broadest stretch of such open land lay east of a rugged coastal range seventy miles to the southwest; some of the mountains in that seacoast formation were mighty enough to hold a blur of snow at their summits. The base of the coastal range was narrow—hardly more than twenty miles. From this the peaks shot up with incredible sheerness to great heights of bare rock that glittered in morning sun like black and red glass. This grandeur, like nothing known on Earth, was clearly visible from the camp above the near hills, especially at midday, when the mists were gone.

And ten miles offshore from that dizzy range, Paul remembered a mountainous island. On his solo exploration two days ago, with the lifeboat's panoramic camera and a head full of puzzled dreams, he had soared above it, noting a peninsular strip of red sand at its southern end, sheltered mountain valleys—one framing a jewel of lake. In the north was a white beach where landing should be easy, and this was protected by a low headland of red cliffs running out to the very tip of the island. Surely a place to carry in the mind, it seemed to invite human living as did no other near region in this continent of Lucifer. Wright thought so: he listened to Paul's description and named the island Adelphi. . . .

North of the camp, the range of low western hills dwindled to rolling land and was lost in a tremendous expanse of unbroken jungle, which ended only at the shore of one of the great lakes four hundred miles away—an inland sea fourteen hundred miles long. Sixty-odd miles to the south there was that large cluster of parallel lines in jungle, and beyond it the forest gave way to more open ground, prairie, red desert, and bare mountains.

Abro Pakriaa dipped her spear in the water; she lifted a handful, letting it trickle away while she spoke a rippling invocation; then she was lithely crossing on the stones after the bowmen. The bottom was pale sand with varicolored pebbles.

Beyond the stream, Pakriaa followed a path a short way and pressed into undergrowth. Spearman grumbled, "Good path for once, and we have to—"

"Path's probably booby-trapped. She expects us to know that."

"Hell . . . " It was difficult passage, stooping on a trail meant for little folk; it ended at a ditch six feet wide and five deep. The ditch made a right angle, both lines stretching away straightly as far as the eye could go; the inner side of the ditch was heaped with dry sticks and bundles of grass. Pakriaa trilled orders to an old black-skirted woman with a whip, in charge of a gang of four women and three men, all totally naked. They were struggling to shove a movable bridge into place across the ditch—two logs bearing a mat of vines and bark. It was grunting work for them, and when the end of the bridge was in reach, Pakriaa's escort made no motion to help. Spearman started to; Paul interfered. "We'd lose face. Those are slaves. Women tied together at the ankles —one of the men a eunuch. Look at the brands on their cheeks. Nan, you're the dominant sex—try to look more like the president of a women's club."

Her finely modeled face had dignity enough, he thought, if she could keep the worry out of it. . . . The old woman in the black skirt bowed arrogantly to Pakriaa; the slaves cringed, with the hating stare of the trapped. All were scarred and young except for the eunuch, who was wrinkled and flabby. One female had a recent chest wound; the effort at the bridge had made it bleed, but she ignored it. Paul saw Spearman's face settle into lines of poker blankness and thought: *Good. And if, to patience and courage, he could add (I hear you, Doc) charity and self-knowledge—Oh, be quiet, critic, be quiet. . . .*

Trees had been felled—some time ago, for the stumps were rotted—and the spacing was such that the tops of the trees left standing provided a gap twenty feet wide, the entire length of the village. There would be two other such gaps, visible from the sky as parallel lines, admitting full midday sunlight but shutting out the omasha. "Nan—let's try to learn something about that big settlement in the south—the other parallel lines."

It was surprisingly easy to convey the question to Pakriaa with the help of signs, but her response when she understood it was a shrill snarl and shaking of her spear, a repetition of a name, "Vestoia," which seemed to be the place, and of another name, "Lantis," a name that caught in her throat and made her spit. Paul said, "We make faces at the south too, and do it fast." It seemed to appease the princess: she even smiled.

The area bordering the ditch had been left wild, a barrier of vines, brush, untended trees. Inside were orderly rows of plants, some broad-leaved, resembling beets, some bushy; another type was rangy with cosmos-shaped blooms of startling emerald green. Near the row of trees was a path which Pakriaa followed; under the trees stood grass-thatched structures. Paul counted thirty, well separated, before the princess left the path, and no sound came from them. The trees were mostly of the same species, thin-trunked towers with dark serrated leaves, blazing with scarlet blossoms like the one Pakriaa wore. They were the source of an odor like frangipani which filled the village, heady and sweet but clean. It was no primitive agriculture in this part-sunny corridor: rich darkness of earth was drawn up about the plants; there was not a weed in sight. And there was no trace of the strangling purple vines.

Pakriaa's male attendants had slipped away; her spear-women accompanied her through an opening into the next corridor, where her people were waiting for her, the soldier women in three formal ranks. There were about fifty in each rank, and here again were dyed skirts of every color but the regal blue that was Abro Pakriaa's. Small faces maintained the flat indifference of the unliving copper they resembled.

Pakriaa's intricate oratory flowed over them. More than two thirds of the stiff soldiers were gashed with recent wounds, ranging from scratches to lost hands or breasts or eyes. Some had deep body wounds so ugly it was amazing that they could stand upright, but there seemed to be no evidence of infection and there was no wavering in the lines while Pakriaa declaimed. Her right hand soared with spread fingers. The lifeboat? The name Torothee occurred; when it was repeated the women swayed with unchanging faces, murmuring it in unison like a breath of wind. Pakriaa faced her guests. Tears were not unknown to her; laughter might be. She clenched and relaxed her hands, the fourteen fingers rising and falling until Paul lost count of the motions—more than twenty. She pointed to the soldiers, repeating the display more slowly and only ten times; then one hand rose alone with the thumb curled under. Paul muttered, "I think she's saying only 146 are left after the war, from—maybe three hundred."

Pakriaa laid her spear at Ann's feet. Paul advised: "Give her your knife, same way." Pakriaa took it and placed it across the spear and stood back, motioning to Ann to do the same. When the three had withdrawn, Pakriaa still made impatient gestures. Paul whispered, "Ed, you and I are trifling males. We stand further back."

"We do like hell," said Spearman in his throat.

"We do, just the same. It's nothing but ceremony. Safety's off on my .38. We can handle anything. Stand back."

Ed Spearman stood back, muttering. At a shrill summons from Pakriaa, a shuffling procession swung out from the tree shadows. These were all men, decrepit, ancient, dirty; some limped and two had empty eye sockets and one, from a pathological fatness, could barely waddle. They were striped and splotched with paint in elaborate designs, mostly of white and yellow, and their skins, either with dirt or age, had darkened to dull mahogany. They formed a hobbling circle around the crossed knife and spear; each grotesque, as he passed the weapons, spat on them and scattered on them a handful of earth until the place became a low mound. As they did this, they muttered and howled and squeaked, performing precise evolutions with twiddling fingers. They carried white thighbones like clubs, and shell ornaments jangled on their raddled throats and ankles. It was, on the surface, a simple ceremony of peace and friendship, but the casual contempt of these male witches cast a foulness over it. Their sidelong glances at the strangers were poisonous with furtive malignancy. "Medicine men," said Paul under his breath. "Distant equivalent of the wise women in some patriarchal groups. Ed, we stay on the good side of those loopy scarecrows, or it's just too bad." And with a certain hunger he studied the mask of the man who had never offered the relaxation of friendship, wondering how far it was physically possible for Spearman to accept a world in which engineering science was the dream and crude survival the reality.

The ceremony ended in a dribble of anticlimax. The hideous old men merely shambled away from the mound toward the shadows after a ceremonial whoop that caused the soldiers to relax. But they did not quite go. They huddled and squatted under the trees. They stared. They spat and scratched and consulted together. Some of the green eyes were close-lidded, veiled; others were wide, making no effort to conceal a hatred compounded of jealousy and fear. The fat monster nursed his obscene belly between scrawny knees and whispered a stream of information into the close ear of a witch with empty eye sockets, and the whispering dark lips wore a destroying smile.

8 Abro Pakriaa motioned her guests to be seated before a large building; the fibers of this structure were dyed the blue of her skirt. The soldiers stalked about in a show of nonchalance. Young men and naked children had come timidly from the houses. The youngest children were disproportionately tiny, large-headed but no bigger than house cats. Perhaps childbirth for this race was no more than a passing inconvenience. There were many pairs of obviously identical twins. The children stayed near the protective men, all but the older girls, who ventured somewhat closer.

It was a village without laughter. No scampering, no horseplay, no evidence of any tenderness except between the men and the smallest children. Curiosity burned in all of them, but its overt expression was limited to the deadpan stare.

Pakriaa entered her blue building alone, greeted by a flutter of voices from within, and she was gone several minutes. When Pakriaa had seated her guests, most of the ancient painted males had shuffled across the clearing— even the fat horror whose walking must have been pain —to settle in the shadows on the other side and continue their baleful watching. Paul noticed that even the spear-carrying women skipped clear to give them elbow-room and never looked directly at them. The fat witch found a place to squat that gave him a clear view of all three visitors; as he gazed he sucked toothlessly at the knob of his thighbone club.

The houses were lightly framed of wood, with walls of interwoven fiber two thirds of the way to the eaves, joints bound and roofs thatched with the same material, a design similar to what Paul remembered from a year spent

in the Republic of Oceania. The modern citizens of that
many-islanded republic, Paul recollected, still preferred
the ancestral savage building pattern to stone or plastic;
it suited the climate and the friendly, unpretentious way
of life. But none of the buildings here was raised on
supports: snakes and vicious insects were evidently no
problem. There were no domestic animals, apparently no
parasites nor self-evident diseases; except for wounds
and the dirt of the old men, the pygmy skins looked clear
and healthy. There were not even any bad smells except
the mildly disagreeable oil the males used to anoint their
bodies.

Pakriaa returned, with her make-up on. She had flowers
behind both ears, and one tied by its stem to Dorothy's
locket. Heavy white circles were drawn about the lady's
eyes and breasts and navel; blue bracelets dangled at her
wrists; her skirt had been replaced by an innocently un-
concealing fringe of shells—similar to snail shells, Paul
thought. Pakriaa's anklets of wooden beads were orange.
The top of her bald head was robin's-egg blue. Two males,
with the brand marks that must mean slavery, followed
her with a seat—a block of wood, cleverly carved with
stylized animal figures. It brought her face on a level
with Ann's. Ann said politely, "Why the hell can't I be
handsome too?" And Pakriaa inclined her head. A boy
without the slave brand came with a wooden bowl; Pakriaa sipped the greenish liquid and offered the bowl to
Ann. Spearman rumbled. Paul said, "Protocol. You gotta,
Nan, but don't offer us any—we're meek males."

Ann swallowed some; her eyes watered; she repressed
choking. "Alcholic, I do mean . . ."

Feasting followed—a laborious hour of it, as food arrived without pause in the hands of branded men from the
other side of the sheltering trees. Wood smoke drifted
from that direction, and a hum of voices. All the dishes
included meat cut in tiny cubes—stewed, fried, boiled, or
smothered in unknown vegetables. Only one course was
aggressively horrid, carrion swimming in peppery sauce,
clearly a favorite of Pakriaa's, for she belched wonderfully
and patted her stomach in self-applause. Ann remarked,
"Another go at that and I start looking for another
planet."

In time even Pakriaa had had enough. She clapped her broad hands. Greasy-mouthed and bulging, the soldiers formed a swaying, stamping line. Spearman burped helplessly. "All that inside, and they can dance?"

Ann suggested: "Maybe it helps. . . ."

It was an hour-long narrative dance, vastly monotonous, a picture of war. Some of those most cruelly wounded pranced into solo pantomimes bragging of how the injuries had been received. In climax, a straw figure of a woman was dragged to the center of the clearing: an image carefully made, brightly painted, the face hideous, the sexual features grossly exaggerated. Shrilling what seemed to be a name ("Lantis! Lantis!"), the soldiers swarmed on this effigy, squealing, stabbing, defiling, tearing it into shreds, which they carried away as treasures or mementos.

When the soldier women had finished in yawning exhaustion, a crowd of dainty men performed another sort of dance, purely an erotic show, indicating that the role of the male was seductive, half infantile, submissive all the way. Occasionally a soldier pulled a dancer out of the line, slapping his face until he stopped the squealing that was evidently required of him, and wandered away with him; but most of the soldiers were too tired, gorged, or wounded to be interested. Later, some twenty soldiers formed a group, and men brought them babies to be nursed, morsels of humanity, quite silent, far smaller in proportion than Earth's newborn. The mothers' arms were careful and competent, without tenderness; they held the infants two at a time, examining them shrewdly, often exchanging them with other soldiers. There were a few cooing demonstrations of affection by the men toward these infants, demonstrations which the soldiers ignored. Ann whispered, "I could spend a lot of time hating these little devils."

"Try not to."

"I know, Paul, but—"

"At least they have a civilization." Spearman was arguing with himself. "A potential technology. That's good gardening. Good tools, weapons."

"Nan, see if you can ask Mrs. President to show us the town."

Pakriaa caught on swiftly and was delighted. . . .

The first of the tree-sheltered areas contained all the dwelling houses, dulled by the splendor of Pakriaa's. Ann was invited to enter this blue palace, Pakriaa making it clear that the men must not follow. Ann emerged, red-faced. Later, when it would not be so patent that she was talking of Pakriaa's house, Ann said, "Couldn't make out much detail. Dim, and no lamps burning, though I think I saw some clay things like old Roman lamps. Clean, funny perfume smells. I met—her mother maybe. Incredibly old anyway, and almost black. Their skin must change color with age."

"Dirt more likely," Spearman said.

"Not a bit of it. Very clean. Just a dry little ghost in a fancy room of her own, with a—a male slave manicuring her toenails. We haven't seen any old women out in the open."

"Sheltered and reverenced, maybe," Paul said. "Natural."

"Her Highness has a—I suppose you'd have to call it a harem. Ten little husbands, or maybe eleven."

"What a girl!" said Spearman.

Ann was amused, though her cheeks were flaming. "I was offered one."

"Hope you explained the rejection implied no lack of merit."

"I tried to, Paul. I think I got over the idea that there was a taboo involved—something like that. Her Majesty didn't insist. . . ."

The ditch enclosed the village. One side of its square paralleled the river, not more than thirty feet from it but making no connection. It would have been easy to flood the ditch, but that was evidently not the intention. When Ann conveyed curiosity, Pakriaa was astonished that anyone could be ignorant of its function. "*Kaksma!*" she said, and pointed west. "Kaksma . . . !" Convinced at last that Ann's puzzlement was genuine, she drew a picture on the earth, with such vigorous art that she herself feared the image and drew back. It was a profile view of an animal larger than a rat, long-headed with a hump on the back. She had given it a tiny eye and a forward-thrusting tooth nothing like a rodent's; the forefoot was broad and flattened, a digger's foot. Giving Ann only

a brief time to study it, Pakriaa spat on the image and
wiped it out with a violent heel. She muttered an angry
incantation and pointed to the dry wood heaped by the
ditch, while her dancing fingers told of flames that would
defend the village. . . .

In the second tree-sheltered area were the industries.
Men, not slaves, glanced up from the shaping of earthenware vessels. They had no potter's wheel, only their hands,
but there was a kiln of baked earth. Pakriaa called a favorite over, hugged him, and sent him back with a pat
on the rump. He was quite old, toothless, and giggling.
They passed a row of dye pots, three women braiding
fiber into flat sheets, a square of ground with part-finished
spearheads, arrow points, other devices, a rack where
deerlike hides were stretched in some curing process.
"They sleep on those," Ann said, "and use 'em for rugs.
The palace was full of 'em. . . ."

In the rear of the village was a stockade of stripped
logs, guarded by two soldier women. In the space before
it, but facing away from it so that the painted eyes
brooded over the village, stood a monstrous wooden idol,
eight feet tall, raised on a low platform. Pakriaa led her
guests before the image and knelt. It was necessary to
do the same, and Ann imitated her gracefully enough.
As he knelt himself, Paul saw in a backward glance
that three gangling male witches had followed and were
observing every motion with a rigid malevolence. It was
difficult to kneel with his back to them; Spearman, he
hoped, had not seen them.

The idol was exaggeratedly female, with huge carnivo-
rous teeth indicated in white paint. A slot representing the
left hand carried a nine-foot spear upright. The right arm,
a natural branch of the log, reached forward and spread
into a rugged table; more wood had been neatly joined
to make the table five feet long, but the whole gave the
effect of a swollen accepting hand, and it was foul with
bloodstains old and new. Pakriaa's long murmured prayer
repeated the name Ismar many times. At the end she
seemed satisfied; her glance at Ann was almost a smile.
Paul saw that the witches had drifted away, but the
pressure of their watching remained.

Pakriaa now took them into the stockade. It seemed to

Paul that the guards were scarcely needed. . . .

These naked men, women, and children had no danger in them. No life. They moved and functioned as if in life: walked, spat, scratched, yawned; a woman nursed a baby mechanically; a man strolled to a trough in the center of the compound and ate a handful of damp stuff like poultry mash, then rubbed his side against the wooden edge as a pig might. Beyond such elemental motions there was no life. A woman followed a man for several paces; both flight and pursuit were dull, unfinished, a fumbling response to a sluggish stimulus. They paid no attention to Pakriaa and the strangers. The slack emptiness of their faces denied the possibility of any thought more than a flurry in response to physical need. They were all over-plump; some of the females were scarred, but the wounds were old and healed. Paul could see no anatomical differences between them and their lively free kindred. A drug . . . ?

Pakriaa walked among them like a farmer in a flock of chickens. She lifted a young girl, who made no effort to escape, and showed her to Ann with contented pride, pinching a fat thigh and middle. The child was limp, unexcited, mumbling a mouthful of the mash. Fighting back a retching, Ann muttered, "Paul, when can we get out of here?"

Abro Pakriaa caught the tone. She tossed the little girl away and led them out of the stockade. She seemed hurt rather than angry—disappointed that her important friends had shown no admiration at this thriving industry. . . .

The soldiers had gathered again in the clearing, but now there was a waiting, a tension with the descent of twilight, and a gloom. A long fire had been built; Pakriaa's wave at her guests appeared to mean that they should sit where they pleased. Ann had not been able to convey the wish for an escort home, and Pakriaa's mind was plainly filled with some other, graver concern, having no more time for hospitality. Pakriaa entered her blue house. While she was gone, the soldiers seated beyond the fire scattered handfuls of earth in synchronized motions and the witches grouped behind them set up a monotone of chanting. Pakriaa returned wearing a white skirt, bare of all her paint and jewelry; she walked back and forth along the line of the fire, praying, until daylight was wholly gone. At her call, old men, neither painted nor grotesque, carried out burdened hides and laid them open beside the fire: white bones, broken weapons, skirts, loincloths, necklaces, arrows, little earthen pots and wooden bowls, many images of clay. The soldiers threw themselves face down, their foreheads on their arms, and wailed.

Spearman's voice was tortured with perplexity: "Eat some, mourn for others. Murder them and love them—"

"Yes, they're human."

"Oh, shut up, Paul. What do you mean, human? These animals?"

"Human mourning, isn't it? Listen to it."

Ann spoke with held-in fury: "At least we're not cannibals. There may still be war back on Earth, but after all—"

"Better to murder in groups of a thousand at long distance? Just listen to it, Ann. . . ."

It was music, becoming after a time the only thing existing under the red moon and the delicate unceasing dance of blue fireflies. It was the music they had heard on the first night in the jungle, a pouring forth of lamentation, wonder, supplication, whatever the spirit may feel in the contemplation of death and its troubling counterpart. A music that was meant to go on unchanging as the song of tree frogs for the thirteen hours of a night of Lucifer. . . . Pakriaa took no vocal part in the ritual, but sat alone, guarding the relics of the fallen. From time to time small man shapes carried new fuel to the fire. And there were stern sidelong glances from the princess: she had not forgotten her guests. Once or twice Paul caught himself dozing off, dragged into a partial hypnosis by the endless lamentation. . . .

"Paul?"

"Yes, Nan. I'm awake." He saw Spearman's head jerk upright.

"Doc asked me yesterday—if I would bear him a child."

Spearman's arm sought for her gently. "Why bring that up now? Can't think with all this damn caterwauling."

"I—did get to thinking. . . . Everything we used to live

by—it's so far away. Paul, you're close to Doc. You understand him, I guess."

Two troubled faces were turned to Paul in the mystery of firelight. A glance from Pakriaa conveyed annoyance at the sound of voices. "Dorothy told me she wants Sears to be the father of her second. It won't take her away from me. Not natural perhaps, but right under the circumstances. Some of the most important laws and customs can't be started by us. They'll be established by our grandchildren, if we can have them."

"I know." But her upward look at Spearman's worried, half-angry face said that her decision would be made by him, no other.

"He mustn't talk. The queen no like. . . ."

It might have been an hour later that Paul saw Spearman's head sag down on his chest. Ann leaned against him, but his arm around her had gone slack. Paul searched for the cause of a sense of danger that prickled his skin. Not the witches: they were grouped as before, chanting a faint counterpoint to the soldiers' wailing. No—it was Ed Spearman himself, and Paul came broad awake in a certainty of what would happen. Too late. Spearman's head twitched, and his unconscious throat let loose a resonant, uncompromising snore, a snore that had been famous on the great ship *Argo*. Sears Oliphant had always claimed that if only Ed could be harnessed in sleep to the reaction chamber . . . But this was not going to be funny. . . .

Pakriaa leaped up and shrieked a raging order. The wailing ceased. The soldiers were staggering upright, grabbing spears, forming a circle of violence around the guests before Spearman could even rise. He gasped, "Wha's matter?" and ten pygmy women were hauling him away by wrists and ankles, clear of the ground.

Paul shouted. "Don't fight 'em, Ed! Keep quiet!" Two soldiers were clinging to each of his own arms, there was a ring of shivering spears around him, and others had dragged Ann out of sight, but she was screaming as if they could understand: "Don't hurt him! He didn't do anything! Let him go!"

Without twitching his hampered arms, Paul moved

slowly against the circle of spears. They had no quarrel with him, he sensed, but only meant to restrain him: it was at least the only action worth a gamble. The spear-women stepped backward away from him. The whole circle moved in slow motion, following where Spearman had been carried—through the tree shelter, on across the next clearing, and into the space before the looming god.

Ed had not been able to snatch his rifle; he still had his holstered automatic. Paul could not see Ann, nor Pakriaa. He could see Spearman's face, a concentration of craft and fighting fury. The pygmy women lifted him and flung him on the table before the idol. He was ready. He bounced like a great cat, gained his feet, and twitched out the pistol, which banged once—at the huge blade of the idol's spear. The stone blade crumbled; the crash of the little gun made his captors wince back in shocked reaction. Then Ed Spearman stooped, grasped the reaching wrist of the idol, and heaved upward with the whole of his strength.

The god swayed, groaned like a thing of life, and toppled over, squashing one of the howling witches—a blind one—like a red bug.

The village dropped into total silence. Paul could see Ann now. The pygmies had let her go. The whiteness of her face had more than terror in it: it had exultation, a glory of excitement and wrath. Paul's own captors had lurched away; his automatic had slipped into his hand without conscious effort; he searched in desperation for something that might restore his friends to steadier sanity. "Walk," he said. "Walk, don't run, to the nearest exit. . . ."

The pygmies allowed it. The god had fallen. They even stood back, too profoundly dazed for any thought or protest. . . . At the edge of the village Spearman jumped in the ditch, reached for Ann, swung her up on the other side. "Did anyone bring a flashlight?"

"Oh, I—I did," said Ann, and began to cry. "Brought flashlight—'stead of gun. . . ."

Paul stayed in the rear. "They won't follow, I think. Not for a while."

The stooping passageway was hard to find. But when they won clear of it there was the guiding sound of the stream. Paul held the flashlight on the line of stepping stones until the others had crossed. Ann was still weeping in reaction. "We'll never win. It's all madness—the ship, everything. All human beings are crazy, crazy—"

"Hush, dear," Spearman said. "We got out, didn't we?"

Now, where was the trail? A madness of groping, blundering, where there was no path, no guidance, and even their little thread of light a mockery and confusion.

Abruptly, ahead of them, there were other lights, then voices—Mijok's soft rumbling, Wright's clear outcry: "There they are! All three, Mijok—"

Paul ran to him. "The others—Dorothy? Sears?"

"Right as rain, son," Wright mumbled. "Except Dot's been frantic about you since we heard the shot. We left Sears practically sitting on her—well, figuratively. Women are odd, you know: they don't like shots in the night when the best boy friend is out on the tiles."

"Had a little trouble. They may come after us—don't know . . ."

Ann was quiet. Paul saw her white hands starfished on the gray of Mijok's chest. She said, "Mijok, I'm tired and sick. Will you carry me?"

Spearman groaned: "Ann, what—Use your head. . . ."

But Mijok knelt at once to make a cradle of his arms, and Christopher Wright said, "Why not? Why shouldn't we need each other?" Mijok went ahead with her on the blind trail.

Paul heard Spearman choke: "I would have carried her." It was not meant to be heard. Paul looked away, hearing also the deep precision of the giant's voice exploring the mystery of words: "You are my people. I will not ever be much time far from you."

"You really have something there," Spearman was cor-

Part Two

The Year One

1 "THIS ISLAND IS EDEN." SEARS OLIPHANT SPOKE DROW-
SILY. Toy bat wings flickered from the woods crowning the
hillside, hovered over a pond: *illuama.* In a scant year of
Lucifer time (seventeen months of the calendar of Earth)
native names had become natural, mostly Mijok's names.

Two red-moon changes ago, in the final jading month
of the rains, the pygmy word "kaksma" had been only a
symbol. Now it woke the image of a village desolate,
bones scraped and scarred. The mind's eye winced in pity
—a sentry careless, a bridge left in place after dark;
thousands of ratty bodies rustling down from the wet hills,
over open ground, swimming swollen streams, finding the
bridge before oil on the rain water in the ditch could be
ignited. Small bodies, not swift, leaping or humping along
like furry worms, sniffing, squeaking, their stabbing teeth
dark with the blood of any flesh that moved. The north-
ernmost of the villages allied with Pakriaa's had already
returned to jungle.

But here, ten miles offshore from the coastal range, no
kaksmas lived; Sears and Paul, in two days of study on this
second visit, had established that. No wide wings lurked in
the sky. The hilly island had no large meadows where omasha could hunt. Three giants had been flown to the island
a month ago—the girl Arek, her mother Muson, and old
Rak. They said it was a place of calm. Their soft talk
could be heard up the slope, where a log building was
growing. Paul stretched, lean and comfortable, on the grass,
glad to be alone for a while with this least demanding of
his friends.

Sears was fatter, but hardened, a round block of man,
with a coarse black beard, kindness of brown eyes un-
altered. Christopher Wright, waiting at the "fortress" by

Lake Argo and no doubt frantic for word of this exploration, had let his beard grow too, sandy gray. Spearman and Paul had stayed clean-shaven, with soap made from fat and wood ashes. "The others must come here, Paul. I suppose Chris won't consent till Pakriaa agrees—damn, you'd think she could see it. She knows her enemies fear the ocean as she does. Lantis' two-by-four army would never chase after us in their lake boats."

"Wait a minute, Jocko. Lantis is no two-by-four proposition."

"Damn pint-size Napoleon with four teats and a grass skirt."

"Lookee: that settlement south of Lake Argo is thirty miles long. Equivalent of two hundred villages, to Pakriaa's six. Say twenty thousand warriors who got their pride hurt a year ago when the crash of *Argo* swamped their fleet and scared the pants off 'em. They'll have replaced the fleet. They'll come overland too. Lantis, Queen of the World."

"If they do"—Sears' heavy voice had the tremor that he himself hated—"the firearms should be at least one ace in the hole."

"Ye-es. Ed's pistol helped in our one bad scrape with Pakriaa herself. But it was his smashing the idol that stalled 'em, not the gun."

"Poor little Abro Pakriaa!" Sears spoke with tenderness. "If ever a lady was pulled seven ways from Sunday! Wants our way of life, doesn't want it. Wants to grasp Chris' ethics, doesn't want to. Afraid of Ed's strength and aggressiveness, admires 'em too, oh my, yes. Tries to believe the god Ismar died or never lived—but can't, quite."

"And can't understand why our women are gentle— Dorothy anyway——"

"Nan's toughening up is conscious effort, Paul. Superficial. She's made herself hunt, shoot well, act hard, because her brain tells her she should. If we could only find something to restring her violin! I think she's given up hope of it: nothing I've found so far has been any good. She doesn't see that Dorothy does more for us by remaining the person she always was. . . . You know, when I go alone to Pak's village, I just set. Even the witches have got used to me, not that they wouldn't gut me if they could."

"Jocko"—Paul looked away—"you told me once you were scared all the time. When you go there alone—or when you tame the olifants for that matter—are you sort of grasping the nettle? And does it work?"

"Don't ask me, friend. Because I don't exactly know. I was never a brave man." Brown eyes misted in what was partly laughter. "Oy, the witches! There's the big enemy in the battle for Pakriaa's mind. Chris may claim they aren't real witch doctors, just advisers, low-grade magicians. I'm not so sure. Priests of Ismar, and when Ed clobbered the idol Pakriaa did consider having 'em all burned alive. Point is, she didn't do it. They gnaw away in the dark at all we try to teach her. That proposed bonfire, by the way, is gossip passed on to me in confidence by Abara."

"There's a dear little man."

"Ain't he though?" Smiling into late sky, Paul envisaged the wizened red midget riding the white monsters that Sears had tamed and insisted on naming olifants-with-an-f. A painting might grow out of that, he thought, squat coppery lump astride of massive white—it might, if the desire to paint should ever wake again and be as strong as it once was on *Argo*, when his mind's eye could remember Earth without distortion. Abara, popeyed and potbellied, a favorite in Pakriaa's harem, had been commissioned by her as a student and go-between at the lakeside camp; Sears had not only adopted him as an olifant trainer, but suspected him of furtively possessing a sense of humor. "Well—the giants. Lantis will always have thought of them as wild animals——"

"Sears"—Paul rolled over and pressed his face in the grass—"can we ask or even permit the giants to tangle in a pygmy war?"

"Ah . . . It's tormenting Chris too, ever since Lantis sent that ultimatum." He snarled in his beard, "Thirty fat meat slaves every two months! There's politics for you. Dirtiest way she could answer Pak's challenge to personal combat, and the automatic refusal makes an excuse to come and clean up. Sounds like home. . . . Mijok wants to help fight—says he does."

"It's still our responsibility." Paul sat up. His eyes kept returning to the towering courage of the trees. Brave as any cathedral spire, scarcely one was free from the clutch of the purple-leaf vine. "As for moving here to the island, Pak sees it, but the idea's too new. You just don't pull up stakes, venture on the Big Water, crossing forbidden kaksma country."

Sears chewed a grass blade. "Anyway we've got to bring Dorothy and the baby here, and Ann. Dorothy won't fuss, will she, son?"

"Since there *is* Helen—no, she won't. I still dream sometimes, as I did during her first pregnancy. Things, shapes, trying to pull her away—or she's where I can't find her, can't push through the leaves."

"She told me. It's something else that's made you blue lately."

"No."

Sears watched him. "Yes. . . . Want to start back tomorrow?"

"Might as well. We've learned all we need."

"Mm . . . Second thoughts about the daddy of Dorothy's second——"

"No no. We settled that. She's proud to be carrying it."

"Good genetics could be damn bad psychology."

"No, Jocko. Don't think that. She's close to me as ever."

Sears waited and spoke softly: "New York late on a rainy night, a few car lights moving, street-lamp reflections like golden fish——"

"Orange paintbrush in New Hampshire meadows—— We'd better stop."

"We better. I want boat whistles—floating city coming out of the fog. Call it a slow-healing wound. . . . And look across the channel."

Paul saw it presently: a cliff formation in the coastal range made a brow, nose, and chin. Below this, rounded rock could be a shoulder straining in heroic effort; then, tumbled reality of mountain—fancy must supply whatever held the figure in bondage. "Yes. He looks west. Past us, at the sun."

"Why, no, Paul. I think he looks west of the sun. . . ."

A red-furred girl wandered down from the woods. "I got tired." Arek had lived twenty-two years; she was seven feet tall, not yet adolescent but near it. In the next Red-Moon-before-the-Rains, ten months away, she might take adult part in the frenzy of love if her body demanded it:

if not, she would go apart with the other children, whose play also became innocently erotic at that time, and help care for the youngest. Sears grinned as she sat down with them. "Tired or lazy?"

"Both. You Charins are never lazy enough." The name Charin, Paul thought, was almost natural now, a pygmy word for "halfway," intended by Pakriaa merely to convey that Wright and his breed were halfway in size between her people and the giants, but Wright took sardonic satisfaction in it as a generic name. "Work and loafing are both good. Why can Ed Spearman never sit still in the sun? Or maybe I like to talk too much."

"Never," Sears chuckled. "Well—his best pleasure is in action. Maybe it's the technician in him—he must always be doing something."

"Like always waking, never sleeping." She sprawled in comfort; her broad hands plucked grass, scattered it over the furry softness of her four breasts. "Green rain. . . . I want to stay on this island. Will they come?"

"We hope so. Mijok will as soon as Doc does."

She sighed. "Mijok is a beautiful male. I think I'll take him for my first when I'm ready. . . . And soon the pretty boat will be no more good. It's sad we can't make another. Tell me again about Captain Jensen. He was as tall as me? He had hair on his head, red like my fur. He spoke——"

"Like storm wind," said Paul, supplying the wanted note in a favorite fairy tale, remembering a brother on Earth who was—perhaps—not dead.

"Hear the ocean," Arek whispered. Paul could hardly separate the sound from the mutter of the pond's outlet. This ridge of high ground ended short of the island's northern limit. A white beach, where the lifeboat was shaded from late sun, faced the mainland. West of the beach a red stone cliff ran to the tip of the island, shouldering away the sea. Wind out of the west allowed no soil to gather on it. Now and then a rainbow flashed and died above the rock, when a wave of uncommon grandeur spent itself in a tower of foam. "Hear what it says? 'I—will—try—aga-a-ain. . . .' Why must the others wait to come here?"

"Pakriaa's people are not ready."

"Oh, Sears!" Arek laughed unhappily and sat up. "I think of how my mother taught me the three terrors. She took me to the hills, beat two stones before a burrow till one blundered out maddened, afraid of nothing but the light. She crushed it, made me smell it. I was sick; then we fled. I think of how she flung an *asonis* carcass into meadow grass, so the omasha came. She wounded one with a stone, made me watch while the others tore it apart. Later still, when I could run fast—ah, through night to a village of the Red Bald——"

"Please, dear—pygmies. That's a name they accept."

"I'm sorry, Sears. . . . Yes, we hid in the dark, waited until a sentry moved—careless. . . . It was wrong. You've shown us how such things are wrong. And memory's someone talking behind you, out of the big dark."

"The laws we've agreed on—— "

"I do honor them," she said gently. "The law against murder was my first writing lesson. But—what if Pakriaa's tribe—"

"They're slower," Sears said in distress, and the distress would be as much a message to Arek as any words. There was no hiding the heart from these people: green eyes and black ears missed no smallest nuance.

"When will they know they must not dig pits, with poisoned stakes—"

"But Pakriaa's tribe don't do that now. Do they?"

Arek admitted: "I suppose not. But the six other villages——"

"Five, dear. The kaksmas. And only two months ago, Arek."

She stared at Paul with shock. " I *had* almost forgotten. But they do still hate us. The day before you flew us here, Paul, I met Pakriaa and two of her soldiers in the woods. I gave them the good-day greeting. Oh, if one of you had been there she would have answered it. . . . Wouldn't the island be better without them? Some of *you* don't like them. Even Dorothy only tries to like them. Since the baby was born, Paul, she—shrinks when they come to the fortress. They don't know it, but I do."

Dimly, Paul had known it, known also that it was a thing Dorothy would consciously reject. "Time, Arek.

You'll live a hundred and fifty years or better—more than three pygmy lifetimes. You'll see them change."

Speaking almost like a Charin, Arek said, "They'd better."

They strolled up the hill; the other giants' labor had ceased. The building was a sturdy oblong, intended as storehouse and temporary communal dwelling for them all, including (Wright hoped) some of Pakriaa's people. Rafters were not yet in place. For that, Rak needed the strength of another like himself: chubby Muson tired easily. Someday a road would climb from the beach, traversing the ridge which was the backbone of the northern half of the island. Here, where spring water filled the pond and rushed on down to carve a small harbor below the beach, would be Jensen City, and the three races of Lucifer would learn to live there in good will and pleasure under a government of laws. So Wright said— peering at photographs, teasing his gray beard, tapping thin fingers on the map drawn on the paper of Earth, on the new maps of whitebark. Paul could see it too—sometimes; glimpse the houses, gardens, open places. South of the pond, a wheat field, for on Lucifer the wheat of Earth grew to four feet and bore richly. Near the field, perhaps the house for Dorothy and himself, with no doorway lower than ten feet.

At other times he could see only defeat—the arrogance and blind drive of genus *Charin*, species *Semisapiens* beating against the indifference of nature, the resentment of other life. He could see his people destroyed, by accident or anger, the giant friends adrift with only hints of the new life and spoiled for the old. Then he would stop trying to foresee and would make his mind's ear listen to Wright insisting: *"Give protoplasm a chance. Patience is the well-spring. . . ."*

The walls were eleven feet in height. Rak and Muson rested on the coolness of bare ground within; Rak pointed at the top of the walls where rafters would rest. "Slow," he said, "and good." Rak could not be sure how old he was. When Mijok had first persuaded him to the camp ten months ago, Rak had won his English with the grave precision of a mason selecting fieldstone. His language had none of the flexibility and scope that Mijok and others had achieved, but it served him. After absorbing basic arithmetic, Rak had deliberated on the problem of his age—squatting at the gate of the stone fortress by Lake Argo, spreading out rows of colored pebbles to indicate years, rainy seasons, episodes of hunting or fear or passion too keen to forget. At last he had come up with the figure of 130 years. "But," he said, "there are two times. In here"—he patted an ancient scar on his belly—"and there." He pointed at the red crescent moon.

"I'll cook supper," Arek said. Muson bubbled and shadowboxed with her daughter. Muson would laugh at anything—the flutter of a leaf, a breath of breeze on her red-brown fur. Paul followed to help Arek trim the carcass of an asonis killed the night before. Hornless, short-legged, fat, the bovine animal was abundant on the island; its one enemy here was what Arek called *usran,* a catlike carnivore the size of a lynx, which could tackle only the young asonis or feeble stragglers. Rak hunted in the old way. Bow, club, spear, even rifle, had been explained to him, but the stalk, the single rush and leap, the grasp of a muzzle and backward jerk that snapped the neck before the prey could even struggle—these were Rak's way still. In the old life, Rak's age would have led him eventually to a few dim years with a band of women, who would have fed him until he chose to wander into deep jungle, preventing any from following. When far away, he would have sat in the shadows to wait—for starvation or the black marsh reptiles or a great mainland cat, *uskaran,* which never attacked a giant in the prime of strength. Rak would have taken no harm from the young men in this weakness: his own territory would have been inviolate, and he would have joined the women, in a taciturn farewell to life, only when teeth and arms had failed. ("We're gentle people," Mijok said, puzzled at it himself. "In the Red-Moon-before-the-Rains we only play at fighting. It's not like what we see the other creatures do at that time. How could one 'possess' a woman? Do I possess the wind because I like to run against the touch of it . . . ?")

The meat hung from a makeshift tripod; Arek jumped back, startled, as a furry thing scampered down. It was like a kinkajou except for the hump on the back (a true hindbrain in the spine: Sears had long ago verified that guess of Wright's). "Little rascal," Paul said. "Let's tame it."

"What?" Arek was bewildered. "Do what?"

"Do these live on the mainland?"

"I never saw one till I came here. Too small to eat. Tame it?"

"Watch." Paul tossed a bit of meat. The visitor's chatter changed to a whistling whine; it elongated itself, grabbed, sat back on stubby hind legs to eat in clever paws; it washed itself with a squirrel's pertness. Arek chuckled, examining the idea, and went on with her work; she had become a hypercritical cook, under Dorothy's guidance. "Jocko, biologist, stand by: I propose to name an animile. Genus *Kink*, species *quasikinkajou*." Genus Kink did not retreat at Sears' quiet approach, but wriggled a black nose.

"Rak asked in solemn curiosity, "For what is it good?"

"To make us laugh," Paul said, "so long as we're kind to it."

"Ah?" Rak moved his fingers to aid the patient mill of his mind.

"Dance-Nose," said Muson, who already understood. She shook all over. "Come, Funny-Nose." It would not— yet, but Muson could be patient too.

Sears whispered in his beard, "Less homesick?"

"Yes. . . ."

After the meal Arek wanted Paul to come out on the cliffs. Though there seemed no danger from the omasha, she carried a long stick and Paul took his pistol. The slope leveled out to the bare rock of the headland; the ocean voice was the humming of a thousand giants. The way was easy, with no crevasses, no peril while the wind was mild. Arek had often been out here alone. Yesterday Paul had seen her standing for an hour, watching the west where unbroken water met a sun-reddened horizon. In her earlier years there might have been dim mention of the sea by her almost wordless people, but no true knowledge: the mainland coast was steaming vine-choked jungle, or tidal marsh, and shut away by the kaksma hills. Paul wondered what member of his race could stand for an hour in contemplation like a thinking tree, not shifting a foot nor raising an arm . . . ?

"Paul, why did you leave Earth?" Arek patted the rock beside her.

Below the troubled water laughed, endlessly defeated and returning. Cloud fantasies gathered below a lucid green, and the wind was a friend. "I have doubted sometimes whether we ought to have done so."

"That wasn't my meaning. We love you. Didn't you know? But I've wondered what sent you away from such a place. Ann says it was beautiful."

"A—drive of restlessness. We took boundaries as a challenge. I used to think that a great virtue. Now I call it neither good nor evil."

"I think it is good."

"Everywhere, we carry good *and* evil."

"What you do here is good. You teach us. You do kind things."

"We can be bad. But for Doc Wright and his dreams that Ed Spearman finds so impractical, we'd have done you harm." Helpless at her innocence, Paul saw she did not believe him. "On Earth, we fought each other. We hunted for lies to make ourselves feel big. We created great institutions built on vanity-tickling lies: imperialism, communism—most of the isms you find so puzzling when we talk of Earth history. The anger of Charins rarely focused itself on the actual causes of unhappiness or injustice. Instead we hunted for scapegoats, easy solutions. We wouldn't study ourselves. Always we itched for something external to take the blame for our own follies and crimes."

"I don't understand."

"As if you stumbled on a root, Arek, and then banged your fist on the tree that grew it, to blame it for your own clumsiness."

"But Paul—only a very small child would act like that."

"Darling, let's watch the sunset." She felt his pain, touched his knee, and was silent until he said, "A poor naughty child . . ."

"There was a thing Ed Spearman said to me—what I wanted to talk to you about. I've never gone to Pakriaa's village. You know, even Mijok won't go there except with one of you. I asked Ed if Pakriaa still kept that stockade for drugging and fattening prisoners—in spite of her agreeing to the laws. He said yes, she did. I said it was not right. I said we made a law against slavery too. He said, 'Forget it, baby—one thing at a time.' I am not a baby. How can the laws govern us unless all obey them?"

"Ed—meant no harm, Arek. He only meant it does take time. The pygmies have more to unlearn. You—started clean. And—well—with the army of Lantis likely to come back at any time—we can't afford—"

Yet it seemed natural that this giant child, who had herself done murder in the old days, should answer his troubled evasions not only with reproach but with command: "If the laws are to govern us they must be respected by everyone. I wish I had gone to that village and torn down the stockade with my hands."

"And they would have killed you with a hundred spears and Pakriaa's people would hate us forever, learning nothing but more hatred."

Arek cried a little, rubbing at the unfamiliar wetness. "Maybe I begin to see, how difficult . . . The sun's going." But they sat quietly in the warm and undemanding wind until the first sapphire glint of fireflies dotted the slope where Jensen City might one day shine. Arek stood, reaching down an affectionate hand.

2 PAUL GLANCED DOWN AT SUNRISE-TINTED SNOW ON
the highest peak of the coastal range, thirteen thousand feet
above the sea. Prairie spread for thirty miles east of its
base; then came a region of forest and small lakes fed by
the outlet of Lake Argo, which was the core of the empire
of Lantis, Queen of the World.

Pakriaa's information on Lantis was a murky blend of
truth and fantasy. Lantis claimed birth from Ismar-Crea-
tor-and-Destroyer. Pakriaa had different theories. Originally
ruler of a single village, Lantis consolidated by conquest.
Instead of annihilating defeated villages she took their
populations captive, sorting out three categories: potential
followers, slave laborers, and meat. Many in the first class
became fanatically converted; those in the second provided a year or so of work before dying of whippings and
other abuse; captives of the third class were forced to eat
the green-flowered weed that numbed the brain and were
bled out at the right stage of fatness. In fifteen years one
riverside village had swollen to a city of sixty thousand,
fed by expeditions far to the east, and Lantis named her
city Vestoia—Country of Freedom and Joy. "Got anything new in the 'scope?"

Sears groaned: "There *are* more boats above the falls."

The boats, they knew, were broad canoes roofed like
sampans against the omasha, but with no sail. "Not moving, are they?"

"No—anchored maybe." Sears mopped his round face.

Without the telescope, Paul could see brownness on the
water of Lake Argo's southern end, near the spot where
the outlet tumbled over a high falls to a smaller lake. It
meant that hundreds more must have been portaged past

the falls from Vestoia during his two days on the island. . . .

The fifty red-green flowing miles became a pain of delay. Sears too would be aching for the gray square of their "fortress" to claim the eye in the north, touched by early sunlight, a brave structure twelve feet high, fifty square, built of split stone by the labor of giant friends. Outside it ran a moat twenty feet wide, ten deep, with a drawbridge of logs, bark matting, grass-fiber ropes, the bottom flooded with lake water. There was room within for living quarters, a supply of smoked meat, dried vegetables.

Lantis understood scaling ladders, Pakriaa said. Lantis had patience for a siege. There was no defense, Pakriaa said, in these measures. The only defense was to attack, to retreat, and attack again. It had always been so in the old wars. It was still so with this Lantis and her Big-Village-Vestoia, this bastard begotten of a red worm and Inkar, goddess of kaksmas. It would always be' so—at least, until . . . Paul remembered Dorothy, cherishing Helen at her brown breast, asking neutrally, "Until what, Abro Pakriaa?"

Pakriaa had studied the giants' walls with contempt. "Until I shame this worm spawn Lantis into meeting me alone. She must respect custom. Her first answer is a— what word?—rejection, because she has fear. I have sent a second challenge. She will meet me, or her own people will condemn her. I will pin her belly to the ground. Her government will be mine." There had been no mistaking it: for the first time in the year since the idol of Ismar fell and was not restored, Pakriaa was making vast decisions wholly her own, with only perfunctory interest in what the Charins might think. In her wrath against the mighty soldier ruler in the south there was natural grief at the outrages of past years, but something else too. Her red face glaring southward said: *She has what I desire; she is doing what I would do*. Pakriaa had finished her answer quietly: "It is *I* who will be Queen of the World."

Three days ago. It could have been a mistake to leave the camp at all. Now—a streak of sunshine on gray at the end of familiar meadow. With fuel for only a few more flights, Paul knew he had never made a better landing. The drawbridge was down. Dorothy ran to meet him. Sears was shouting, "Chris! It's perfect—no kaksmas —everything Paul said it was—"

Paul stammered, "You look like a million dollars."

"Dollars. What're those?"

"I forget. What's news?"

"Your funny mouth is tickling my ear."

"That isn't news, Dope. Helen—"

"Full of the best gurgles. Come and see." He thought: *How do I tell her of the boats, the thirty-mile hive of savage hatreds*—but Sears was already talking of it. Wright had no smile for Paul, only a warm gray-eyed stare and pressure of the hand. Paul asked, "Where's Ed? Mijok and the boys?"

Ann looked up from cutting a square of hide. She had not come to meet them. Ann's way nowadays; one's mind insisted: *It doesn't mean anything.* "Ed's hunting. Should have been back last night."

Dorothy added: "Mijok's off missionarying, with Elis and Surok. They took Blondie—Lisson, I mean: moral support."

Wright was hag-ridden. "Sears, if it were only Pakriaa's tribe—but—not fuel enough to fly all the giants over. We cannot abandon *them*."

"Then let's get the women there and the rest of us go overland."

Ann said, "I'm going overland."

Wright muttered, "Damn it, Nancy—"

Sears patted her shoulder and ignored her speech as she ignored the touch. "Chris, I've labored, myself, over that damn knotty little brain of Pakriaa's. She can't see things our way. We need a hundred years."

The conference lengthened into the morning. Sometimes it seemed to Paul that his teacher's stubbornness degenerated into the obsession of a man who won't leave a blazing house until the rugs are saved. Wright longed for the island, which he had seen only in photographs. There had always been some compelling reason why he must stay by the fortress, if only to hoe voracious weeds out of the gardens. Yet to Wright it was unthinkable that the island community should start without the pygmies: he returned to it with haggard insistence. "I know—*I* can't actually like Pakriaa—she's got a mind like a greased eel; but we've made a beginning. They speak our tongue—well. A people intelligent as they are—"

Paul thought: *It's not Lucifer that's aged him—it's us. We are not big enough.* Aloud he suggested: "Doc, can't we make a start without them and just keep the door open? Bring them in when we're stronger ourselves?"

"Oh, son, if we desert Pak now, she's finished. Overconfidence. Lantis will go over her like a tide. We might just turn that tide. If not, we *must* be ready to help her escape with—whatever's left. . . . Well, at least we agree on this: Helen and the women must go to the island, at once."

"Tomorrow." Dorothy choked. "If the boats haven't started yet—"

"All right, dear. Tomorrow. And one man should go with them."

"You," Paul said. "You."

Wright said inexorably, "No." His stare groped at Sears Oliphant.

Sears was nakedly desperate. "Chris, I beg of you—you must not ask me to go away from this battle." He was sweating, white. "I am—in a sense—a religious man. The —Armageddon within, your own phrase—please understand without my saying any more. Don't ask me to go."

"Ed won't go. . . . Paul?"

Leave him, with Sears' inner torments and Ed's arrogance? "No, Doc."

Ann Bryan said, "I'm staying for the show."

Dorothy lowered her cheek to the brown fuzz of Helen's head; the baby's absurd square of palm found Paul's finger. Helen was almost eight months old—Lucifer months. The new life in Dorothy had been conceived in the last month of the rains. Dorothy said, "I'm going, Nancy, with Helen. As a valuable brood mare, I can't afford heroism. Neither can you."

The giant women crossed the bridge; they had lingered outside, knowing the Charins needed to talk alone. Ann said, "I've heard the argument. I'm not pregnant yet. I've learned to shoot damn' well."

Wright asked, "Will you abide by a vote when Ed gets back?"

Ann pushed her fingers into black hair, cut short as a man's. "I suppose I must. . . . If no men get to the island, how do two women and a girl child increase and multiply, or shouldn't I ask?"

Wright mumbled inadequately, "We'll reach the island."

Ann said, "Then you already see it as a retreat?"

Wright was silent. He tried to smile with confidence at the giant women and children, who were sober with reflected unhappiness—all but nine-year-old Dunin, who trotted to Paul and hugged him with her large arms and announced: "I learned six words while you were gone. Hi, listen! 'Brain': that's here and here. 'Me-di-tation': that happens in the brain when it's quiet. Mm—mm . . . 'Breast': that's these. And 'breath': that's ooph, like that. 'Breeze': that's a breath with nobody blowing it. . . . I forgotten six."

Dorothy murmured. "Tem—tem—"

Dunin hopped up and down. "'Tempest!' Big *big* breeze—"

"That's perfect," said Paul. "Perfect. . . ."

Before the five-month rainy season had made travel on the sodden, gasping ground too miserable, Mijok had explored a half circle of territory forty miles in radius east of the hills, for others who might be willing to learn new ways. It was slow work, often discouraging. He had located two bands of free-wandering women and children —twenty in all—and stirred their curiosity and friendliness. But he had been able to recruit only three other males. There was Rak. Blackfurred Elis and tawny Surok were in vigorous middle years, hard to convince but quick to learn once the barrier was down.

Kamon was accepted leader of the women. White with age, gaunt, flat-breasted, stooped but quick on her feet, Kamon rarely smiled, but her good nature was profound. "Ann," she said, "you ought to go. We—if we cannot fight off these southern pygmies, we can escape. But you? One of us would have to carry you. And as Mashana Dorothy says, your womb is needed." (Mashana—sweetheart, mother, hunting companion, friend.)

Wright said, "You, Dorothy, Helen, and the giant children."

That brought murmuring. Kamon checked it: "Only four children still need milk. You, Samis, your breasts are big: you will go." Kamon turned with gentle deference to one authority she felt to be stronger than her own under the laws: "Doc?" Paul found it comfortable, no longer even amusing, that Wright should be known to the giants by his inevitable nickname. The pygmies disliked the short sound, and initial *D* always bothered them. To them he was Tocwright, or more often Tocwright-Who-Plays-with Gray-Fur-at-His-Throat.

"Yes, Kamon. Samis too. Paul, how many trips will that take?"

"Three—leaving fuel for about three more of the same length."

Wright nodded. "Ed has a notion of using the lifeboat for a weapon. Hedgehop, scare 'em to hell. But with fuel so low—"

There was shadow at the drawbridge. Ed Spearman flung aside the carcass he had brought. Ann's white face was still, though she clung to him briefly when he kissed her. It had occurred to Paul that Ann's image of love would not be given reality anywhere in the galaxies: she wished moments to be eternities and a human self to be a mirror of desire. *But Dorothy and I —somehow we've learned to let each other live. . . .* "More news," Spearman said. "I stopped at the village. A spy of Pakriaa's came home last night—must be a sharp article: did the sixty-odd miles up the lake shore in nothing flat, with facts and figures."

"Lantis is moving." Wright dropped his hands to his bony knees.

"No, Doc, but will in a day or so." Spearman sat down, holding Ann's fingers till she pulled them away. He nodded to Sears and Paul. "Good trip?" He had grown even more rugged in a year of Lucifer. He wore only shorts and Earth-made shoes; months of handling a heavy bow had made his upper arms almost as thick as the narrow part of Mijok's forearm. His face had deepened its lines; he had never smiled easily.

"Very good," Sears said. "The island is—" He was silent.

Spearman grunted. "You're sold too? Well, here's the news. One: you remember Pakriaa's second challenge, sent by two warriors, correct and formal—trust Pak for that. One of those messengers is returning. The spy ran on ahead—with part of the body of the other ambassador." He studied the sickened faces. "Two: the spy says Lantis plans to send four thousand on the lake boats, another six thousand overland. Pakriaa—who is in a state of mind I don't know how to describe, not jitters exactly—Pakriaa thinks we may feel the lake-boat drums tomorrow. She doesn't know what they are, by the way—invention of Lantis, I guess. From her description they must be drums, maybe hollow logs mounted on boats. She heard them last year in the war we interrupted. You feel them before you hear them, she says: she thinks it was a lake devil consulting with the Queen of the World. Three: the spy wasn't sure, but thinks Lantis has already sent six hundred east of the lake to make a big circle, come down on the settlement from the northeast."

"Smart," Paul said. "To drive us into the kaksma hills?"

"The kaksma hills." Spearman's gray eyes squinted in a sort of laughter. "They're not so bad. The critters may be all they say, after dark, but—I'd better own up: I've gone that way on my last three solo trips. Safe enough in daylight, when they're half blind. I killed a few today."

Sears asked quickly, "Bring back specimens?"

Spearman teased the fat man with waiting and chuckled and nodded at the asonis carcass. "Tied to one of the hoofs. Don't look so worried, Doc—I waded plenty of streams on the way back." He rose with heavy grace and strolled out on the bridge. "Come a minute, some of you." Paul joined him; Wright stayed as he was; Sears was examining the kaksma's gray, thick-tailed body, holding back its pinkish lip. Paul caught a repellent glimpse of the jutting upper canines; the molars were shearing tools like a cat's. He saw the spade claws of the forefeet. The jet eyes were like a mole's. "Look," Spearman said, "the hills. Notice that hogback at the southern end—it's five miles long. Riddled with burrows. They must live on small game on the meadow below and hunt the other side of the hills too, where it's jungle." His fingers dug at Paul's shoulder. He spoke loudly enough to be heard by all: "Listen: the earth at the burrows is red ocher. Understand? Hematite."

Wright let out his breath sharply. "So—"

"Yeah. Just a five-mile mountain of iron ore. Merely what I've been looking for ever since we crashed. For a start. From iron to steel to—ah . . . And just when we've *got* it—God! with organized pygmy labor—" He strode back into the fortress, glancing obliquely at the silent giant women. "The pygmies do understand work, you know. Well, never mind it now. Of course we must get the baby and the women to your island right away. As a temporary refuge, we must use it." He watched Wright with unqualified sadness. "Apart from that, you know what I think of your Island of Lotos-Eaters—"

"That's not just, Ed."

"Adelphi then. Well, the women and Helen—"

"And the giant children, with Samis to nurse the youngest."

Spearman asked evenly, "Paul, how's the charlesite?"

"After the trips Doc mentioned, enough for three more."

Ann's keen ears caught a far-off sound. "Mijok's coming back."

The music grew slowly manifest: Mijok, in an Earth song more than two hundred years old. Long-flowing chanteys and slower spirituals suited him. He had teased Ann to teach him all she knew, even after she lost interest. Swift melodies and rapid syllables were beyond him—the depth of his tone rendered them grotesque. More than a mile away, he was wallowing in "Shenandoah"—Mijok, to whom the ocean was only a word and a river steamboat the cloudiest of legends. Other voices, true on pitch, followed his solo:

"Away—we're bound away. . . ."

Paul asked, "How many, Nan?"

Ann shut her eyes. "Four, besides Mijok and—yes, Lisson's singing. At least two new recruits. Ah—they can sing before they talk." She hurried into that thatched house-within-a-house which was her corner of privacy on Lucifer. The giant women were smiling, though Kamon's eyes followed Ann with trouble and pity. They hummed in three-part counterpoint. Their voices had the range of a Charin baritone; Paul missed Muson, who could approach the tenor. Sears' bass moved in, a well-behaved trombone teasing a crowd of bassoons. Dorothy's alto added a warm thread of sound. . . .

The tall children and women poured out over the bridge when Mijok and his companions were still distant. Musical thunder in the woods pulsed along the ground. Spearman smiled indulgently. "Just like a bunch of kids."

"Yes," Wright said. "The pygmies are more serious. They have wars."

Sears stopped humming and mumbled, "Don't, Chris. . . ."

Mijok brought in his triumph, beaming and warm. "And my smallest woman?" Dorothy placed the naked morsel that was Helen in his waiting hands. Mijok was bemused. "How can anything be so small?"

Dorothy claimed: "Seven pounds at birth—that ain't hay, Mijok."

"Growing too," Elis said. The golden-furred girl Lisson tickled Helen's chest with the tip of a forefinger, and Mijok introduced the newcomers. One was timid. "Just a boy," Mijok explained. "Knows some words already, though. Danik?"

The giant boy whispered, "Good day." The other was older, black like Elis, trying to display stern indifference, but Surok eased him into relaxation with a few words in the old language.

For Mijok, speech had still the brilliance of newness but was wholly flexible; he reveled in colloquialisms, acquired mainly from Sears and Dorothy. "While the boys and I were out having a hell of a time, what's with local industries? The island, gentlemen?"

"Good," Sears said. "Better than I dared dream."

"And those tough babies in the south—anything new?" Sears winced. "That part ain't good."

Mijok fondled the fat man's arm with a hand mild as silk. "Now, Jock, now. We'll give 'em hell, that's what we'll do. Hey, Paul?"

3   ABARA TROTTED BETWEEN SEARS AND PAUL IN THE
forest aisle, a silent ugly man with popeyes, bulging underlip, jutting ears; thirty inches tall. He was twenty-six. His
potbellied softness had the beginning sag of middle age.
There was politics, Paul guessed, in his presence at the
camp—it was not because the queen had tired of him
that he was temporarily detached from the harem. His
body was agile for all its pokiness, his mind even more
nimble; his English, when he stooped to use it, was good.
After the noon meal Abara had appeared, crossing the
drawbridge like a wisp of red smoke, ignoring the giants,
reminding Sears obliquely that it was three days since he
had visited the clearing near the camp, where the white
olifants had learned to come.

Sears' love for the great leaf eaters had deepened with
familiarity. He had easily persuaded the others to guaran-
tee their permanent protection in the laws. He had taught
the pygmies to call them olifants, a shrewd stroke, conveying to the Neolithic mind that the animals were of
Sears' totem. Even during the long ordeal of the rains he
had gone alone for whole days and nights, following olifant trails, sitting in patience where a broad-leaf tree
they enjoyed was abundant. Deep forest was no place for
a man who moved slowly and shrank from discomfort
and danger, yet Sears held to this undertaking as stub-
bornly as Wright to his dreams of a community of good
will under a government of laws. And before all except
Paul and Wright, Sears was able to preserve a manner
like the face of Lake Argo on a still morning. That calm
gave him, in the eyes of the pygmies, more puzzling di-
vinity than they found in the others. Abara worshiped
from behind a mask of cynical blankness. Pakriaa seemed

almost to love him openly. She was not arrogant with him; when he spoke she listened. She assigned soldiers to collect the insects, fish, small animals he wanted for study; she brought him gifts—an earthenware vessel with ritual painting, odd flowers, ornaments of wood and bone and clay. She liked to sit by him when he was at the microscope and peek, mystified, into the country of the lens.

Sears had let the olifants grow used to him. He talked to them. He learned they like to be rubbed above the tip of the trunk and on the vast flat tops of their heads—for this luxury they would kneel, rumbling and sighing. Eventually he dared climb into the natural saddle between hump and skull: they allowed it. They were never excited nor in a hurry. The kaksmas they probably avoided by keen scent and flight in times of danger; they kept clear of the omasha by going into open ground only at night.

The clearing was silent except for muted trilling of illuama. The ground was trodden; purple-leaf vines hung dead and brown, ripped out by trunks and tusks. Sears said that once, with no notion of conveying the idea, he had tugged peevishly at a vine under the nose of his favorite cow. "So, she came and fetched it loose—tired of watching me act like a damn fool."

Abara said, "I will whistle, me. . . ." Two came, spectrally calm. "Susie!" Sears called. "Been a good girl, hey?" The old cow let down her many tons to have her head scratched. Another arrived on fog-silent feet; then two bulls together, munching leaves. The five were placid, enjoying the hot stillness and Sears' purring talk. The largest bull stood ten feet at the shoulder, Paul estimated, as Abara's two-feet-six approached him, seized a lowered ear, and climbed up. Abara piped: "We walk now, Mister Johnson."

Mister Johnson's pale eyes noted Paul's bulging jacket; the boneless finger of his trunk groped suggestively till Paul produced a melon-like fruit. "Hoo-hee!" Abara crowed. "We thank you." They vanished in the shadows.

"Susie, want to dig some vines?" But Sears halted in the act of climbing her neck. Spearman had joined them, with a good hunter's quiet.

"You really have something there." Spearman was cordial and flushed. "Pygmies still make the best wine. Ours is no damn good, yet."

"Meant to ask how the last turned out."

"Needs ripening, like everything else."

"In fact," said Paul, "you're slightly plastered."

"But slightly." Ed grinned. "How if I climb on one of those?"

Sears was doubtful. "Have to get acquainted first. Mister Smith over there—he shook me off the first time. Not rough—just wasn't ready."

"They pull vines at command? You can steer 'em?"

"Sure. If they like you. Knee pressure."

"Abara's good?"

"They prefer him to me. Arek is better still. I miss her."

"Mijok rides, doesn't he?"

"Mijok and Elis. Surok's a bit skittish. I guess Pak thinks it's undignified—or else the damned witches disapprove."

"Hm . . . We have, maybe, three days before Lantis hits us—"

"Lantis—I'd succeeded in forgetting her for three minutes." Sears drooped his head against the column of Mister Smith's foreleg; eyes closed, he cursed without humor. He dredged up almost forgotten words from the old years of Earth, from bars, docks, dissecting rooms, at least four major religions. He cursed Lantis root and branch, ancestry and posterity, heart, body, and brain. Regaining a trace of mirth, he outlined a program of correction that would have kept hell under forced draft for a thousand years. Still with closed eyes, he asked, "What's the point, Ed? What's the damned point?"

"How many of these critters have you tamed?"

"Five. There's another smelling around, not ready yet."

"And five riders—you ride 'em, don't you, Paul?" Paul nodded.

Abara and Mister Johnson returned in silence, under the trees behind Spearman, who was unaware of them. Sears said, "Paul's good. Good balance."

"So you have a rider for each mount. . . . Well, I talked it over with Doc—he says it's your department. What if a bunch of those animals, with armed riders—"

"No," said Sears. "Quite impractical."

"Why?"

"Well . . . They won't go in the open—omasha."

"They will at night, you told me."

"They are not fighters."

"If they go where you order 'em—"

Sears said, "No. If Paul and I and the two strongest giants were trying that, what's left? You, Doc, Surok, and the giant women."

Spearman snapped: "Then use only three—Abara, Mijok, Elis."

"Mijok will fight beside Chris. You know that. So will I."

Spearman turned away, noticing Abara and Mister Johnson for the first time and ignoring them. Popeyes watched him from a mountain of white flesh. "All right. Oh, I almost forgot: Doc wants you back at the camp for another conference. It has just occurred to him that since we're about to be wiped off the planet we ought to have a military commander. For the look of the thing, you reckon? You know, I dreamed of space travel from the time I was five. Never imagined I'd do it with a Sunday school. Don't hurry of course. Just come when it damn well suits you."

Paul caught up with him on the trail. "Look, Ed—"

"I'll recite it for you: mustn't lose my temper. We mustn't divide; mustn't quarrel; Doc's word is holy at all times—"

"No one says that."

Spearman wasn't listening. "Goddamn it, why do you think I've gone away alone so often? To explore, sure, to find things we need. By God I've found 'em too, haven't I? Also to get away from the Sunday school. Beating my brains out to win a little advance—you people can't see—"

"What do *you* think we should do? I mean right now—Lantis."

Spearman fretted in silence, striding as if speed and heavy steps could ease his distress. "Why, we ought to have gone to live at Pakriaa's village a year ago, after the reconciliation, while they were still dizzy from the fall of the idol. You remember—Pak was almost humble. Ready for big changes. We could have done anything with her —then. Eliminated the witches. Taught and trained the best of her followers. We'd have ironworking now. We'd have a competent army. Why, we could take the initiative, drive south, break up anything Lantis may have while she's on the march. Yeah—a year ago. Sure—Mijok wouldn't approach the village, so *we* mustn't move there. Every day is an opportunity thrown away, wasted."

"You think we should have abandoned the giants?"

"What've they *got?*" Spearman cried. "Don't even understand work—throw things around at a great rate, and then somebody sees a new bug or has a funny idea or starts singing. Or asks Doc to explain a point in philosophy. Or they decide to just sit and look at nothing for two hours. Fight? Mijok talks a good fight. You couldn't make 'em fight with a kick in the rear."

"Never tried it."

Spearman smiled miserably. "One doesn't, with a critter eight feet tall. . . . All right, they're people. They're intelligent. If we had all the time in the world and nothing threatening I'd like to study 'em myself. But look at the numbers. Three on the island. Six grown women here. Twelve flutterbrained children. Elis, Surok, Mijok, and the two tenderfeet they brought in today. Is that an army? As for right now—Hell, I've given up making suggestions." He tensed and stopped short. Paul glanced behind; Sears and Abara were catching up. "Thought I heard something."

"What?"

"Drums. . . . Guess I imagined it. . . . Lantis must have a terrific organization. Bound to, Paul, in a community of sixty thousand. Hadn't you thought of that at all? Communications, laws, disciplined army, a forest agriculture at least as good as Pakriaa's. Why, from something Pak said, I think they even have a monetary system—anyway something more elaborate than the barter that's good enough for Pak's little cluster of villages. Stone Age—but that's partly an accident of ecology, isn't it? I mean, they have to avoid the hills and open ground—wouldn't be easy to get a start in metalworking when you have to stay in the woods. I believe they're a people under strong internal pressure toward the next stage of civilization. With labor, organization, a few modern ideas, there would be ways to clean the kaksmas out of the hills. Then metals.

We know the omasha breed on rock ledges wherever the kaksmas can't climb. They could be exterminated too. There's a whole world for the taking. Doc is right that the new culture has to be a blend of ours and theirs. Oh, the giants too, maybe, sometime. But it won't be done by piddling around with the kind of pretty idealism that never worked even on Earth."

Paul groped for the unspoken thing. "You'd have us join forces with Lantis?"

Spearman halted to stare at him. There was a flush of blood around his eyes, the visible pain of frustration that never gave him rest. He waited till Sears and Abara had come up. "I'm a minority. I haven't suggested a damned thing." He was silent until they reached the camp.

Abro Pakriaa was there, with seven of her soldiers. All seven wore purple skirts, insignia of leadership—"captains" was the nearest word. With makeshift pigments and brittle whitebark, Paul had recently painted such a group. The effort was for Pakriaa; she had been gravely delighted with it, seeing how prominent in it were her own vivid blue skirt and taller stature. To Paul's eyes the colors had sworn horribly, and he had been glad when the princess carried the daub away, balanced joyfully on her bald head.

Pak's seven captains made it a visit of state. Wright was soberly intent, and Ann stood by him, regally silent; play-acting for Pakriaa's benefit, but Ann sardonically enjoyed the pose. Pakriaa had gradually accepted the fact of Tocwright's leadership, but her view of the status of Charin women remained addled by contradictions; the idea of social and mental equality between the sexes eluded her completely. Dorothy sat watchful at the opening of the "home" room—Helen would be sleeping inside; Dorothy's fists were pushed into her cheeks, dark eyes upturned to Pakriaa's explanatory monologue. Abara effaced himself. Mijok loomed with folded arms on Wright's other side. The rest of the giants kept to the background.

"Abro Samiraa, Abro Kamisiaa, Abro Brodaa—" Pakriaa was naming the heads of the five northern villages. A loose alliance, but those villages had fought powerfully against Lantis a year ago and each could provide a hundred and fifty first-line soldiers and fifty of the skittish male bowmen. "They are with me, my sisters," Pakriaa said, with sad gravity and not much of her natural swagger. "The wormseed Lantis has broken custom—her own people must spit on her. For the death of my messenger I spit on her heart and loins, I spit on her footprints."

The arithmetic was simple, Paul thought. A scant twelve hundred fighters against a three-sided attack from over ten thousand. Four Charin men with rifles, automatics, scanty ammunition, heavy bows. A handful of giants who knew nothing of war but theory and whose basic nature would revolt at the reality. Spitting wouldn't help. He forced himself to attend to what Wright was saying: "There must be one commander."

"I give no orders to Abro Samiraa and her sisters, my equals."

"Would you and she and the others accept direction from one of us?"

Pakriaa murmured, "I have never seen you fight."

Spearman laughed. Wright said, "You will, Abro Pakriaa. If you will accept one of us as commander, the army can strike as one soldier. There would be less confusion. And Lantis will not expect it."

That brought shrewdness to the little red face. "But you can do nothing hiding behind this pile of stones."

"A temporary shelter while we shoot. You know our fire sticks. This building commands the upper part of the lake and this end of the meadow. We will not be trapped here. There will be no siege. If it is necessary to retreat, we'll know the right moment to do it."

The oldest captain, Nisana, a wiry, quiet woman, said, "Abro Kamisiaa herself spoke of a thing like this."

Pakriaa murmured absently, "Did I give you leave to speak?" But she was not angry; she was considering it. "This is better, Tocwright, what you say now. I will send, learn if my sisters agree. But who will be the leader?"

"That should be decided now," Wright said, and Paul thought: *Here it comes, Ed—you get what you want at last.* And he remembered that obscure thing which might not have been in Spearman's mind at all: *desertion*—the thing was a dirty word, and the mind would not speak it. But Wright was staring at him—at him, not at Spearman.

"There's only one of us," Wright said, "who ought to lead, in this trouble. That is *my* feeling, Abro Pakriaa, but I alone cannot decide it. All of us here should vote on it."

Pakriaa understood the nature of a vote. Under her iron monarchy, minor village matters were often decided by that method if her own attitude happened to be neutral. Once made, and approved by herself, a pygmy vote was binding as magic. Her gaze touched the giants with a sour smile. She was visibly counting; then she was studying Paul with new curiosity.

Of the giants, only the two new recruits were not in evidence. Paul glimpsed the red-furred boy peering from the doorway of Mijok's private room; Surok went in to soothe him. Pakriaa said, "I will consent. After the vote I will inform my sisters as quickly as I can."

Wright's fingers were frozen in his gray beard. "Then I ask that Paul Mason take command, his orders to be followed without question."

Paul could not speak. *How did this happen? How can I . . .* He heard Ann, imitating the formality of Wright's words, but with an undertone of passionate protest: "I ask for the leadership of Edmund Spearman."

Spearman frowned at her, flushed, proud, perhaps amazed. He said doubtfully, "Other nominations . . . ? Voice vote?"

"Voice vote, as you wish," Wright said.

"M-make it voice vote," Dorothy whipered, and her face was begging: *Is it too much? Can you stand it? Is it what I ought to do . . . ?*

"Satisfactory," Spearman said. Paul nodded helplessly.

Dorothy said, "Paul Mason."

Wright glanced at Pakriaa. When Spearman was nominated she had abandoned her patronizing air; she said with enthusiasm, "Spearman."

Mijok's voice rumbled in the depths: "Paul Mason."

The voting went quickly after that. Abara slipped into shadow and shook his head before Wright could call his name. Sears voted for Paul with a wry attempt at a grin. Surok hesitated; his tawny face smiled at Paul with apology and he said, "Spearman." Golden Lisson voted the same way. The other giant women and Elis voted for Paul. The children were quiet, not needing to be told that this was grown-up business. When one of the smallest boys started to hum, little Dunin squatted behind him and covered his mouth.

All the pygmy captains but one had followed Pakriaa's lead, after a pantomime of meditation, probably for the record. Now, with a vote of 10-10, this one captain was full of trouble. She understood that she would be the last to vote and must break the tie. This was Nisana, taciturn, with the white scar of a wound that had destroyed her lower left breast and run jaggedly down her side; Paul had seen her often but knew little of her. She was studying the candidates with a manifestly honest, tormenting effort to decide, and she avoided Pakriaa's astounded glare. The green eyes fixed themselves at last on one candidate with a blinding innocence.

"Paul Mason."

Pakriaa started as if slapped, but recovered quickly. She said, "Tocwright, is Abara not to vote?"

Abara shuffled a step backward, two steps forward. It brought him nearer the bulk of Sears Oliphant. His bulging eyes tried to escape Wright's look, and Pakriaa's; his ugly lips wobbled. He squeaked: "Paul Mason."

"Twelve-ten," Wright said. "Abro Pakriaa, I am grateful—"

Pakriaa ignored him. She was saying with acid sweetness, "Abroshin Nisana, perhaps you wish to remain here?"

It seemed to Paul that a mechanical force within him was taking over, unsought, at a moment of greatest need. "That would be excellent, Abro Pakriaa. If I am commander, I need one of you here: I am glad to select Abroshin Nisana."

The princess faced him. Her eyelids flickered—usually a sign of pygmy amusement more revealing than laughter, but one never knew, exactly. The machine labored, weighing dangers and advantages. A direct order now might win over Pakriaa or lose her completely and all the twelve hundred. She understood and admired aggressiveness; she was also a bundle of touchy personal pride. And—the slim spear in her hand could strike like a cobra. Paul said, "Abro Pakriaa, you will tell the other leaders our decision, and if they agree, have them come here at once."

There was a gray-white shadow at his left. The balance, swinging delicately, was visible in Pakriaa's almost sleepy eyes. He thought: *One thing quicker than a pygmy's arm —a giant's.* At least he would not be pierced with white-stone, while Mijok stood there.

Pakriaa's arm swung—the harmless right arm, a harmless beckoning gesture to six of her captains, who followed her out of the fortress, leaving Abroshin Nisana staring at the ground and very much alone.

Spearman came alive. He spoke plainly, cheerfully: "Paul, count on me for anything. Do whatever I can." His voice had full sincerity. If his eyes were a little too steady, too candid—never mind it. It was a pleasure to take his hand, thank him, turn to immediate needs.

"Two lifeboat trips right away, Ed, in what's left of day-light. Ann, Samis, and the four smallest giant children on the first. All the carpentry and garden tools. Third trip in the morning." Wright's sudden relaxation was praise. . . .

Ann left, with no more protest than a backward look. But at the last moment she ran back to kiss Wright on the mouth. . . .

And when Ed was returning from the second flight, which had carried Dunin and four other giant children to the island—when it was night and the red eye of the life-boat was slipping down from above the hills, then the drums began.

4 PAUL HEARD THE DRUMS FROM WITHIN THE ROOM
that was his and Dorothy's—merely a section of the
thatched lean-to inside the fortress wall, but Dorothy had
given it the reality of a living place. There were no chairs:
one sat on a rug which was a cured uskaran pelt, a gift
from Abro Brodaa, whose people had hunted down the
tigerish beast after it raided her village. The bed was only
a clumsy framework with an asonis hide stretched across
it. But the shelter had become dear with use, and Dorothy
had hung a few of Paul's paintings on the walls—a portrait of Mijok, one of Christopher Wright which had
caught something of the old man's brooding alertness. The
red jungle flowers were too cloyingly rich to be kept here,
but Dorothy had found a blue meadow shrub, and a
white bloom that hid in shady ground and recalled the
scent of jonquils. . . .

It was too dark to see her plainly; Paul knew her eyes
were open on him. Barely audible against his shoulder,
she said, "I thought I'd be insatiable. I only want to be
near and not think." Nevertheless thought goaded her.
"Ten thousand—ten thousand—What can you *do?*"

All he could say was rehearsed, mechanical, and she
had heard it before. "Frontal attack first, because the
pygmies couldn't be led into anything else. But I shall turn
it into an ordered retreat—to the island. Drive south,
skirt the southern end of the hills, then straight for the
coast. We'll be at the island in—oh, soon—"

"But the range—the coastal mountains opposite the
island—you can't cross them—they rise so sheer—"

"Remember the river that flows almost due west from
these little hills? It comes to the sea north of the range.
We'll make rafts to get down that, I think. There aren't

any falls. At the coast we'll contrive something—dugouts
with outriggers. I've already shown old Rak how to make
one; he may be working on it now."

Dorothy pressed a hand over his mouth. She stammered,
"Make this moment last." But even during the fine sharp
agony there were words: "I shall keep—a bonfire on that
beach—night and day . . ." and when his hand was slack
in her hair and she seemed to be hardly breathing, Paul
heard the drums.

They were far off and everywhere. Only the remembering brain insisted they were on the lake. They were not
sound at all, at first. A pressure pain in the back of the
skull, a rasping of nerve endings. Nothing but drums.
Hollow logs with a hide membrane, rubbed and pounded
by tiny painted savages. "You must go tonight after all."
Dorothy could not speak. He put Helen in her fumbling
arms; he hurried out to the open space, saw the eye of
the lifeboat returning. The drums took on a rhythm, a
throbbing in ⅝ time, rapid, venomous. But far away.
Still not quite sound—*Ah*-ah-ah-ah-ah, *ah*-ah-ah-ah-ah—
growing no nearer, no louder, but gaining in vicious
urgency, relentless as a waterfall, a runaway machine.
Ah-ah-ah-ah-ah. . . .

Paul hoped that Wright and Sears might be sleeping. It
would be an hour yet before Pakriaa could return with
the other leaders, if indeed she ever did. Elis and Abara
were on sentry duty. The three giant children still at the
camp—would they be sleepless, keyed up to vivid fantasies
of the island, like Charin children before a great journey?

Kamon sat alone by the gate. A small figure drooped
at the other end of the enclosure. Since there was no immediate task for her, Paul had told Abroshin Nisana to
rest, but he knew her little bald head turned to follow
him. "Kamon—I'm going to have the third flight made tonight. There would be room for you too in the boat.
Will you go?"

Black lips and ancient white face smiled up at him. "If
you wish."

"I do. Stay close to Dorothy. That will leave four of
you giant women here. I wish they could all go. Tejron's
sober and wise—she'll keep them together. You're more
needed on the island. Don't let Dorothy be much alone."

The old woman mused: "This Charin love is a strange thing. It isn't our natures for two persons to come so close. But I see something good in it, I think. . . ." Paul struggled to hear her over the almost subsonic yammer of the drums. *Ah*-ah-ah-ah-ah—it seemed not to trouble Kamon much, though she would be hearing it even more plainly. "I will stay with her, Paul," she said, and watched the long glide as Spearman brought the boat in.

On the drawbridge Spearman cocked his head at the drums. "That's it." He read Paul's thought: "The rest tonight, huh? Better, I'd think."

"Yes. Get something to eat, why don't you? Kamon is going too."

Spearman nodded, unsurprised. "Not hungry. . . . Wonder how long they keep it up. . . ."

Wright came from his room with sleepless eyes. "Till they attack, probably. All night, maybe all tomorrow. To soften us up. Damn them. . . ."

Somehow Paul was walking to the boat, carrying the baby for Dorothy. He climbed in with her, adjusted the straps. Helen waked and was fretful till she found the breast. "You bore her alone—without any—"

"Alone!" Dorothy was astonished. "I had you. Doc's a fine medical man, whatever he says. Don't you remember how Mijok held out his arm for me to grab when it got tough? He said, 'I am a tree.'" Now she was holding his look with an indestructible smile until the rest came and Paul had to back out of the cramped cabin to give them room; then had to stand aside while the bright relic of twenty-first-century man spat its green flame and hot gases at the lake and leaped to soaring and slid into moonless darkness above the hills. The drums wept, raved, obscenely whispered.

Paul did not know Sears Oliphant was with him till he heard the voice: "I think, Paul—the drums defeat their purpose. They make me sore instead of scared. I think you won't need to worry about me, Paul."

"I never have." He glanced at the fat man's holstered automatic, remembered the cleanness of the rifle hanging in Sears' room. "My father used to say most men are good watchdogs, who know they're scared but stand guard in spite of it; only a few are rabbits and possums." Paul turned his back on the hills. Nothing was there to see, nothing at all. "I wish you'd known my father. He was a tall man. Nuts about animals—always brought 'em into the talk—illustration, example. Couldn't stand to see even a wasp beating against the glass; you never knew when a deer mouse would climb out of his pocket and run down his pants leg." Paul laughed. The drums fretted in ⅝, passionate, soft, cruel.

Sears watched blue fireflies over a lake so peacefully still that the sapphire reflections were as real as their cause. "A teacher, wasn't he?"

"For a while, till he settled in New Hampshire. They wouldn't let him teach nineteenth- and twentieth-century history as he saw it. He saw it in terms of ethical conflict, the man versus the state, self-reliance versus the various dreary socialisms, enlightened altruism versus don't-stick-your-neck-out, and he didn't give a good god-damn whether the first atomic submersible was built in 1952 or '53. Doc would have loved him too: he knew what was meant by a government of laws. He made his students search out not only theory but the actual dismal consequences of the doctrine that the end justifies the means— Alexander, Augustus, Napoleon, Lenin, Hitler. That was regarded as 'wilfully minimizing the significance of technological advance.' He didn't minimize it; he just recognized that other matters were vastly more important, and he didn't care to see the machine built up into one more mumbo jumbo. So he sent me through college by breeding children's riding ponies and selling hatching eggs. Not a bad life, or so he said. . . . Jocko, will Pakriaa come back?"

"I believe so. . . . Ah, Chris—nice evening for the month of Charin."

Wright was a paleness in the dark; stern, weary, tall, watching the lake, talking to himself: "The month we named for ourselves—end of Year One—oh, I do call that a pardonable vanity. . . . Paul, I was wholly selfish in choosing you. I've given you a burden no one should have to carry."

"We're all carrying it."

"Thank you, son." Wright moved away to stand alone at

the rim of the lake, listening to the crawling thunder of the drums. Twice, Paul heard him speak, with an intensity beyond pain: "No one is expendable. No one is expendable. . . ."

Sears exclaimed, "Look!" There were five white cloud-like shapes at the edge of the woods. "Oh, they've never done this before. Susie! What's the matter? There now, girl, come tell the old man—"

Paul followed him. "It's the drums—don't you think?"

The five had been complaining softly, but that ceased as Sears moved among them, patting their legs, soothing them. "But Paul—their grounds are mostly north of here —there now, Mister Smith, you old bastard—so why didn't they travel away from the sound? Take it easy, Millie, Miss Ponsonby—"

"The wild ones probably did. But these had to come to you."

"Oh . . . That detachment of Lantis—the one in the northeast—"

"Don't think so, Jocko. Pakriaa's spies are all around up there—we'll have warning. Elis is posted half a mile north of us—he'd know—smell 'em if he didn't hear 'em. However, I'll go talk with him. . . ."

The depth of forest muted the drums—a little; they were still a cumulative torture of anger in the inner darkness of the mind. Paul saved the fading power of his Earth-made radion flashlight by following his sense of the trail. He had learned to move as softly in the jungle as any Charin could hope to do—more softly than Spearman, softly enough to steal within spear range of the asonis. There was not much danger here, unless it might be from the uskaran, a beast Paul had glimpsed alive only once and then dimly, a striped thing slipping snakily out of his vision in a sun-striped afternoon; the rug in his and Dorothy's room could almost have been a tiger pelt. The black reptiles were lovers of hot sun and shallow water, never going inland. The squeak and rustle of a kaksma horde, it was said, could be heard far off except during the rains, when all noises were smothered in the long rush and whispering of waters. For all his silence, black Elis was aware of him before Paul knew he had reached the sentry post. "Paul—isn't it?" The night vision of the giants was better than the Charins' but not like a cat's; they hunted at night only if the moon was strong.

"Yes. Everything quiet?"

"Quieter than my heart."

Paul still could not see him. "Saving my flashlight. Where are you?" Elis chuckled and slipped an invisible hand around Paul's. "The olifants came to the meadow. We wondered what disturbed them."

"Drums. Nothing in the northeast yet. But a great many of the pygmies are moving from the upper villages. I heard, and smelled the red flowers." The people of Lantis, Pakriaa said, never wore those flowers, and it would not be the nature of Elis to exaggerate his powers of smell and hearing.

"I think the animals wanted Sears. Could that be, Elis?"

"Alojna—" Elis murmured the old word for them: it meant "white cloud." "Two things nobody knows—the thoughts of Alojna and the journeys of the red moon and the white moon when we cannot see them. So we used to say. You give us a hint of knowledge of both things, and more than a hint of much greater mysteries." Elis had always been tireless in questioning Wright; more than Mijok, he was haunted by a need to grope after intangibles, push outward the uneasy border between known and unknown. "So there's never an end of mystery?"

"Never." The hand was warm. "What is the nature of courage?"

The giant's breathing was too quiet to be heard. "To go out, away from a world, in a little shell—that must have needed courage."

"Perhaps only a response to a drive of uncomprehended forces. But I think courage is a known thing, Elis, an achievement of flesh and blood—to hear the drums in the dark and stay at the post as you are doing, as I hope I can do myself. I must go back. Lisson will come and relieve you soon. . . ."

Pakriaa had returned, with her five equals. Wright had lit one of the clay lamps. It burned pleasantly with an oil from the carcasses of the same reptile that had once nearly destroyed Mijok, a thing which pleased Mijok, for he liked to think that a creeping danger could also be a source of light; and the use of this oil had been taught them by the pygmies, who made almost monthly expeditions to marshy regions and butchered the beasts by the dozens for the oil alone.

Pakriaa was almost meek. Her smile for Paul could have been a Charin smile; there was a tremor in her hands, and once they flew up to cover her ears. The drums, he thought, might be a worse pain for her than for his own breed. There was unconscious pathos in the precision of her English: "I did not make clear that I will obey you. I may have been angry; for that I am sorry—it is past. My sisters have agreed."

Squat Abro Samiraa; lame, thin Abro Kamisiaa; sober Abro Brodaa—these three Paul had met before. Abro Duriaa and Abro Tamisraa were from the farthest villages, and shy; Duriaa was fat, with a foolish giggle; Tamisraa had a feral furtiveness—the painted bones of her necklace looked like human vertebrae. In Abro Samiraa Paul saw competence as well as smoldering violence: the green of her eyes was dark jade; she was a flat pillar of muscle from shoulder to hip. Paul guessed her to be a devil of bravery, good in the front line and intelligent. Lame Kamisiaa's bravery would be shrewd, vicious, and careful. In fat Duriaa he thought he saw a politician, not a fighter; in Abro Brodaa—there might be a thinker, even a dreamer, in Abro Brodaa.

The princesses had brought news. A scout from Brodaa's village had succeeded in locating the northeastern detachment of Lantis' army; it was camped twelve miles to the northeast, on the far side of a deep but narrow stream. The scout had shown the kind of nerve the pygmies took for granted: she had crossed the creek to listen in the reeds and had drifted downstream the entire length of the encampment. The Vestoians were careless, overconfident, their dialect enough like her own so that she could grasp the essentials; their unit was six hundred strong, with no bowmen. The scout had heard discontented soldiers' talk: the spearwomen missed their subject males, who were camp followers as well as second-line fighters. Returning, the scout had located and stalked a Vestoian sentry, stunned and gagged her, and brought her to Brodaa's camp, where she was made to talk. Brodaa had been about to describe this when Pakriaa glanced at Sears and interrupted: "They plan to cross the stream before daylight, move straight west, and try to push us down into the open ground, where the rest of the army will roll over us."

The sentry is probably dead. I don't want to know, not now. . . . The machine in Paul took charge of the council of war, rejecting compassion, rejecting everything beyond immediate need. "Abro Samiraa—take the soldiers of your village and of Abro Duriaa's. Abro Duriaa, you will be in command of your own people, but accept Abro Samiraa's orders as it they were mine." Pakriaa intervened to translate for the fat woman, who showed no hostility but rather relief, and placed her hands formally under the spread fingers of Abro Samiraa in token of subordination. "Abro Samiraa, take those three hundred and the bowmen to the stream as quickly as you can with silence, and attack. The important thing is to scatter them before they are ready to move. If they retreat, follow them only enough to confuse them and then return here at once. If you can take prisoners, bring them here, unharmed. But do not be drawn into any long pursuit. There are still eleven hours of darkness. I hope to see you return long before sunrise."

"Good!" Pakriaa exclaimed, and Samiraa grunted with pleasure. Brodaa said, "Take my scout, sister. I have given her the purple skirt; she is Abroshin now, and my friend." Duriaa waddled behind, and Paul sent Abroshin Nisana to relieve Abara from sentry duty. Nisana was glad to go, for Pakriaa still sent her sour glances, remembering the election.

Sears was fretting: "My pets. Damn it, Paul, I dunno— they're huddled out there in the meadow—just get in the way, get hurt."

"Would they follow Abara?"

"I think so. . . ." Abara slipped in and puffed with pride when he learned what was wanted. "Certainly they will follow Mister Johnson, and Mister Johnson will follow me."

Pakriaa laughed. She caught him by a prominent ear and hugged him to her leanness, grinning at Brodaa over his head. "So ugly!" Pakriaa nibbled his neck. "And he leads olifants! Don't be afraid, little husband—I was never angry

with you. Look at him!" She spun him around for the
lewd admiration of the other royalty. "I couldn't do without him. When the war is over I'll have him back in my
bed. But now he leads olifants. Hurry, Abara—and don't
hurt yourself." And she sent him off with a pinch.

"Keep them in the woods," Paul told him. "And stay
with them."

"Good." Pakriaa sobered. "He could do nothing. He
never learned the bow. . . . Ah, look!" The red dot of
the lifeboat had caught her eye. "Look, Abro Tamisraa—
you never saw it fly at night." It moved with apparent
slowness, like a mad star, not toward them but toward
the lake, perhaps ten miles away; it was still high when
the searchlight beam stabbed down, probing from northeast to southwest, and vanished. "It's all right," Paul said,
"I suggested he scout the lake on the way back. . . ."
The red eye silently tumbled; Wright gasped. "Still all
right," said Paul. "A dive. He can make it talk." But the
moment dragged out into an ugliness of waiting.

Then orange fury glared against the underside of clouds
and the clamor of drums abruptly ceased. Paul said
loudly, mechanically, "I think he gave 'em the jet—set a
few boats afire. I didn't order it, Doc. And wouldn't try it
myself. . . ." Now the red dot was shooting upward,
disappearing as the boat circled once, then growing larger.
Briefly the searchlight illuminated the meadow, and Spearman came in, overshooting slightly, driving almost to the
moat before he checked. He swaggered in, satisfied. "See
it?"

"Uh-huh. What did you learn?"

"Those were drum boats. Why, my God, they opened
out like little orange flowers . . . ! Well—the main fleet
is 'way behind them, say thirty miles down the lake, coming slow. Couldn't spot the land army—no campfires."

"All right. Sit in on this, Ed. . . ." And the plan was
drawn up, so far as there could be a plan when the odds
were ten to one in a world that never asked for them.

Paul, with Mijok and Pakriaa, would lead three hundred
spearwomen and a hundred bowmen south before daylight, in the hope of disorganizing the advance with sur-
prise and gunfire, but unless the Vestoians were demoral-
ized beyond expectation, this could be only a skirmish.

They would fall back, try to avoid losses. The remainder of the army would stay at the edge of the woods until Lantis was in sight: Wright at the fortress with the giant women, now only four, who could handle rifles; Abro Kamisiaa and Abro Brodaa in the center; Sears and Abro Tamisraa on the right flank in the west, with Elis and Surok. Spearman in the lifeboat would follow the advance party at first-light. Paul said nothing of the second drive, to the southeast, the retreat that would seem like attack. When the time came for that, he must have in one unit all that remained after the first wrath had spent itself—and even then the pygmies would have to believe that they were attacking singleheartedly, or they could not reach the southern end of the range, but would probably be driven into the trap of the kaksma hills.

The drums began again. They began after the council was ended and Sears had gone to take charge of his command on the right flank, with Elis and Surok and shifty Tamisraa. The other small red sovereigns had gone too, and Wright had stalked into his room—to sleep, he said—and Paul had followed Spearman out to the boat, where Spearman would sleep until it was time to go. Spearman tapped his elbow. "You're surprising me, boy. Better than I could have done, I think. We'll knock 'em over." And the drums began.

Spearman stared off at the lake; after a while he grinned, and the lamp burning in the fortress caught the grimace. "Yeah," he sighed, "well, I knew I only singed 'em." He climbed into the boat and glanced down with a half salute, which Paul answered mechanically. But as Paul walked away the thought stirred: *That was like goodbye. . . .*

Paul went along the path at the edge of the woods. It was wide and easy, broadened during the Year One by much travel between the camp and Pakriaa's village. There were occasional small-voiced greetings from the woods: these were Kamisiaa's and Brodaa's people, who knew him. Brodaa cherished a painting he had made of the singing waterfall above her village in return for that uskaran pelt. Many of these soldiers would be chosen by Pakriaa to bring up the number of the advance party to four hundred.

There was no red moon tonight. The white moon was half the size of the planet Earth, so far away that its glow was scarcely more than that of a star, but Paul knew that by what light it gave the pygmies could see him smile in response to their greetings. They would be studying him, trying to weigh the tone of his answer. *One of them might save my life tomorrow; certainly I shall have to see some of them die. They are people.*

There were two visible planets to follow the wandering of the no longer alien star that was the sun. One was hidden tonight; the other, red like Mars, hung over the eastern jungle in tranquillity. A little shape detached itself from the trees to meet him. Abro Pakriaa. "Will you not sleep tonight, Paul, before we go?" It was a human question, sweetly spoken and meant kindly.

"Later, I think." He stood by her awhile; in the blackness from which she had come there was a steady mumbling, and Paul knew what it was: the witches also had their part to play in these heavy hours, although long before battle was joined they would be cowering in the villages. Somewhere in the tree shadows they were squatting, muttering the antique prayers. He wondered whether to go on and visit with Sears awhile. *No: Elis is a rock, better company than I would be at the moment. . . .* There was much, he thought, that would be good to talk about with Pakriaa tonight; there ought to be words that would reach her. Perhaps on this night a glimpse of Wright's vision would meet with something better than amusement and distrust. But in the end he only said, "We'll always be good friends, you and I."

He thought she might take hold of his hand in the Charin gesture. She did not—undignified perhaps. But she said, "Tocwright says we are all one flesh." She said it thoughtfully, without contempt.

"Yes. We are all one flesh." And lest he become a true Charin and spoil a moment of truth with unnecessary words, Paul turned back to the camp, seeing that she remained there in the open, looking south, the grumbling witches behind her, before her the long night of drums and no red moon.

Mijok was not asleep. He sat cross-legged by the lamp. "I wanted to thank you. Doc's gone to sleep at last, and before I could find the words I wanted. It will be difficult to talk in the morning."

Paul sat by him, puzzled. "To thank me?"

"Because I've learned so much. And had so much pleasure in the learning." Mijok yawned amiably, stretching his arms. "To thank you for that, in case you or I should be dead tomorrow."

It would have been easy to say: "Oh, we'll be all right —" Something like that. Paul buried the words unspoken, knowing their triviality would be a discourtesy, a dismissal of the insight and patience which made it possible for Mijok to speak so casually. Mijok loved to be alive; there was no moment of day or night that he did not relish, if only for its newness and from his sense that every gift of time is a true gift. "I thank you for being with us." Mijok accepted the words without embarrassment or second thought.

"Why, you know," he said, "in the old days I never even knew that plants were alive. But look at this—" He lifted one of Dorothy's white flowers from his knee. "It was in your room, Paul. She put it beside that painting you made of me, before she left." He peered into the white mouth of the flower, touched the fat stamens, and stroked the slim stalk. "Everything it needs. Like ourselves. But I never knew that. We are all one flesh."

Paul glanced over his shoulder. The red planet like Mars was still high over the jungle. He thought: *When that is hidden, it will be time to go.*

5 ALL NIGHT PAUL HEARD THE DISTANT BARBAROUS thunder of the drums. In the hour before first-light his advance company formed; a furious serpent, it stole two miles south through grassland following the pallor of the beach. Near first-light, Paul knew, they would see a thread of new moon. In this present darkness the Vestoians might be slipping north on the lake; there would be no betraying sound above the passion of the drums. As for the land army, that could be miles to the south or over the next rise of ground.

His mind fought a pressure of alternatives. Better to have kept the army in one unit? To wait in the forest for news of Abro Samiraa's thrust in the northeast? *Never mind: no time now.* At least his body was meeting the challenge without rebellion. His wiry legs carried him in silence; his senses were whetted to fineness. Rifle, pistol, field glasses, hunting knife made a light load. Ahead of him Mijok loomed against a division of two shadows, sky and earth. Not first-light: only a sign that five thousand miles away on the eastern shore of this continent there might be the shining of a star now called the sun. Mijok carried a shield of doubled asonis hide; his only weapon was a seven-foot club, since his smallest finger was too large to pass the trigger guard of a rifle. Though keeping watch with Paul, Mijok had spoken little during the night—brooding perhaps, trying (Paul imagined) to see a new world in the matrix of the old. But there was no guessing a giant's thoughts. Lacking the stale burden of human guilt and compromise, they had the strength as well as the weakness of innocence; the country of their minds must wait on the explorations of centuries.

Abro Pakriaa, close to Paul's right, moved like a breeze

in the grass. She and her small soldiers despised the use of shields, despised the arrows of their own bowmen as fit only for timid males. They never threw their spears but kept them for close quarters; their only other weapon was a white-stone dagger. . . . The army groped through the meadow in three ranks, widely spaced at Paul's order; beyond the right flank the archers were concentrated. Four hundred fighters altogether—against six thousand.

A wooded knoll grew into silhouette fifty yards from the beach, ten feet above the level of the meadow. "We meet them here," Paul said. By prearrangement Pakriaa halted a hundred of her spearwomen between the knoll and the beach, the other two hundred on the west side, the hundred bowmen out beyond. Paul and Mijok penetrated the blackness of the knoll, pushing through to its southern side, where Pakriaa joined them. Even in that short passage the heaviness of dark had altered with a promise. There were few clouds. The day (if it ever came) would be hot, windless, and beautiful. No more blue fireflies were wandering. The planet Lucifer had become three gray enigmas of lake and meadow and sky, but in this blind hush when morning was still the supposition of a dream, the shapes of the trees were attaining a separate reality; in the west Paul could find a hint of the low hills standing between him and the West Atlantic.

Seventy or eighty miles over yonder Dorothy's brown eyes would be watching for first-light on the sea, watching for it not on the great sea, he knew, but on the channel that shut her away from the mainland, from himself. With his child at her breast, another unknown life in the womb. Ann Bryan too, her troubled secret mind still full of protest at the contradictions and unfulfilled promises which made up the climate of life on Lucifer as well as elsewhere; and the ancient giantess Kamon, and Rak and Muson, Samis, Arek, and those giant children perennially puzzling and lovable. . . . *No time.* Mijok was peering out on the west side of the knoll. "Nicely hidden. Your soldiers are very good, Abro Pakriaa," said the giant, whose knowledge of war was almost as dim a product of theory as his knowledge of the planet Earth, where his Charin friends had been born.

The pygmy princess did not answer. Paul thought with held-in anger: *Can't she understand even now that Mijok is one of us, the best of us . . . ?* But Pakriaa was staring south; she might not have heard. She pointed.

Thus, after a year of waiting, wonder, rumor; a year when Lantis of Vestoia, Queen of the World, had been a half-mythical terror, symbol of tyranny and danger but not a person; a year that Ed Spearman spoke of as "lost to the piddlings of philosophy"—Paul saw them at last.

Saw rather a waving of the grass, a cluster of dots shifting, bobbing, advancing. Pakriaa's tree-frog voice was calm: "They come fast. They want to reach our forest before the light makes the omasha fly. Your plan is good, Paul: we hold them in the open, the omasha have good meat."

A man could dourly accept it, somehow. Bred to gentleness, undestructive labor, study, contemplation, Paul could tell himself that a certain spot (even as it bloomed like a nodding flower in the telescopic sights) was not flesh and blood and nerve, only a target. *Would it be so if I were fighting only for myself . . . ?* He held the spot in focus; he said, "Your soldiers are prepared for the fire stick? They know they must not charge till they have the order from you?"

Her voice had warmth: "And they know you are my commander."

Paul squeezed the trigger.

Too soon—and too damned quiet. The clever makers of twenty-first-century firearms on Earth had cut down the shout of a .30 caliber to a trivial snap. The savage eyes out there might not even have caught the flash at the muzzle. There ought to have been the glare and circumstance of a rocket. How could they be panicked by a silly pop and a spark? Even though—well, one of the dots had vanished, true enough. Maybe he had killed his first human being.

He glanced westward, wondering how soon the gray must change to saffron and crimson. The new red moon—there it was. A bloody sliver of a sword above the far shore of the lake.

And he saw the boats.

They were half a mile out. No others were visible north of them, but that meant nothing: these might or might not be the lead canoes of the fleet. The noise of drum boats in the south was constant: those would stay anchored in hiding, letting their wrath appear to come from all parts of the world.

The leading boat jumped to clarity in the sights. Forward the bark roofing reached the gunwale; aft, the sides were open to leave space for two paddlers. Paul saw the tight mouth of the one on the port side: she could have been Pakriaa's blood sister. Now it was necessary to think of Abro Pakriaa's ambassador torn in quarters, head and arms sent back as a message from the Queen of the World—until the mind of the student of Christopher Wright rebelled: *Vengeance was one of the ape's first discoveries.* It became more necessary to think: *Make it a good head shot—she won't feel it.* . . .

It was not a very good shot. The scream came weakly across the water. The paddler tumbled, an arm dangling. The starboard paddler seemed not to understand and labored stupidly, making the canoe lurch to port. The prow of a following boat rammed it, tore away the matting, revealed the huddled soldiers who became splashing legs and arms in a sudden foam. While the land army came on. . . .

Dots that were bald red heads, white specks that were spear blades. A simple arithmetic: less than a hundred rounds for the rifle; four hundred soldiers; a heart divided but angry, and the devotion of an eight-foot giant with a big stick. Against six thousand in the land army alone. "Pakriaa, it's a single column—the fools! Send your bowmen out west, catch them on the flank." Pakriaa ran down the knoll.

Paul shot twice at the head of the column. A flurry. No halt. Some of the boats were no longer sliding north, but driving down on the beach, forty or fifty, like hornets from a torn nest. *Another mistake—no, not if it diverts them from the camp.* Pakriaa's hundred on this side of the knoll were holding firm for an order. Paul's wave was enough: they spread out in the grass at the edge of the beach, quivering like waiting cats. The light was changing their bodies from vagueness to familiar copper, black skirts, white body paint. . . . Mijok tore a half-buried rock from the ground and hurled it out to splinter the nearest boat. But the soldiers would merely swim ashore. "Mijok! Stay with me!"

The head of that column was less than two hundred yards away. Paul fired mechanically, seeing life tumble backward and lie still. "Let them see us now, Pakriaa, Mijok——"

They strode down the south slope of the knoll in plain sight under the beginning of morning as the bowmen in the meadow released a harsh flight. The beach on the left became a seething of yells, snarling, trampling, clash of white stone. *First-light—first-light—and where in damnation is Ed Spearman with the lifeboat . . . ?*

The column was confused by the many pressing up from behind. A few dozen spearwomen streamed out toward Pakriaa's archers; a second and third flight downed most of them—the little men had skill. No Vestoian bowmen had appeared. "Now, Pakriaa——"

Her one cry brought the spearwomen out of the grass west of the knoll, skimming forward like red bullets, spears low in the left hand until they crashed into the column; then weapons rose and plunged and rose.

The Vestoians wore no white paint. Their leaders had caps of green. Their grass skirts were mere fringes. They died easily. They killed easily.

Some distance down the column—for it was still a column, still a rolling machine that could not halt—a tall structure was swaying, hard to assess in this tortured twilight. A litter? Lantis of Vestoia, the Queen of the World herself? Paul checked his own running advance to send two shots at it. Then he and Mijok were surrounded by a writhing of arms, white-stone, and blood, Mijok raging but bewildered. Paul saw Pakriaa's spear drive down below naked ribs and withdraw from what sprawled on the ground. She was untouched. Her lean little body dripped with sweat, her teeth gleamed in a devil's grin. Two purple-skirted captains joined her; the three smashed into a cluster of shrieking souls who only began to understand what was happening.

Arithmetic still ruled. This column might be only one of many pushing up between lake and hills, bent on reaching Pakriaa's forest before the omasha soared in from those hills to feed on living and dead.

Mijok brushed through the fighters with his shield and down the line till he was clear of Pakriaa's white-painted demons. His stick swung, destroying everything in a half circle before him. He was not confused now, not even shouting, but saving breath. He worked stolidly, like a man beating at a swarm of rats. . . . Pakriaa jumped on a fallen thing to point at that clumsy framework down the line. "Lantis! That is Lantis——"

The litter wobbled toward the center of confusion on the shoulders of six women. Paul fired twice again at it. He had a glimpse of a scrawny figure with a high green headdress leaping down, snatching a spear, vanishing in an improvised protective phalanx. He shot into that, dropping one of the outer soldiers. Mijok saw; he changed the course of his attack, a bulldozer aiming at a new clump of brush. Pakriaa screamed in frenzy, without meaning. Her spear was still a part of her. She was bleeding from a thigh wound; her bright blue skirt had been torn away; she glittered with sweat and paint and blood, a dancing devil mindlessly happy. Then she was down once more in the press, squirming toward the phalanx, and Paul could not shoot.

But it was the toiling giant, Paul thought, who made Lantis break. Again he saw the snarling face of the Queen of the World and heard her squeal an order. Before Mijok could cut his way to her the phalanx was running, sheltered by the mere mass of soldiers. It was necessary to call Mijok back.

The whole Vestoian army was running. "Pakriaa!" Paul plunged after her, caught her shoulder. "No pursuit!" Her eyes glazed in mad rejection; he thought she would bite his wrist. "Turn your soldiers! Bring them down on the Vestoians from the boats—*the boats!*"

She could understand that. Her order was the shriek of a rusty nail on glass, and it turned them. It brought them howling down to the beach to aid what was left of the first hundred. The water was a jumble of abandoned boats —even the paddlers had struggled ashore to kill and die.

Mijok ploughed in a second time. . . . That ended it. Some of the Vestoians might have glimpsed what he did to the land soldiers. A few forgot all custom and threw their spears, which Mijok's shield carelessly turned; then they stared with sickness at their empty hands and waited for the club. Meanwhile the strengthened crowd of pygmies worked on till the sand was redder than the sky and there was no more to be done. "Back!"

Pakriaa screamed "No!" and pointed south. Paul stumbled on something slippery. He stooped to her, yelling, *"Omasha!* The sky will be full of them. Let them fight Lantis. We've lost a hundred already——"

Her face became sane and blank in agony. "My people —my people——"

"Yes! And other boats are still going north. Your soldiers must pick up the hurt and run for it."

There were not many living wounded in this sudden quiet. A spear has scant mercy. And the lifeboat had not come. . . . Mijok was holding out his shield on both arms; he had tossed his stick aside. "Put them on this. I can carry six—seven." When the shield could hold no more he lifted it, his face contorted and changed. "Paul—I told myself I was back in the old life, when we always killed them if we could. But the new laws—oh, Paul, *the laws*——"

"War perverts all laws. But the laws are true. It is— climbing a mountain, Mijok: we slip, fall back, try again. Nothing good in war, only necessity, choice of evils. Now make the best speed you can, friend—don't wait for us." Mijok ran with his vast strides, holding the shield out in front so that the motion of his body would not jounce it.

Pakriaa would not move till the last of the survivors had stumbled past her. They were disciplined. Already some of the soft bowmen had taken out arrows of the whining, glittering type that sometimes frightened off the omasha. They were ready. Paul tried to count, gave it up. Less than three hundred. The archers had not suffered much. Paul said, "Your leg is hurt, Abro Pakriaa. I'll carry you."

She was indifferent. "I thank you." He slung his rifle and caught her up, naked and slippery with blood and acrid-smelling paint. Her weight was less than forty pounds. Her head lolled back; she whispered to the sky, "No one should call me Abro. I am Pakriaa the child, weak as a male, a fool. I could have followed. I could have brought her to the ground. I let her go. I am a red worm. I blame you for it, Paul-Mason. You and your friends. All of you—

except Sears, who is a god with a window on another world."

"Hush! The world Sears shows you in the microscope is this world, Pakriaa. He tells you so himself. And I tell you there'll be a new way——"

She was not listening. Still he saw no threat of brown wings, and no lifeboat. But time was a deception; dawn on Lucifer was abrupt on cloudless mornings. The battle which had seemed long as heart-break had been a skirmish, a brush of advance parties lasting perhaps ten minutes from his first shot to the retreat. Pakriaa's head twitched from side to side; her eyes were dry. "I have betrayed Ismar, Creator-and-Destroyer-Who-Speaks-Thunder-in-the-Rains——"

"Pakriaa——"

"My people are to burn me in the pit for the kaksmas with lamp oil. I will order it. I would have been Queen of the World." Making no effort to escape from his arms, she burst into rage at him; a rage pitiable, not dangerous: "Why have you come, you sky people, you speakers of new words? We had our life, no need of you. We were brave—you weaken us with words, with words. Your friendship is the green-flower weed that kills the self. You make children of us. You break our beautiful image of the god and tell us she never lived. You say that now?" She slashed her fingers down her side, drawing blood.

Firing? Firing at the camp?

She clung to him, wailing: "And now you carry me. I cannot even hate you. You steal our strength. The priests were right—the priests——Ismar, help me! *Ismar!*"

Paul forced himself into a run. It was firing, rapid and sharp, pistols and rifles. The ammunition would melt fast at that rate. He could hear yelling. Catching up with the running soldiers, leaving them behind, he could see Mijok, far ahead, swerve to the left.

And the lifeboat was in action.

It curved grandly from near the surface of the lake, which was dim with smoke. It circled over jungle, descended in another swoop at the canoes. Red bodies tumbled overside; the silver nose tilted as if in disdain; the jet spoke for one second, blasting the near canoes into nothing, sending up the further ones in yellow fire, driving the life-

boat into its seeming-careless leap. But there was still
firing from the gray stone fortress, a human tangle on the
beach before it, a high long screaming.

Forward detachments of the lake fleet must have passed
in the dark. Paul ran on, only his arms remembering
Pakriaa. She slipped down, grabbed a spear as her soldiers
caught up with her, and ran straight for the beach.

That part of the agony was almost done. No more boats
were coming in—Ed Spearman's sky weapon had seen to
that. There were more canoes, many more, but they were
holding off, grouping clumsily at a distance. Paul waited
for the lifeboat to slip over him and waved to the south.
Spearman altered the course of the glide, dropping after
one more group of panicked boats but heading south.
A longer burst of the jet, and Spearman's weapon lifted,
straightened, shot out of sight across the meadow.

Paul could picture the big man's intent and mirthless
grin, the cold gray eye alert on the fuel gauge. And when
this fuel was gone—no more. It might stand for a while,
somewhere, a decaying artifact. . . .

Those left alive on the beach were bringing in casualties.
The boats were still withdrawing. Christopher Wright was
in the fortress with the wounded, his narrow face tight in
the misery of a doctor who can do almost nothing. "Doc—
how many have we lost here?"

"You! I had almost—Oh, Mijok, what've you got there
. . . ? Paul, they jumped us at first-light. No time even
to remind Ed to go after you——"

"No, he did right. More needed here. We've stalled the
land army, but they'll come on. They have to." In the sky
the brown dots had appeared at last, pouring from their
foul rock ledges in the hills. All of them were flying south.
"Pakriaa, look! Lantis has two wars now."

She stood naked and stiff, watching, her underlip thrust
out, despair giving way to a glare of satisfaction at the far-
off wings, the beasts who ate everything, feared nothing.
The southwestern sky was heavy with them. Paul had been
right; he sickened at his own cleverness. "How many,
Doc?"

"Forty or worse. This defense on the beach was by
Kamisiaa's people and our giant girls—who can shoot."
Paul saw the golden-furred girl Lisson smile uneasily at

him; there was a sober stare from brown Tejron. The other two giant women, old Karison and young Elron, seemed more deeply disturbed, Elron studying her rifle as if it were a living thing. Wright said, "With Abro Brodaa's help I made the others stay in the woods where you posted 'em. Surok ran over from the right flank—I had him run back and tell Sears and the rest to sit tight. . . . Pakriaa"—Wright strode out to her—"let me bind that up—you're bleeding." She permitted it. . . .

The boats were clustering a quarter mile away. Paul fumbled for his field glasses; they were lost. Little Abroshin Nisana, whom he had ordered to remain at the fortress, spoke beside him, slowly and carefully because her English was not good: "Commander, Abro Samiraa is return. The plan—good. She crossed the stream, catch them in blackness. A few escape. We lose twenty. One was Abro Duriaa —I am not know how she is killed." She scuffed her little seven-toed foot in the dust; there was nothing alien in her smile. "Those who return Tocwright is send west." She was puzzled, not disapproving. "Why are we most strong in the west? The Vestoians follow lake shore."

He said, not quite honestly, "Their straightest approach to Abro Pakriaa's village—your village—is in the west. Were there prisoners?"

"Abro Samiraa is not like to take prisoners. We took not any on the beach. Wrong?"

He smothered a sigh of exhaustion. "It may not matter." With Mijok, the stout giantess Tejron was moving among the wounded. Paul noticed a heap of torn cloth, all that remained of Earth-made shorts and jackets and overalls, ripped for bandages. Wright's idea, no doubt, and good: the pygmies' pounded-bark fabric was a poor second best. *After the war we can go naked—fair enough.* . . . He saw a pygmy woman shrink from Tejron's approach; she might be from one of the northern villages, her stoicism unequal to accepting the touch of the huge beings she would always have regarded as wild animals. Paul knelt, hoping to reassure her, as Tejron eased a bandage around a pierced abdomen. There would be internal bleeding. "You are from the north?"

She looked hurt that he did not know her face. "I am of Abro Brodaa's village." Then in spite of her shrinking her question was directed at Tejron: "Abro Brodaa has say to us—we are all one flesh. That—that——"

Tejron was able to say, "That is true." And while Paul searched for other words that might affirm, comfort, ex- lain, the soldier died.

The only omasha now visible were soaring stragglers. The swarm would have found the army of Lantis—which must and would continue to advance. There was a limit to the gorging of the bat-winged beasts; they too could die on the spears. Meantime the lifeboat was gone, the boats were landing, in a moment of darkly sweet quiet which was the eye of the storm.

Paul checked the giant girl Lisson from firing at the landing party. "Save ammunition." He indicated a tall blue-flowered shrub a hundred yards out in the meadow. "We wait at the edge of the woods until they pass that bush, then charge them. If they break us down here, everyone is to fight west, away from the lake—*west*. Now run down the line, pass on these two orders." Lisson sped away, her golden fur bright and unstained. "Doc— get the wounded together, have the other women and Mijok take them west, beyond Sears' group; well back in the woods. Try to find out where Abara's got to with the olifants but send a runner back (if there's time)—don't come back yourself. And keep Mijok with you. I don't want him to do any more fighting if we can help it—it's tearing him up inside."

"I——" Wright checked himself, nodded, hurried back into the fortress.

"Pakriaa, Abro Kamisiaa, get your soldiers at the edge of the woods."

They vanished. The meadow was empty of life; the many open eyes on the beach would not see what was to come. Wright's party left the enclosure, Mijok carrying the shield. Wright could not look back nor wave, for his own arms were full, his head bent in some consoling speech. Paul was striding for the woods when Pakriaa met him and murmured in contempt, "We hide too, Com- mander?"

He answered out of a moment of black indifference. (*Probably we all die and everything I have done is a mis- take.*) "Pakriaa, they may break easier if they don't see us till we charge." She shrugged, following him into the obscurity, pointedly ignoring Nisana, who came to his other side, perhaps still hating the little captain for her independence of yesterday, when Paul was chosen commander of this grotesque army.

The Vestoians from the boats were rising out of the grass and coming forward. Steadily now, with no more apparent haste than the first breakers leading a destroying wave. It was possible to think with amazing leisure of the high meadows and wooded roads of New Hampshire. Paul's brother had always been a little too fat and fond of ice cream. There was a bookstore in Brattleboro. And the waves of the South China Sea were moving mountains with snowcaps of foam as they came in on Lingayen. Why, there was a war there once, more than a hundred years ago, when the Republic of Oceania was hardly even a thought. Yes: they called it a Second World War. . . .

The Vestoians passed the blue shrub. The breaker was red, with a foam of white-tipped spears.

Paul was swept into the open, not only by the howling drive of his own pygmy army, but by the machine within, relentless again, briefly free from the compromise of thought. He was firing with precision in the scant time available before the white-painted bodies crashed into the unpainted and churned up a froth of battle.

He had time to wonder why Nisana was here with him a few yards back of the hand-to-hand frenzy. She was not afraid; her spear was balanced. A break in the line of fighters let through a Vestoian soldier, dark mouth squared in a yell. Nisana's spear widened the mouth to a death mask and withdrew. Paul stepped into the breach and sent a few shots toward a trio of green-capped leaders. Something slapped and gouged at his chest—*nothing serious*. But his own fighters to the left of him were going down, outnumbered. He shouted at a brief gleam of Pakriaa's face, "West! Fight *west!*"

Golden Lisson was running back from her errand, her rifle waving, her lips straining in wild laughter. She passed him, trying to bring her rifle into use as she ran; it did not fire. A Vestoian was forcing Nisana away from Paul and beating down her spear. "Why, damn you!" The Vestoian face dissolved in pulp and strangeness under his rifle butt, and Paul reeled back, believing for an unbounded second that ghosts from a place only a few light-years away had swirled across this stinking battlefield to shriek at him: *"Yes! Your people always fought that way—the ape picked up a stone. . . ."* But Nisana was alive; Nisana was unhurt and alive. He could look up again and see the girl Lisson also using her rifle as a flail.

She was between him and the beach. Three pygmies had caught the butt, and now she swung them absurdly high; she had almost shaken them off when a spear pierced her arm and hung there. The rifle dropped. She was down, under the leaping spears and red bodies. She did not even cry out again; the golden fur was reddened and defiled. Paul beat his way toward her, scarcely seeing what his swinging rifle hit, knowing it was too late, forgetting his own order to drive west. Aware too of another tawny shape flashing toward him.

Surok, who had loved Lisson, who would have been her playmate in the next Red-Moon-before-the-Rains. Paul tried to stop him—but if any sound came out of his own throat it would have been lost against Surok's mindless crying. The giant tore into the press around Lisson's body and fell almost at once, crushing a few as he rolled. . . .

"West! Stay behind my rifle, Nisana——"

It had become a methodical insanity like Mijok's, a cutting of red hay that spouted blood. He noticed blood on his right hand too—nothing: front sights of the rifle gouging him. The Vestoians in this direction were thinning out and giving way. He caught up with a white-splashed back and bandaged thigh—Pakriaa, ploughing her way west. Abro Samiraa drove across his path in the wrong direction, chasing an isolated group of three; squat and heavy-faced, she looked happy and more than life-size in the moment of her death, as she took a spear thrust over her heart and lay down with the enemy to grin at the sky and cease hating.

A rifle barked ahead of him. That could only be Sears Oliphant: Wright would surely follow orders and keep Mijok and the giant women with him to protect the wounded. . . . Abro Brodaa was fighting through to aid Pakriaa, not yelling, not excited, keeping somehow an air of dreamy contemplation, as if the arms driving her spear and dagger were not quite hers. Nisana cried out, "They are not following! They go back——"

It was true. Partly true. Here in this patch of bloody meadow there was not much left to fight. The defenders had functioned like a single organism, forming a new semicircular line. Behind it was a quiet, where Pakriaa was gasping, pounding her foot into a body that felt nothing.

And this dear monster, this fat naked grotesque, panting and smeared with red—this must be Sears Oliphant, late of John Hopkins University. The monster smiled in a black beard. "Few got by, oh my, yes. Tamisraa's girls fixed 'em—had to club m' rifle—dirty cave man—no fear, Paul—*no fear!* Muscle man with an empty head. They had—couple bowmen with 'em—no harm done." No harm? Was he unaware of the broken arrow shaft below his ribs, deeply bedded, with dark blood oozing around the wood? "They quit, Paul?"

"They haven't quit." He looked south, seeing why they wouldn't quit.

"Tamisraa got a bad one—throat." Sears coughed painfully. "I sent her to Doc—he's just back of those trees. And my pets, Paul, my olifants, why, they're standing fast, boy. With Abara, bless him—'bout half mile north. You can't beat 'em. We must figure some way to ferry 'em over to the island—must—they're people, those olifants——"

"You go to Doc yourself, Jocko, and fast. That——"

"Oh, that, that. Mere prac'l dem'stration nobody loves fat man——"

The Vestoians would not quit because of what was coming half a mile away in the south under a cloud of brown wings, coming fast. The horde would be ignoring the omasha, striking them aside, spearing them when there was time, granting them the necessary toll for passage, and coming fast. Oh, they would be less than six thousand now—somewhat less. Meanwhile the remnant from the boats was waiting, regrouping, drawing breath, readying itself for the climax of massacre, maybe deliberately postponing it until Lantis of Vestoia, Queen of the World, could arrive to enjoy it. Paul tried again to count his people in the sturdy half circle. Black Elis was striding among them, a great stick in each hand, rumbling comfort and encouragement, and none of them shrank away from him.

It looked like less than seven hundred. A hundred lost at the knoll; forty, Wright said, in the first skirmish at the camp; twenty in Samiraa's night expedition. Perhaps three hundred in this last wave of the battle. And Samiraa herself; Duriaa; Tamisraa wounded, Pakriaa insane with grief; Lisson and Surok dead. Lame Kamisiaa—Paul could not find her. Abro Brodaa—still calm, unhurt, competent. Very well—seven hundred against somewhat less than six thousand of the land army, somewhat less than four thousand from the boats.

How I dreamed! There would be no southward drive to the island. The omasha alone made it an absurdity. He had been idiotic to imagine it.

Pakriaa broke her spear across her knee. She walked out into the meadow toward the advancing swarm. She looked back stupidly at Paul's shout, and Nisana ran to her, crying out in the old language. Pakriaa, with no change of expression, lunged at the captain, striking flat-handed across her face, forcing her back until Paul reached them to interfere and Sears caught Pakriaa's wrist, mumbling, "Come now—come with me, princess."

"I am no princess."

"I call you so," Sears said clearly, and speaking with sternness for possibly the first time in his life. "Now come with me."

Paul stammered, "Have Doc get that damned arrow out of you. Then he's to start north with the wounded—at once."

"North." Sears nodded.

"There are no gods," said Pakriaa.

"Yes, north. We'll catch up with you."

"I thought of you as a god."

"Think of me as a friend who loves you. It is better." She went with him, stumbling as Paul had never seen her do, and when the leaves closed behind them it seemed to Paul that there was surely the cloud of another world. She might have been a small girl going for a walk in the woods with her grandfather. . . .

There was no lifeboat above that rolling swarm. Ed

Spearman must have——*No time to think about it.*

But he had to, a little. Spearman was forced down by lack of fuel and killed. Or forced down, isolated somewhere, miles away. Or he had kept good watch of the fuel gauge until there was just enough for another trip to the island and had gone—right, reasonable, what he ought to have done, what Paul would have ordered him to do if he could have. . . . Paul turned to Brodaa. "Your sister Kamisiaa—I don't see her——"

"My lame sister is dead." Her eyes were shrewd, counting. "We have more than seven hundred. Two hundred of them bowmen."

"Bring them all to the woods. Spread the bowmen at the edge: they will meet the first charge with arrows, nothing else, and then join our retreat. Send a hundred spearwomen to guard and help Tocwright's group: they will go straight north. Send another hundred through the villages to save what they can—the children, the old—and take them west and north to join the others. All the rest will stay with you and me and Elis to fight in the rear—delay and confuse—fighting retreat, Brodaa. I see nothing else."

"Nothing else," she said evenly. "As you say. . . ."

Elis was with him, waiting under the trees, and Nisana, who said, "No gods? There must be other gods. Not Ismar. . . ."

Elis watched the meadow over the crouching bowmen. "Within you, Captain. The god within you made you save the life of my friend. I saw that. I even think I begin to understand. But that might be vanity."

6 A SORRY DAY MOVED INTO EVENING, AND WHEN
evening became an approach to moonless dark, this day of
retreat was in Paul's mind a passage of distorted images,
true or false.

True that he was now limping through forest stillness
between Nisana and a skinny ghost who was Christopher
Wright and Wright carried Pakriaa, who moaned at times
like a child with a nightmare, and up ahead were five white
drifting mountains, one of them ridden by a man who was
silent in pain, Sears Oliphant. It might or might not
be true that at some time during the day Paul had thrashed
on the ground with a broken head in front of some squall-
ing danger until black arms swept him up away from—
whatever it was.

Tejron and the two other giant women Karison and
Elron, and Mijok, still lived. Elis was walking behind Paul,
unhurt; therefore the mind of Elis would still be probing
at the borderland of known and unknown, searching and
incorruptible. All true. Apparently true that the gash in
Paul's side had stiffened, his right leg was knotting itself
in some unimportant distress, and his bandaged forehead
no longer throbbed.

The first contact with the Vestoian land army had been
a swift skirmish and ordered withdrawal. Abro Brodaa's
archers had crumpled the first enemy charge. After that
the Vestoians had crashed into the woods with no caution,
driven by the horror of brown wings that still pursued
them. Paul had had a final glimpse of the green headdress
of Lantis, Queen of the World; his two shots before the
rifle jammed had not touched her. Once, under cover of the
trees, the Vestoians had paused to reorganize, giving Paul's

retreating force a little time and distance and the help of forest obscurity.

The spearwomen sent ahead to clear the villages had poured through Pakriaa's settlement and Brodaa's, rounding up old people, children, and the chattering pack of male witches, sending them west to join Wright's group of wounded—if they could find it. But at the third village upstream—it had been Abro Samiraa's—there was delay. Perhaps the people had refused to go where there were giants. Paul's rear guard had halted south of the village to protect the evacuation; here the Vestoians caught up with them.

They had fought it out for two hours in the misery of bush and brier and purple vine outside the village ditch, while the jungle world steamed in the growth of midmorning. Paul's horizon had narrowed to the knot of fighters who stayed with him—Nisana, Brodaa, Elis, an unknown black-skirted soldier who fell at his feet with a bleeding mouth. Somewhere in that hell he had lost his rifle. It was Brodaa (this must be true, for it was Elis who told him of it)—Brodaa who had guided them out of the trap, regrouped the remnant of the rear guard north of Samiraa's village while the Vestoians paused to set that village afire and rejoice over its dying.

Paul could remember that regrouping: black Elis had set him on his feet, supporting him till he could walk. There were many twittering, mad-eyed bowmen among the survivors. Brodaa had sent runners to give the other three villages a final warning; she herself decided against trying to reach them with this fragment of an army numbering less than three hundred. The only way to save anything at all was to flee north, join Wright's group, hope that the remaining villages would delay the conquerors and that at least some of their non-combatants could scatter before Lantis, Queen of the World, took them for slaves, meat, and sacrifice.

The rest of the day had been a running, a harsh drive into country unknown even to Elis. There had been, for Paul and Elis at least, a breath of second wind when they found the tracks of the olifants. They had caught up with Wright's refugees in the early afternoon, but there could be no pause, even though it was quiet here at the edge of forest and western meadow and the sound of screaming in the villages was an hour behind them. . . .

Paul noticed that he was naked except for ammunition belt and an empty holster. Perhaps his present clarity of mind was the true madness, the earlier fog of pain and anger the mind's more natural climate. But one might as well reason and take stock. He remembered the map. Was it saved? No matter: a copy had been flown to the island with Dorothy and the baby.

I have a woman who loves me; I have a daughter. I have my life.

On his left, just visible in twilight beyond a meadow turning brilliant with blue fireflies, there were the low western hills, the hills rotten with the burrows of kaksmas, and they were nearer, much nearer than he had ever seen them except from the lifeboat. (*But Ed Spearman went there; he walked in the hills alone and found iron ore, and now he is——Never mind where he is. If the charlesite was giving out he did right to fly to the island and abandon us. What else could he do?*) Well, it was right too that the hills should be nearer: the edge of the forest slanted northwest, narrowing the meadow. And this far north the hills were smaller, more broken up. Yet it would not do to approach them closely: even the least of the hills (so pygmy and giant tradition said) could be the dwelling place of day-blind ratlike killers numerous enough to destroy this entire party and still be hungry. The retreat must struggle north until the hills were well behind, shut away by level jungle—where the kaksmas still might come, to be sure, but only to the distance of half a night's journey from their burrows. "Doc—can you estimate what distance we've made since we caught up with you?"

"Maybe twenty miles," the old man said. "In more time than *Argo* once needed to travel twenty million miles. What is man?"

"Man? A mathematical absurdity. . . . Aren't you tired? I could carry Pakriaa a while."

"No, I'm not tired, son. I like to have her. . . ."

Rifles—in the beginning there had been only five, and one shotgun. The shotgun had been taken to the island. Dorothy and Ann had their pistols there, too. Paul's rifle was lost. Lisson's had been lost when she died. That should leave three. Wright had one slung at his back. Peering up ahead, Paul saw another in the red-brown hand of the young giantess Elron. Sears must have lost his. So two at least remained. And one automatic—Wright's. "Those two new recruits Mijok brought——I'm in a fog—I only just remembered——"

"Lost," said Wright, staring ahead. "The boy didn't understand. He ran into the mess on the beach like a horse running into a fire. That was before you got back from the south. The other had more sense. Saw the pygmies spilling out of the boats and ran for the woods. Naturally we didn't try to hold him. Perhaps he's reached his home territory. I hope so."

Behind him Elis spoke softly: "It was not very far, Doc. When we reach the island and start the new settlement——"

"Oh, Elis——"

"When that has been done I'll come back and find him, give him the words—him and many others. I promise you that. Let me believe it."

"Believe it, Elis. But the boy Danik is dead. He was bright, curious. He should have lived 150 years."

"We overtake mystery," Elis said, "and leave it behind."

"Men have never overtaken the mystery of untimely death."

"There is chaos," said Elis. "Chance. Mystery is great jungle around a small clearing. I accept that. We make a wider clearing."

Paul felt Nisana's finger hook over his. Pakriaa groaned, perhaps in sleep. The darkness had blotted away the hills; even the small shape of Nisana was growing too dim. Elis said, "You're limping, Paul. Abroshin Nisana is tired. There are still three of the animals without riders. You and Doc——"

"Yes," Wright said. "We might make better time." Nisana trilled an order to Abara, who rode the colossal bulk of Mister Johnson at the head of the line. The animals halted without sound. "We must go on all night, Paul—right? What became of your—prisoner?"

"My——" the mental clarity must be a fraud, Paul thought, if new memories could flash into it so abruptly. At some time—it must have been after Elis had carried him clear of the nightmare at Samiraa's village—he had stumbled on a Vestoian soldier unconscious from a head wound and loss of blood but not dead. He had still been carrying her when they caught up with Wright. With this, the memory of that reunion became whole—the wordless suffering on the shield that Mijok carried, the improvised stretchers, the bewilderment and exhaustion in the red faces, the very smell of defeat—with this also a picture of the horribly fat witch from Pakriaa's village carried on a litter by two spearwomen, and one other witch, a lank skeleton with white and purple lines emphasizing the prominence of his ribs, striding beside his colleague and shooting glances of wrath from left to right and back. Someone had gently taken the unconscious soldier. "She's safe, Doc. Tejron took her—still has her, I'm sure."

"Good." Wright added with a harshness canceling humor: "Now if only friend Lantis will initial a copy of the Geneva Convention . . ." He was fumbling in the twilight before one of the white beasts, uncertain what to do.

The old cow olifant Susie, carrying Sears, fretted at the delay, sampling the air and rumbling. Paul petted her trunk to soothe her; Sears' voice came down to him: "Paul? Take this, will you?" He was reaching down the case that held his microscope, safe somehow out of the inferno of the day. "My grip's not too good, got nothing to tie it to—bare's a baby's bottom, like you. We look like the last days of a Turkish bath, hey?"

"How d'you feel?" Nisana tore shreds from what remained of her purple skirt; she looped them about the case, fastened it to Paul's ammunition belt.

"Feel good," Sears said. Each word was a thick struggle for normal speech. "Arrowhead came off; Chris got it out. Manicure scissors for forceps; you may slice me crossways and call me ham and eggs if it ain't so. Right, Chris? You there?"

"I'm here, Jocko," Wright said, and under his breath to Paul: "Medical kit lost. I don't think the spleen is injured, but——" Aloud he said, "Of course, with your gut what I needed was a hook and line. Paul, how do you make one of these ten-foot roller coasters kneel down?"

"Let me—that's Miss Ponsonby—she knows me." At Paul's order, tons of gentleness knelt on the earth; Paul held Pakriaa while Wright struggled into the hollow between hump and head, and Pakriaa was either asleep or not caring. . . . "Abro Brodaa?"

"Here, Commander."

"Form your people in three lines with linked hands. The giant women Karison and Elron, and Elis, will guide them at the head, because their night vision is better than yours and mine. Mijok and Tejron will walk beside us. We must travel all night. I think the Vestoians will not."

"They will not," the princess Brodaa said. He wished he could see truly what was happening in her little face. "They will not because they have no giants or Charins to help them." It carried no hint of the obsequious.

"Thank you, Abro Brodaa. Wait here a moment." He patted Millie's trunk—she was a young beast, nervous but fond of him—and made her kneel. "Help Nisana climb up to me. . . . Abro Brodaa—the people of your village——"

"Most of them lost." It might have been the oncoming night itself speaking temperately. "These remaining are a few from all the villages. I think they will follow me. And I will go with you. . . ."

In the rest of the night—a silence and a drifting, on the surge and thrust of the great animal under him—it was possible to reach a kind of sleep, knowing his body would not relax enough to fall or to weaken his hold on Nisana, who trusted him. She was deeply asleep in the first part of the night, occasionally snoring, a comic noise like a puppy's whine. All day she had never been out of his sight; she had fought like a hellcat, but singlemindedly, saving her strength to deal with those who threatened him.

It would have been possible to abandon these people; at one time, Paul remembered, he had almost favored it himself, and Ed Spearman had very nearly hinted that it might be better to join forceś with the tyranny in the south. . . . Life seemed cheap to Pakriaa's tribe—others' life. Devil-worshipping cannibals, capable of every cruelty, committed for thousands of years to all the superstitions that ever crippled intelligence. You had to look beyond that, said Christopher Wright the theorist, the doctor, the anthropologist, the impractical daydreamer. *Anyway I*

*saved a Vestoian—if she lives. One balanced against how
many that I destroyed . . . ? No answer. . . . Unless you
can see a world where the ways of destruction become
obsolete under a government of laws. With the devils of
human nature—the vanities, the greeds, the follies and
needless resentments, the fear of self-knowledge, dread
of the unfamiliar, the power lust of the morally blind, the
passion for easy solutions, scapegoats, panaceas—how
do you see such a world . . . ? You say, Christopher
Wright, that no one is expendable. I believe you. But—
when I must choose between the life of myself or my
friends and the life of the one whom the stream of history
has tossed against me as my enemy——*

*When I do that, I only discover once more that I am
caught in the same net with the rest of my kind and cannot
escape until all of them escape—escape into a region of
living where men do not set traps for each other and the
blind do not lead.*

Therefore——

"Are you awake, Nisana?" Her even breathing quick-
ened. It seemed to Paul that there was faint color in his
glimpses of sky; he remembered the silver moon that had
appeared over the jungle with first-light so long ago—
yesterday morning. The passage of the red moon around
Lucifer was swift: tonight it would be rising two hours
before first-light and would be something broader than
the gory scimitar he had seen from the knoll.

"I am awake."

"I think the red moon has come back."

"Yes." She pointed over his shoulder; he glimpsed it
through a gap in the leaves. "A good moon. Begins the
Moon of Little Rains. The small rains make no harm,
make the ground sweet. Is better than the moon past—that
we call the Moon of Beginnings." She moved restlessly
against him. "This country—all forest? How long have I
sleep?"

"Most of the night. We're past the open land."

She whispered, "No one has ever come here. We have
think always there are bad—what word?—tev—tevils in
the north."

"Tomorrow—rather, today—we turn west and then
south on the other side of the hills, to the island."

"Ah, the island. . . . I cannot see this island."

"You'll like it, Nisana. You'll be happy there."

"Happy?" And he remembered that the old pygmy language had no word for happiness.

Wright's voice came thinly in the dark: "Abara, stop them! Sears——"

Millie halted and knelt without an order: Nisana jumped down. Paul saw the shapes of Elis and Sears suddenly bright under Wright's flashlight—the only radion light left. "Easy," Elis said. "I have you." And he lowered the man's bulk to the ground as Susie moaned and shifted her feet. Sears had said nothing, but he was smiling, his face red and vague above the disorder of the black beard.

"Paul, hold the light for me." Wright removed the stained bandage. There was a wide area of inflammation; the lips of the arrow wound were purple. "Pakriaa! You said once you never heard of poison on the arrows——"

Pakriaa gaped, rubbing her eyes. It was Brodaa who answered: "Our people never had it on the arrows. But in the war with Lantis last year some of our soldiers had wounds like this."

"And what happened?"

"Ismar——" Pakriaa stumbled forward. "Ismar took——"

"My sister," said Brodaa, "be quiet, my sister."

"Elis," Paul whispered, "have Tejron and the other women keep watch—we must stay here a while. Where is Mijok?"

"Here." Mijok spoke behind him. "I have put my shield —over there." His voice became a whisper for Paul: "There are only three on it now. One little man, two women. They might live. Paul—is it happening, Paul?"

"I can't say it. I don't know. . . ." Sears was talking, ramblingly, very far from this patch of earth. One could only listen till he was silent. Then Paul said, "I think so, Mijok. He needs to speak; we need to remember."

"What is this—Tel Aviv——"

"The place on the other planet where he was born."

"And there were the vineyards, oh my, yes—the little white and tan goats——" Sears could see it, Paul thought, that small country, a quiet corner of the Federation, where every grain of sand might remember blood spilled in the follies of hatred, where a teacher of mercy had been crucified. But now for Sears it was not a place of history: he saw gardens defying wasteland, the homes and farms, centers of music and learning where he moved, thoroughly at home, discovering the country of his own science, himself a citizen of no one place except the universe. Later he was recalling the hot white streets of Rio, the genial clutter of London, Baltimore, the majestic contradictions of New York.

"Why, yes, Doctor," he said—and he did not mean Christopher Wright, but some friend or instructor whose image might be standing in front of the shadows of Lucifer, "yes, Doctor, you could say I've traveled a great deal, in my sort of blundering fashion. And I would not exactly say that people are the same everywhere, but you'll have noticed - yourself—the many common denominators are much more interesting than the seeming-great differences, aren't they, hey . . . ? What? Sorry, Doctor, I've got no damned use for your abstraction Man, and why? Because he doesn't exist, except as a device in a brain that wants to prove something—which may or may not be useful. In any case it's not my dish. There are only men and women. They get born and love and suffer and work and grow old and die; or sometimes, Doctor, they die young. Men and women I can love and touch; sometimes I can even teach them the few things I know. You may take Man to the library; feed him back into your electronic brain and don't bother me with the results so long as I'm alive to see a child discovering his own body—or for that matter a bird coming out of the egg, a minnow in a spot of sunlight, a blade of grass."

Pakriaa wailed: "What is he saying? He is not here." She squirmed past Wright, dropped to the ground, her cheek pressed on Sears' tangled hair, her free arm wandering over his face and shoulder as if she wanted to cover him like a shield. "He talked to me once. Sears, you said—you said——"

He was back among them, gazing around in sane bewilderment. "I should be riding. . . . Pakriaa—why Pak, I'm all right." Paul moved the torch here and there to pick out his own face, Wright's, Mijok's, the white bulk of Susie looming close by, the pouting ugly mask of Abara, who had stolen up close, his underlip wobbling in an effort to speak. "I fell asleep—took a tumble?"

"Almost," Wright muttered. "Just lucky chance I saw you tottering. You need to rest a bit."

"Oh no." Sears frowned. "Can't stop." He smiled at Pakriaa, who had lifted herself to watch him pleadingly. "What's the matter, Pakriaa? What's the time?"

"First-light before long," Paul said. "We made good distance, Jocko. The Vestoians won't have traveled in the dark. Plenty of time and we all need rest. Take it easy a while."

But Pakriaa could not hide her knowledge that he was dying; Sears touched her cheek with a curious wandering finger. "You liked looking in the microscope, didn't you?" She nodded. "Remember—must be sure you've got the best focus you can before you make up your mind about anything. But this is more serious, Pak—because I think you love me and you have trouble. I tell you again, you must go to the island with the others. You must live. Now I expect to go there too, but—"

Abara moved away. Paul glimpsed him striding back and forth, striking the air with little fists. When he returned, Paul made way for him.

"—for a teaching is a gift, Pakriaa, not to be thrown away—"

Abara stammered. "You have talk to me too, Sears—"

"Why, to all of you. Certainly to you, Abara. . . . What's the profit of any effort if the result is thrown away in a time of weakness? You discard only if what you have is proven false. We haven't much—we never have much. Some things appear to be empirically certain. Not many . . . You know, I believe I've given a few people—call it a wakening of curiosity. I think that's good. Curiosity and patience. Good as far as it goes. I'm not ashamed." He was trying to see Wright's gaunt face. "You picked a tougher subject, didn't you, Chris? Don't worry—give you an A for something more than effort. . . . Now look, this hanging around here won't do." He caught Paul's hand and heaved himself upright. "I remember—map—damn it. Need another whole day before we pass the hills. Susie— down, Susie—"

But Susie, fumbling at him with her trunk, would not kneel. Paul heard Mijok's agonized whisper: "She knows."

Sears laughed. "All right, make the old man climb." And before anyone could stop him he had tottered a few steps and burned out the last of his strength in a heaving jump toward her neck, which barely lifted him from the ground and dropped him at Paul's feet. Groping for him, Paul saw that he was dead, saw also, above the arching of the trees, a lucid cruelty of morning.

7 TWICE THAT DAY ELIS DROPPED FAR BEHIND TO LIS-
ten and reported there was no pursuit. It was hard to judge
their distance from the foothills of the western range, for
now there was no open ground—only Wright's compass,
the memory of the map, and treetop surveys that Mijok
made from time to time. Abara rode Mister Johnson in the
lead, making the beasts travel slowly since the pygmies
were faint with weariness. Susie trailed forlornly; she had
not been willing to abandon the grave till the others went
on without her.

The pygmies carried only half a dozen makeshift
stretchers; the number of unwounded had diminished too.
"They slip away," Brodaa said to Paul. He saw three men
carrying children too small to walk; no old women. The
fat witch rode his litter, unconcerned at the fatigue of its
bearers; the other old man, smeared with white and purple
paint, stalked beside him. Brodaa said, "My sister Tamisraa ended life with the white-stone dagger. While Elis and
Mijok made the—what word?—grave. We left her body
looking north to help the spirit journey. There are many
lost who will have no prayers—bad—they may follow us.
What is this—burial, Paul-Mason?"

"A Charin custom. Most of us believe the spirit dies
with the body: different parts of the same thing."

"Ah?" She did not seem shocked. "Maybe true for your
people."

"We live in others," Paul said. "Sears lives so long as we
remember him. That will be always. . . ." It seemed to
Paul there were scarcely a hundred in this worn line. "We
mustn't try to hold them if they want to go. If you, Brodaa, or any others want to leave us, you know you are
free."

Her answer was firm and considered: "I will not leave you. . . ."

Wright had not spoken since the burial, nor had Pakriaa. They kept together; Paul was with them sometimes. Behind them Mijok carried his shield. It was Elis who heard the bleat of asonis and stole off to bring back meat for an afternoon meal. It was Elis, before that, who said, "We have done what we could, Paul. We could not have made these people retreat in time to save themselves. If we had abandoned them Lantis would have left no more than a fire leaves in the Red-Moon-of-Dry-Days. Pakriaa is too sick to understand that, yet. She carries a grief like a little one swelling in the womb: it must grow greater before she is delivered of it."

In the afternoon halt, it was Elis who tried to make Wright eat something and sleep, but Wright could do neither.

The giant women Elron and Karison also refused the meat. They sat apart with stout brown Tejron. She was eating, keeping close to her the still unconscious Vestoian, whom the pygmies had given no more than disgusted glares. Tejron might be listening to Karison's undertone—it was in the monosyllables of the old language. The girl Elron held her eyes downcast, fondling the rifle. She and Karison had been much together in a peculiar loneliness since the children were flown to the island: Karison was old, her children grown and gone away before the Charins came; Elron was too young to have given birth. Three of the children at the island were Tejron's; the others were children of Muson and Samis and of a mother who had died in the old life. Tejron wiped her lips and grunted impatiently; she took up her charge in careful arms and left the two. Paul sensed what was to come when Elron set her cherished rifle at his feet. Karison approached Wright, humble but determined: "We must leave you."

Before Wright could speak, Mijok answered her with a sullen anger Paul had never heard from him: "I brought you from the jungle with empty heads. We gave you the words, the beginning of the laws we must make together. You lived like the uskaran, furtive and cruel—"

"No," Wright said. "Mijok, no. . . ."

Karison had winced, but she repeated: "We must go. The old way—we need it."

"Then you must go," Wright said, his spread fingers white-nailed on the ground. "And remember always that you go with our good will."

"That is so." She was torn two ways. "But the old life—"

Elis rumbled: "Elron, come here." The girl would not. "I hoped that in the next Red-Moon-before-the-Rains—"

She muttered, "When the change comes you will return to us—"

Elis laughed, roaring at her, "You're a fool, a child!" The harshness, Paul knew, was calculated, in the hope of changing her mind by shaming her. "You think the old life was a freedom. Freedom to live like an animal without an animal's peace, Elron, because of the thing in you that struggles for knowledge—oh yes, in spite of yourself, and always. Freedom to hunt all day or else sleep on an empty stomach, jump with fear at every creaking branch. Freedom to cram yourself with moss root and slugs from the streams—never enough—in the bad moons when the asonis go north. Freedom to kill the pygmies and be hunted by them, never an end to it—that's your freedom without the laws, without the words. No, so long as you're a fool I don't want you." She turned away, speechless; he shouted after her in a different voice, "He said you go with our good will. That is true. You can't forget us, Elron. You're not the wild thing Mijok brought out of the woods. You'll feel us pulling you back—you feel it now—and you will come back." But she was gone in the shadows, Karison following her, and Elis rubbed his broad forehead on his arms.

Wright whispered, "If they wanted it—it had to be so."

Elis waited for his angry breathing to calm. "Mijok, do you remember? In the old days I couldn't even have been your friend. Remember how angry *I* was—only a year ago? You stepping over the border of my territory, telling me—I've wondered how you did it with our few stumbling words—telling me every being should be free to go as he pleased anywhere in the world? You were in danger, Mijok. I am older, bigger, heavier—I nearly went for your throat. Long ago. So—don't be angry with these two."

Tejron sat by Wright, holding the Vestoian like a nursing baby. "Maybe," she said, "maybe they will take some of what you teach us to others. Maybe it will be like the thing you showed us, how a little seed no bigger than the eye of illuama can become a tree. . . ."

Pakriaa had watched indifferently; Paul hoped he was right, that her face was not quite so tightly set in lines of rejection and despair. Wright came stiffly to his feet, a hand on Tejron's shoulder, the other wandering into his gray beard. "Abro Brodaa, interpret for me—some of them have no English. Tell them we turn west soon, then south through bad country—swamp, heat, uskaran, marsh reptiles maybe, maybe the kaksmas swarm on the west side of the hills. Tell them we go through that. When we reach a river we have seen from the air—it has no falls and flows southwest—we shall make boats."

Brodaa put it into the high music of the pygmy tongue. Paul could see no change in the saddened faces; by rumor, most of them would already know this much. But the thin witch was muttering to his gross colleague, and some soldier faces turned to overhear that instead of attending to Brodaa.

"Tell them, Brodaa, this river will take us to Big-Water. We go south along the coast, to the island where our friends are, where we believe Spearman has gone in the winged boat. Tell them, on this island there are no kaksmas, the omasha never come, nor the lake boats of Lantis. There is game, good ground, room for all. Tell them— No, wait. . . . Oh, Brodaa, tell them in your own way that we hope to live there in peace."

The lean witch interrupted Brodaa's translation with a wailing diatribe, twitching his twigs of arms, lashing the battered soldiers with his oratory. Brodaa turned to Wright in misery: "He says—he saw Ismar change Spearman back to a marsh lizard and the boat to an omasha."

Mijok laughed savagely. "When did he see that? Ask him."

Brodaa did, on a thin shout. The scarecrow flashed her a glare of resentment and a snapping answer. . . . "He says he saw it in sleep picture."

Paul snarled, "Yes, a dream's as near as he came to a battlefield."

Brodaa was shocked, but Nisana laughed. The fat witch

on the litter was fuming. Coming from Pakriaa's village, he probably had enough English to understand it; he leaned forward, embracing his hideous belly, croaking at the soldiers. Nisana translated in swift whispers: "Says —you Charins all marsh lizards, changed by Inkar-Goddess-of-Kaksmas. . . . Says we lose to Vestoians because image was broke; Ismar punishes. . . . Will I kill him, Paul-Mason?"

Brodaa choked: "You cannot touch Amisura. Your spear will turn—"

"My spear is lost," said Nisana, loudly enough for all to hear. "But Aksona, Amana, two other men of magic— those I saw killed at Abro Samiraa's village. Vestoian spears was not turn in the hand—I saw." She stepped forward, fingering her white-stone knife, and the fat Amisura cringed, squeaking.

Wright cried, "I forbid it, Nisana. Let them go. Brodaa!"

Brodaa said quickly, "He asks sacrifice—you, Paul, Pakriaa—"

Nisana laughed again. She dropped her white-stone dagger on the ground and slapped the thin witch in the face. The crowd gasped and shrank back. Such a man, Paul knew, was altogether holy, never to be touched; one must not even look him in the eye. But Nisana slapped him again and shoved him sprawling. She caught a pole of Amisura's litter, heaved at it, and he tumbled like a red melon. "*Now* let them choose!" She came back to Paul with grin and swagger, patting her scarred chest. "I am little Spearman. I break images too."

And the pygmies were choosing, not as she or the witches had hoped—choosing headlong retreat from this sacrilege, dissolving away into the forest with sick-eyed backward looks. Paul saw Amisura weeping, humping pitiably back to his litter on all fours, and heard Pakriaa laugh. The two soldiers who had carried Amisura brought the litter nearer, not daring to touch him; when he flopped on it they bore him away. The other witch had run blindly, covering his insulted face, and Wright said like a machine, "Let them go—let them—"

Sardonically, Pakriaa had watched the whole incident without rising; now she seemed to want to catch Wright's eye, lifting a skinny shoulder as if to say: "What can you do with fools?"

When the panic was over, thirty followers remained. . . .

In the early evening Mijok reported, after another treetop survey, that the last of the kaksma hills was about three miles southwest. West of them the jungle was level; it was time to turn. Elis had slipped away and returned with two heavy carcasses like wild boars. Sears had named these stodgy animals pigmors. The *mor* suffix, he had insisted, was an intensely scientific shorthand for "more or less, damn it." The meat was high-flavored and coarse but safe. . . . Hearing Mijok's news, Brodaa sighed, thinking perhaps of the long history of her people, the groping for a narrow path of survival among endless perils. "We say the great uskaran hears a leaf fall to earth from a thousand paces away but the kaksma hears the leaf divide the air as it falls. Oh—three of your Charin miles, that is great length. Maybe enough."

The tremendous sheer spires of the coastal range, Mijok said, were visible in the southwest though nearly a hundred miles off; it would be a clear sweet night, he thought, with no clouds and many stars. They should go at least fifteen miles due west; then the course would be southwest rather than south, to miss the hills. . . .

In the crowding darkness Mister Johnson's leading was again a thing of wisdom; his lifted trunk and sensitive eyes avoided dense growth and drooping vines that could endanger the riders. From each necessary detour he came back willingly to the course, under guidance of Abara's sense of compass direction, and the other four followed him as the arm follows the hand. Tonight Paul rode old Susie—she seemed to feel happier for it—carrying Nisana again; Wright was on Miss Ponsonby, with Pakriaa. Tejron, unfamiliar with the beasts but ready to learn, had climbed on Millie's back and kept her balance without trouble, holding the wounded Vestoian, who stirred and whimpered but was not truly conscious. Behind Paul was the more nervous bull Mister Smith without a rider, and Elis and Mijok walked beside him, Mijok with his shield, Elis holding Brodaa's hand. The thirty who had dared to choose the forbidden unknown trailed behind Brodaa with linked fingers, nine bowmen among them; there were few weapons, no wounded except on Mijok's shield, and this held only two, for one of the women had died. The wounded archer was yellow-faced with loss of blood from a hip injury, but that was clean and closed; he was free from the signs of fear, almost cheerful. The woman was a sturdy black-skirted soldier of the ranks, gashed in the face and with a leg torn from knee to ankle.

Another night of silence and of drifting—for a while. Wright's voice floated back: "I am thinking of Dorothy and Ann, and your daughter."

"And not of Ed Spearman?"

"Oh. . . . The fuel must have been getting low, Paul. Nothing the boat could do for us after we were back in the woods. He must be at the island."

Paul could only say, "I hope so." The thing Spearman had almost said when his anger and disappointment were high, the hint at joining forces with Lantis in abandonment of everthing thus far achieved—nothing could be gained by speaking of that now. But some of Spearman's words murmured on in darkness: *"Lantis—terrific organization . . . monetary system . . . whole world for the taking . . . pretty idealism that never worked even on Earth . . ."*

There had always been strain and mutual exasperation in argument with Ed Spearman—long ago, on the ship *Argo.* The Collectivist Party, surviving as an innocuous political group after the horrors of the Civil War of 2010-13, lived strongly in Spearman's mind, not only because his father had fought for it. Lacking the frenzied dogmatism of the antique communism it resembled, it was nevertheless communism's natural heir, a party of iron doctrines simplified for minds that resented analysis and magnified Man out of a dislike for men. Like communism, it needed to imagine a class war and felt that it had a tight vested monopoly of the underdog. The C.P., said one of its late twentieth-century prophets as humorless as his predecessors, "believed in Man." You could always fluster a collectivist by asking for a logical breakdown of that— and make an enemy: they were usually good haters and made a virtue of it. The years following the Civil War had been troubled though materially prosperous, darkened by the build-up of yet another monolithic state under Jenga the Mongol, who had inherited the desolation of the Russo-Chinese war of 1970-76; in those years the Collectivist Party in the Federation, unsupported by any conveniently foreign deity, had become not much more than a serio-comic decayed socialism with a dash of bitters. But it was alive; at the time *Argo* left the spaceport it had had ten senators and a larger handful of delegates in the Federation Congress. It was respectable, no longer subversive, and owned a small hard core of the aggressively sincere. . . . Not Wright nor Sears nor anyone had ever been able to convince Edmund Spearman that evil means breed a further evil, which swallows up any good that may have been imagined in the beginning. Spearman could admit that (himself in no way an evil man) he would not do evil—if he could help it. But in the region of theory Spearman held quite simply that you can't make an omelette without breaking eggs, and that settled it. . . .

"They should be safe," Wright said. "You and Jocko saw the island."

"It's beautiful. I know they're all right."

"Yes. . . . Would you say it was a place where Ann might—oh, how shall I say it?—might attain tranquillity? Not cry too much for the moon?"

"If there is any such place in the Galaxy."

"Time," Elis said. "Little Black-Hair needs time. She is like grass I have seen growing in too much shade. She is not like our Mashana Dorothy who will make sunshine if the other sun is clouded."

"Listen!" Brodaa's voice. "Listen. . . ."

Paul heard nothing, at first. Up ahead Abara sputtered: "Mister Johnson—hoo-hee—be quiet. Is nothing—be quiet—"

Nisana came broad awake in Paul's arms. Wright's mount halted, as did Susie, but Susie was trembling, raising and swinging her head in a way to make balance difficult; Paul saw the white writhing of her trunk lifted to explore for a scent. . . . He heard it then: a long rustling, like a repeated tearing of paper behind a closed door; nothing else. . . . A wet howl from Mister Johnson sent a spasm through Susie's mass; her muscles bunched; Abara's voice wailed back: "Mister Joh—I cannot hold him—*kaksmas!*"

Transition from realization to stampede was a flash like the pain of a blow. Paul heard Mijok: "My shield—it will hold more." Elis cried something to Brodaa. Then Susie had plunged ahead, uncontrollable; Paul could only bend low above the clinging of Nisana, hold on with hands and knees, hope that no trailing vine or branch would sweep them off into death. Mister Johnson could make no careful choice of a trail now—he would be parting the jungle like a six-ton bullet. "Don't be afraid, Nisana—we can outrun them—"

"My people—"

"Elis and Mijok can outrun them too. They'll carry all they can." In spite of the agony of mere hanging on, mere straining to stay alive, he had to think: *They were loyal and we got them into this. . . .* Branches slashed across his back, stinging and scraping. Once Susie stumbled and recovered as the group went splattering across some invisible mud, and Paul wondered if Mister Johnson in his terror would run them into quicksand or marsh.

That ended; there was more thick jungle whipping his back for—five minutes?—an hour . . . ? This too ended.

Crazed or purposeful, the beasts charged out into open land through a soft roaring of torn grass. Paul could twist his head to glance upward at a field of stars. He could not win a backward look for Elis and Mijok: his neck and arm muscles were stiffened in his grasp of Susie's ears, and he dared not risk disturbing Nisana's clutch of him. But to left and right he could make out other shapes under starlight and hear a frantic thudding of hoofs—fleeing asonis, other innocent woodland cattle with a hunger to live. Once he glimpsed a long-bodied thing pass off to the left in wild leaps lifting it above the grass tops: uskaran, he thought, the huge tiger cat, no enemy but a brother in panic.

The open ground ended at water; here at last the olifants slowed to a halt, unlike the lesser desperate brutes, for Mister Johnson was still wise, considering the stream, aware of his leadership. Paul could shout to the others now, and they all answered. But his backward staring found only the stars, the white mass of Mister Smith, the disturbed darkness that must be meadow. "Elis! Mijok!"

No answer could have reached him above the bleating and thunder of terrorized harmless things crossing the field and hurtling blindly into the river. Mister Johnson was wading in deliberately. There was splashing at first, then silence, as cool water came up around Paul's knees and Susie's motion changed to a smooth throbbing and heaving; he saw small foam where the curve of her lifted trunk cut the water. He whispered to Nisana, "We're safe, dear. Big river. Kaksmas won't cross it. . . ." Mister Johnson was leading them in an upstream slant, bearing well to the right while the bobbing frantic heads of other creatures let the moderate current press them away to the left. This way—whether by Mister Johnson's wisdom or Abara's guidance—they might be able to come ashore clear of the dangerous passage of the stampede.

"My people cannot go through the water. We never—"

"Elis and Mijok can swim. They'll get them across somehow. Maybe the shield will float, Nisana."

The madness behind them dwindled into the faraway. In growing quiet, Wright's voice came back, not loudly: "I am a murderer."

Paul wondered what insight made him call out words not his own: " 'What's the profit of any effort if the result is thrown away in a time of weakness?' "

The even motion became a clumsiness of wading in mud. Then there was solid ground. Paul said, "Halt them here if you can, Abara." Mister Johnson must have shared the sense of safety; they all calmed, heads drooping, shaken breathing slowing to sighs. "Down, Susie. . . ." All but Abara descended. This was still open grassland, but there was a black velvet curtain of jungle not far off. "Doc— still got your flashlight?"

"Eh? No—lost somewhere." The old man spoke vacantly; he stumbled to the edge of the water, sat with his head on his knees. "Mijok—Mijok . . ."

Tejron still had her Vestoian, but now the pygmy woman was panting, fully conscious in Tejron's arms and witless with fear. Tejron said, "She's trying to break away. Can't someone talk to her?"

"Pakriaa!" Paul searched for the princess. "Here— please."

Nisana whispered, "I will talk to the Vestoian—yes?"

"Not yet. If Pakriaa—"

Pakriaa said thickly, "I am here. What to say? She is nothing."

"She is nothing to you, Pakriaa? Then Sears chose a poor student. Brodaa would have spoken to her. I ask you to tell her the war is over and she is among friends."

"Friends? She is Vestoian." Pakriaa approached Wright, who did not look up. "Tocwright—I must speak to the Vestoian kaksma? I owe you my life—will obey you."

He groaned: "I do not want you to obey me. If there is nothing inside to tell you what you should do, then I have nothing to say to you."

Pakriaa flung up her arm across her eyes as if struck. Tejron muttered, "I can't restrain her much longer without hurting her." It was Nisana who gave the Vestoian the message in the pygmy tongue, a ripple of sound that must have conveyed some reassurance, for the struggling ceased.

"Look!" Paul dug his fingers in Wright's shoulder. "Over there—"

The dark spot under starlight was surely the floating shield; behind it, another purposeful splashing, rise and fall of a driving arm.

"Mijok!" Wright was on his feet. "This way! A little upstream—"

Both giants were bleeding from small double stab wounds of the kaksma teeth. There were four pygmies on Mijok's shield. Elis had carried Brodaa and another in his arms and one on his back; they had clung to his fur as he swam the river. Mijok plucked a sodden thing from his thigh; its jaws had clenched in flesh when he smashed its body. He flipped the ratty thing into the water and remarked like a Charin, "Damned if I could ever care for 'em."

"The others—"

"We tried to help them into the trees," said Elis. "Could be some safety in that if the swarm passes by. But most of them ran blindly, so—beyond that, Doc, don't ever ask us.

We must forget some things. We've all done what we could, so—let's rest a while and go on."

"Oh, we go on," Wright said. "Chaos, or maybe a little bit of light from time to time. What—sixteen of us now . . . ? Which way was the swarm going?"

"North. Our flight was west. I think this place is safe." Abara called down: "Mister Johnson says it is safe."

Paul said, "No more travel tonight. Wait here for daylight. This is not the river we wanted, but we know it reaches the sea somehow. Let's think about that in the morning. And—if you will, Doc—I'd like to make that my last order. Let Elis be our commander till we reach the island."

"I!" Elis was shocked. "But Paul . . . I am a big baby, I wonder and wonder and never find the answer to anything."

Wright laughed; it sounded like laughter. At any rate when his voice found words it was warm, relieved, more like his own than it had been at any time since the drums sounded on Lake Argo. "That doesn't matter, Elis. Paul has done all anyone could, done it well, and leadership's a wearing thing. But you can carry it."

Paul wished he could see the black face in the dark; he might learn from it, he thought, so far as a Charin was capable of learning. Elis said dazedly, "If you all wish it—"

"I wish it," said Abro Brodaa.

"Yes," Mijok said. "Let's not trouble to vote. We know you, Elis."

"I'll do my best. . . ."

Most of the pygmies collapsed in sleep. The bites the giants had received were not numerous enough to be a danger, but both were in some pain, and wakeful; Abara also said he would prefer to watch out the night and not sleep. Paul stretched on the damp grass, aware of Nisana, sitting near him. He tried to make a mental refuge of Dorothy and the island; for a time it was possible, but twice, as he thought he was drifting into true healing sleep, the present pulled at him and the thought was not of Dorothy, but of Pakriaa, throwing up her arm across her eyes as if Wright's words had been a deeper wound than any she had received in these days of calamity and defeat.

He woke while it was still night. The red moon had risen, changing the river to deep purple; the stampede was all ended, and stillness was everywhere, underlying the low voices of Wright and Elis. He saw the small silhouette of Nisana beside him; he could make out none of the others, but he heard the soft breathing of the olifants, and at least some of them must have gone to the jungle and returned, for there was a steady munching of coarse leaves. He thought: *Sears' pets—one of his ten thousand gifts we can never live long enough to assess. His laughter was another. . . .*

Wright was talking placidly: "We suppose it must have been a similar story on this planet, Elis. The major patterns are the same. The small and simple forms must have grown to greater complexity through their millions of years, undoubtedly in the seas, the good saline medium for our kind. Then other millions of years, while the first creatures to try the land were clumsy amphibians, still needing the sea but developing ways to carry it with them, venture a little further. There's no hurry in history."

"And before the beginning of life?"

"Difficult, Elis. We think (there are other theories) that each star with planets was once two—a binary, our astronomers called it—"

Someone thin and small came near to Paul, speaking delicately, in an extremity of pain, and not to him. "Nisana," Pakriaa said. "Nisana—"

Nisana was looking up, a little afraid, uncertain. "Princess?"

"Only Pakriaa. . . . Nisana—I saw how you spoke to the Vestoian, how she was quiet. If you will bring her—and Tejron too? And we go and listen—Tocwright is talking about the stars—the world—I think, maybe, we tell her what he says? Will you come with me, Nisana?"

Part Three

The Year Ten

1 *Argo IV* ANSWERED DUNIN'S BROWN HAND AT THE tiller, sliding south under a following breeze. Her chief designer Paul Mason liked to call her a sloop, admitting that on no planet would any sloop have cared to be found dead with a pair of twelve-foot oars amidships. She was thirty-six feet fore and aft. Without a sawmill, shaping boards for her strakes had been harder than trimming and placing the single tree trunk that was her keel. Much of her joining was with wooden pegs; there was iron in her too, from the single deposit of ore on the island of Adelphi. Her building had started seventeen months ago in the Year Nine. One month ago Paul's daughter Helen had cracked across her bow an earthen flask of wine brought to maturity by Nisana and *Argo IV* had slipped out of the mouth of the Whitebeach River for a maiden voyage—a forty-mile circuit of the island, including the passage of a strait where a current from open ocean ran formidably between Adelphi and a small nameless island in the south. Since then she had journeyed short distances up and down the coast, learning her own fussy ways and teaching them to her makers.

Argo II had been a clumsy oared raft of heroic history. Nine Lucifer years ago, roughly the equivalent of twelve Earth years, *Argo II* had not only brought fifteen survivors of a war to the island, she had also, broadened and repaired, returned to the mainland over the ten-mile channel to pick up a sixteenth survivor, Abara, and the gentle white beasts he had refused to abandon. He had guided them south, through seventy miles of unknown terrors, and ten miles further along the beach, until it came to an end at sheer cliffs; here *Argo II* found him. One by one—probably no one but Abara could have coaxed them aboard—*Argo II* had ferried all five of the olifants across. During the rains that came for a dark ending of Year Two, the swollen Whitebeach River had torn *Argo II* from her moorings and she had been swept away down the channel. Now she would be driftwood scattered over the infinity of the unexplored; she was remembered.

Argo III, still in existence and more often called Betsy, was only a boxed platform with outriggers and two pairs of oars. With four giants at the oars and a favorable current she could approximate three miles an hour and carry several tons. She had been built in the Year Four and was still busily bringing slabs of building stone from the base of the coastal range. The stone was red and black or sometimes purple, heavy, already smoother than marble without polishing; unlike any common stone of Earth, it was so hard that wind and sun and water over the centuries had done little with it. Wright believed that was why the coastal range could rise to such heights from a narrow base. While the years in their millions had turned other mountains to level ground, the glassy rock remained: it could be broken for use but defied erosion like a diamond.

Argo IV was unequivocally a ship; after her trial Paul had carved for her bow a figurehead with the dreaming face of Pakriaa.

"Maybe," Dunin said, "with a few more like this the first explorations could be around the coast instead of overland? If we had two or three more ships when Kris-Mijok is old enough to go?"

Paul knew Dorothy had winced, though her face was turned to the evening-reddened field of water. "If he still wants it, when he's old enough to go. . . ."

Kris-Mijok Wright, her third-born child and only son, had been born in the Year Three; in Earth years he was only nine. His hunger for the long journeying might be mainly a reflection of his devotion to Dunin, herself full of visions and not yet a woman. A tentative half joke, a means of channeling a child's fantasy into patience, had somehow become a sober adult plan: that the first major explorations would begin when Kris-Mijok would have a man's strength to take part in them.

"We might have such ships by then." Paul tried to sound judicial. "Say the Year Eighteen or Nineteen. Yes, a coastal exploration might be better than trying to cross the continent. Not a circumnavigation though, at first."

Dunin's big face blossomed in a grin. "Only about thirty-six thousand miles, by the old map made from the air. Open water at north and south poles, plenty of it. Could do it in less than a year."

"More like fifty thousand, allowing for deflections, tacking, pull of currents we don't know. Storms, flat calms, contrary winds, repairs, expeditions ashore for provisions. You pull your horns in just a bit, my girl. Do you remember a desert plateau the map shows in the southern hemisphere? Solid cliff rising out of the sea for over seven hundred miles, and on top of it roasting sand all the way across the continent—and that plateau is only a small part of the coastal desolation down there. From the equator to the 30th parallel I don't think you'd have a chance to go ashore—and nothing to help you if you did."

Dunin still grinned. "Just sail past it."

"Yes—well out to sea, with the equatorial sun at work on you. Very few islands in that region, some of them bare rock." And he thought: *If I might go myself . . . ! I am fifty now, in Earth years, a young fifty. . . .*

He knew also that Dorothy would not prevent him. She would not go herself: she would remain at Adelphi, faithful to the daily things, undramatic labors and loyalties that make civilization something more than a vision. She was a young thirty-eight, though she had already borne five children. If he went away, she would mind the watch fires on the beaches, as she had done nine years ago; she would work in the school, the house, the gardens, stand by Christopher Wright during the depressions that sometimes overcame him. She would grow old waiting. Therefore, Paul knew, he would never leave her. "The explorations will come in good time, Dunin," he said. "You'll have 150 years to watch and take part. I think you'll live to see the other continent too, and the great islands in the southwest. In the meantime—there's so much exploring to be done right here!" He watched the water too, aware of Dorothy's face turned to him, sober and appraising. "You know, Dunin—that island we visited today—that could hold a community of a thousand between its two little hills. And I'm remembering the one forty miles north of us. *Argo II* was swept ashore there: get Doc to tell you that story sometime. I was sick for a week and laid up in one of the limestone caves while the others repaired the raft. A round island less than five miles across. We might sail there next trip."

"The other continent," Dunin murmured, and she watched the rising blue-green mound of Adelphi in the south. "The islands of the southwest . . ."

Dorothy leaned against the hand-hewn rail, looking northeast, saying lightly, "There he is. . . ." The stone figure in the coastal range grew visible as the channel current pressed them a little too far eastward. The vast features were not clear; one could find the line of shoulder. "And Sears said, 'He looks west of the sun.' Was it long ago you told me that, Paul?"

"In a way it was. . . . Penny for 'em, Dorothy?"

"Oh——" Her brown face crinkled in the way he hoped for. "I was climbing down off philosophy with my usual bump—wondering what hell the twins have been raising while we're away. Brodaa's patience with them passes belief. With her own three sets of twins she's had practice. I wish Pak could have had children. Twenty-nine—late middle age for her people. . . . Helen's going to make a better med student than ever I was—don't you think, Paul? Seems like more than just a kid's enthusiasm."

"I think so." And Sears' plump daughter Teddy (Theodora-Pakriaa) would no doubt find herself too, sometime: there was no hurry. Even Christopher Wright no longer seemed to feel that time was hounding him, though his years by the Earth calendar were sixty-five, his hair and beard were white, his wiry thinness moved deliberately to save the strength he had once been able to spend like unconsidered gold. . . . "Look!"

Dorothy said carefully, "But that is impossible." A column of smoke on the flank of the coastal range, above one of the beaches where building stone was found. Blue-gray against the red and black, it rose straight in untroubled air. "They weren't taking Betsy out till we got back."

"Too high anyway," Dunin said. "No need to climb so high for the stone."

Dorothy whispered, "I have *never* quite believed that Ed and Ann——"

"Oh, Dorothy! Well, we——"

"Yes, I saw the lifeboat go down on the channel. It didn't sink." She shut her eyes. "It was a misty evening, lover, more ways than one. Remember, Dunin?"

"I'll always remember."

"Paul, I know that when the open-sea current below the island took the lifeboat it must have been smashed against the cliffs—oh, of course—and for nine years the sea spiders will have used the pieces of it for their little castles and hideaways. All the same—Ed and Ann could have managed to swim ashore. Cross the range somehow or go around it."

"Nothing to eat. Barren rock straight up from the beaches, where there are any beaches, for ninety miles south of the only place where they could have landed and for twenty miles north of it."

"But no kaksmas in the coast range either; no omasha, this side. There *are* beaches here and there. They might have found—shellfish— blue seaweed."

"Nine years——"

"It *is* smoke. Our people wouldn't be up there. . . ."

"You've never wanted to talk much about that day."

"No, I—haven't. I didn't behave too well myself. Yes, there are things I've never told. . . . Paul, Ed Spearman was like somebody I didn't know. He did say in so many words that he planned to go to Vestoia, not to—to throw himself on the mercy of Lantis, but to 'give her civilization'—he said. We tried, Ann and I, tried to reason with him against that. I think he had some alternative plan— maybe flying south of Vestoia as far as the fuel would take him and starting a community of his own—with Ann and me, you know, and himself the old man of the tribe."

"And without us," said Dunin mildly.

"Yes, dear, I recall that. He put that in words. . . ." In a way, Paul did not want her to go on, living it over again, but she had a need to speak of it. "I suppose his plans made a kind of sense if you accepted the premise. As I couldn't, of course. When he said you were all lost,

I believed (I had to believe) that he was—not lying perhaps, but telling something he hadn't truly seen. I know that was where I let go—I raged and screamed, and when he grabbed my arm (probably just wanting to quiet me down)—well, if he's living he'll have two or three white scars down his cheek. Uh-huh: the Dope comes clean. I ever think I was trying to get hold of my pistol when Arek took it away, and took his away too. After that she forced him to give a precise account of everything that had happened, every detail. She made him tell it five or six times, watching for contradictions. She was—justice embodied. I was afraid of her myself even while I loved her for it. I knew what he told us then was the truth: the fuel was low, he'd come direct to the island with no real knowledge of what had happened to you. He was saner after the telling. He lost a—a certain look of exalted listening, as if somebody behind Arek's shoulder were telling him what to do. Arek never gave back his pistol. We were on the beach. The giants had been bringing wood all day for a beacon fire. I remember the exact shape of a big shell at my feet, the look of a bit of driftwood tossed in by the channel breakers. . . ."

"And Ann——"

"Oh, Ann! Torn two or three ways as usual. She was very much in love with him, you know, from our first days on Lucifer. But her mind was a battleground with no armistice. I think Ed always knew that. When he pleaded with her—reasonably too—she couldn't think, she could only cry and say: 'I won't go with you—I won't go.' He stopped trying—suddenly, as if he'd knowingly turned off a light inside himself—unsteady light and the only one he had, I reckon. He said, 'So much for the human race: but I'll see what one man can do here before I'm dead without issue.' And he walked off to the lifeboat, while Arek let his pistol dangle from her finger—and, Paul, I shall always think he knew Ann would run after him. I saw her tugging, trying to pull him out of the boat—but she was pulled in and it was gone."

"And I remember," said Dunin, "what you did after we lost sight of it."

"What I did . . . ? What was that, Dunin? I'm blank there."

"You went to the beacon fire and put on more wood."

"Well," she said vaguely, "of course. We all did. . . . That *is* smoke, Paul. Lantis' pygmies or the wild giants couldn't be there on the cliffs."

Dunin said, "Oh, there are no giants in that country, Dorothy. Those low hills I remember west of the first camp—those kaksma hills were an impassable boundary in the old days. The country west of them—nobody went there, ever. And south of them—Vestoia. My wild kindred are all very far north of here. . . ."

Argo IV eased up to the wharf, where Elis and Arek handled her like a toy, making her fast with ropes of a fabric as good as linen. Wright was there with them, and Tejron, and Pakriaa and Nisana, who were inseparable. "Too far," said Wright, and handed Paul the field glasses. "Just smoke."

Elis grumbled, "What's up there to burn? No vegetation. Rock."

The smoke seemed to be thinning. "How long since our last trip over?"

"Eight days, Paul," Tejron recalled. "My impatient eldest wanted to see if he could handle Betsy's oars, remember?"

"He could, too." Paul remembered. "Sears-Danik pulled his weight, my lady. Yes, that was the last time. And we saw nothing unusual."

Only Nisana thought to ask, "Good voyage today, Paul?"

"Fine, darling. You should have come."

Wright was carefully calm. "I'll go over, with Paul, Elis —and——"

"And me," said Dorothy, not smiling.

"Well . . . Okay, Dope."

Pakriaa's thin wrinkled face turned to him. "Nisana and I? Miniaan—she would remember the Vestoian dialect— but she is at the city. It would need an hour to send for her, and then it would be getting dark."

"Yes, come with us. . . ."

The site of Jensen City was not where Wright and Paul had originally dreamed of it but two miles south, where the radiance of Sears Lake hung in the hills. A gap in the west admitted ocean winds; the outlet of the lake ran for a mile to the edge of a red stone cliff and tumbled over in a waterfall five hundred feet high. There would one day be houses along that mile of river. Already, near the waterfall, there was a temple of red and black stone devoted to quiet without ritual, thought of sometimes as a memorial to Sears and to the other dead, more often simply as a place to go for the satisfactions of silence. It had no name; Paul hoped it would never have one.

Miniaan of Vestoia was an eager citizen. The old wound had left one side of her head cruelly scarred; from the other side she was beautiful, by Charin as well as pygmy standards. Younger than Pakriaa, she was the mother of four, by Kajana—the archer whom Mijok had once carried on his shield, who would never walk again nor live a day without pain, and who was more cheerful as a permanent habit of mind than any of the other pygmy survivors of that war. The fifty-four pygmy children of Jensen City were all fathered by Abara and Kajana—a fact which caused old Abara to draw dead-pan comparisons between himself and Mister Johnson and to grow darkly desperate when Kajana wistfully asked him to explain why it was a joke. . . .

Elis shipped the oars; Paul let down the anchor, a heavy block of stone, in two fathoms of blackening water; Elis lifted the dugout over the side and held it for them. He himself swam the short distance to the beach and eased the canoe through the shallows. Even now at low tide there was barely a quarter mile of gray sand between water and cliffs. Chipping away of building stone had created a fair path a hundred feet up; beyond, natural irregularities made it possible to climb another two hundred to the first setback of the great sea wall—a ledge which ran only as far as the next patch of beach, five miles south. Sunset had been ending when *Argo IV* came home; here there was a depth of evening quiet, no sign of smoke or life, no sound but the long hiss and moaning of small waves. "We might make a fire here," Wright said. "But there's enough light. They—they?—must have seen *Argo*."

"There," Dorothy said, and ran up the sand.

The others watched in frozen helplessness as the woman came down the crude cliff path, gaunt, seeming tall only

because of the gauntness—flaring ribs, thighs fallen in,
every arm bone visible. Her hair was black disorder to her
waist, her body a battleground of bruises, dirt, scars old
and new, and she winced away from Dorothy with pro-
testing hands. "You mustn't touch me because I'm very
dirty, but I know who you are. Besides, I had to burn the
last of my clothes. My baby died. I know who you are. You
see, my milk stopped. You're Dorothy Leeds. I left him
on the cliff. Matron would not approve. You see——"

"Ann——Ann——"

"I have two other sons, but this one died. On the cliff.
I used to know a man who called me Miss Sarasate, but
that was just his way of talking—I don't happen to be in
practice." Still trying to fend off Dorothy's arms, Ann
fell on her face. . . .

Pakriaa was speaking softly, in the room where Ann
was sleeping—Wright's room. "She will be healed," Pakriaa said. "I can remember—and you remember it too,
Paul—how my own mind refused to be my servant for
a while." Since Ann had been brought to Jensen City,
Pakriaa and Nisana had never left her: the little women,
both now far from youth, took on the duties of nursing
with a fierce protectiveness, so that there was little for
even Dorothy to do. Ann had slept heavily all night and
morning. At noon the stone-walled house remained cool;
mild air entered at the screenless window openings, stirring
the wall map of Adelphi and the three of Paul's paintings which were the only decorations Wright allowed in
this ascetic shelter. There was glassmaking now, but in
such a climate, with no serious insect pests, it seemed a
waste of effort to make windows; a long overhang of the
eaves was sufficient against the rains. The house was
large, U-shaped around a garden courtyard open toward
Sears Lake; the walls were of black stone, the roof of a
material indistinguishable from slate, carried by hardwood
timbers. Wright shared this house with Mijok and Arek,
Pakriaa, Nisana, Miniaan, and their children and Arek's.
There were five other such communal houses overlooking
the lake; a seventh was building. The children were everywhere: it was, and would be for many years, a city of the
young. Rak had died in the Year Four, a matter of falling
asleep without waking, but Kamon lived, sharing a house

with Tejron, Paul and Dorothy, Brodaa and Kajana. Lately Sears' daughter had taken over the task of caring for Kajana in his helplessness, lifting him to and from a wheel chair that Paul and Mijok had contrived or carrying him to a hammock slung near the waterfall, where he could watch the ocean and its changes. In middle age, Kajana had taught himself to write, and kept a journal of the colony with a sober passion for detail.

Ann had not waked when Dorothy and Nisana washed her and clipped the dreadful tangle of her hair. "She will be healed," Pakriaa insisted. "Maybe in the next waking." And when Ann's gray eyes came open an hour later, they did show a measuring sanity, recognizing Dorothy and Paul, but wincing away when Nisana smiled and touched her.

"Do not be afraid of us," Pakriaa whispered. "We are still proud. But our pride now is that no one is afraid of us. . . . You came to my house in the old old days, remember? My blue house, and I thinking I would be Queen of the World? I laugh at that now. Do not look at what I was, Ann."

"Pakriaa . . . Paul, you haven't changed much."

"One of our other friends is about to bring a man-sized meal——"

"Why, Paul, you must be——"

"Fifty, Earth calendar——"

Dorothy said, "We measure it in Lucifer years, pretty please."

"Nicer," Paul admitted. "That way I'm around thirty-seven. Ann, you—let's see: one Earth year, one point three eight—damn mental arithmetic—let's call you half past twenty-seven."

"Imagine that." Ann achieved a smile. "And—Pakriaa?"

"Twenty-nine. See—already I am an old woman and ugly."

"Don't be absurd, Pak," Dorothy said. "And this lady——"

"You would not remember me," said Nisana.

"Oh, but I do, I do. You—voted for Paul——"

Pakriaa chuckled with unforced gaiety. "Politics," Nisana chirped. "P.S., I got the job." Paul pinched her tiny ear lobe and stepped out to the kitchen, where he found Wright with Arek. The children were at school, with Brodaa, Mijok, and Miniaan: ordinarily Wright would have been there too. When the youngest of this house were through with lessons they would go wandering in the hills with Mijok and Muson, so that Ann might have quiet, with only distant sounds of the laughter and playing in sunlight. "She's awake," Paul said, and Wright hurried to the bedroom, but Arek lingered, filling a tray.

Arek had grown almost to Mijok's height, filling out, a red mother goddess still bemused by inner discoveries. Her fine soft-furred fingers fussed at the earthen dishes on the wooden tray. "No ambition, no achievement—nothing, I think, could be worth the price of what's happened to her. Whether she recovers completely or not. There's human right and wrong. I think sometimes, Paul, it's not necessary to do much wondering. You can look straight at a thing and say: 'This ought not to be.' "

"Granted," Paul said, watching the garden through the broad kitchen window. His eldest, Helen, must have elected to do a little work after school instead of strolling away with the others. She was weeding, her brown head sheltered from the sun by an improvised hat of leaves; but for that she was prettily naked as the day she was born, and though she was humming to herself, she restrained the sound so that Paul could hardly hear it. She saw him in the window and grinned and waved. She had most of Dorothy's warm coloring, with Paul's long-legged slimness.

Arek saw her too and smiled. "What Ann should have had too. . . . Paul, I told you once, we love you. All the good new things we have—your work. All the same there's a devil in—some of you. As in us too, of course. Need of the laws is obvious. If Spearman is responsible —the Vestoians too, maybe?—then I think we live in too much seclusion here." She took up the tray. "Too easy to live all the time in Paradise and—leave things undone."

"Yes. Vestoia is big, Arek—or was, when it almost destroyed us."

"True. But you tell me that over there on the beach she said, 'I have two other sons.' Living, did she mean? We must find them, and Spearman too."

"I believe she can tell us about it soon."

"Understood that I go with you when you find them."

"Yes. Yes, Arek. . . ."

In the bedroom Arek's manner was altogether changed. "Observe: this is asonis *rôti à la mode Versailles,* whatever that means. All I did was roast it. These are (Paul says) lima beans Munchausen, and here we have could-be asparagus. And by the way, the cheese tastes better'n it smells."

"Cheese——"

"Asonis milk," said Wright. "They moo, too."

"Oh, you've tamed them." Pain fought with interest in the haggard face. "Yes, Ed wanted to do that, but we —somehow we never——"

"If you're good," Arek said, "and eat all that, there's cake."

"You found something for sugar?"

"Can't tell it from terrestrial," Dorothy chattered, "only it's pink. From a tree fruit sort of like a plum. We have a plantation of 'em across the lake. You boil it down to nothing and the sugar crystallizes out. We make another kind from sap, not as good as maple. Flour—that's from the same old wheat that came from Earth. Miniaan—oh, you don't know her yet—Miniaan and Paul have experimented around with the local grass grains—nothing yet that measures up to wheat." Ann picked at the food, crying weakly at the first mouthful. "Ah, don't do that," said Dorothy, looking away. "You came home, that's all."

Later she ate ravenously. "I want to tell you——"

It took a long time in telling. Once she fell asleep but woke an hour later, obsessed with a need to continue. . . .

The lifeboat drifted south, its last remnant of fuel gone in a mad effort to leap the coastal range. Water sneaked in at the seal of the floor window, damaged in an earlier landing, and Ed Spearman talked to himself. "Fugitives from a Sunday school—we'll live." Like a hurt boy he said, "We'll show 'em. . . ." When the current beyond the island swept them toward the cliffs, he opened the door and pulled Ann into the water, dragging her, forgetting that she was herself a strong swimmer. Later, on the beach, he was tender, trying to comfort and reassure her with a vision of the future abundantly real to him. They had no food, no way to light a fire of driftwood. They would go to Vestoia, he said, convince Lantis that they were friends, with something to offer her empire; they would "bring her civilization."

From this beach there seemed to be no passage north. They could have found one by climbing high into the range—Ann did so, nine years later. But Spearman found a ledge of sorts running south: it might take them the eighty-odd miles to the lower end of the range or give out at any point, trapping them. It did give out twice; both times, rather than clamber higher on the cliffs, Spearman hurled his famished body through the breakers and swam south, aided by the current until it was possible to continue along the rocks. Ann followed, not quite wishing for the death the ocean could have given easily. They kept alive with shellfish and seaweed washed ashore and small crustaceans that hid in the tide lines and in crannies of wet rock; there were pools of rain water and violent small streams plunging down the range. It took them fifty days to cover the eighty miles. ("I think I spent a hundred coming back," Ann said. "Couldn't swim, with the baby. It would have been against the current anyway. Climbed—sometimes went back miles from a dead end to try again.") In the afternoons the sun pressed on them with total fury; then they could only crawl into what shadow the rocks gave and wait for the torture to cease.

But at last there were trees. Level ground. In a few miles, a rapid friendly river. ("Are there rivers here? I've forgotten. Nothing prettier in the world. I let that one close over me. Ed pulled me out—we had to go on.")

There were five more of those bright leaping coastal streams in a journey of another fifty miles southeast through good country, where the great range thinned out into rolling jungle and meadowland. There were asonis and small game. Spearman made himself weapons. Ann could remember these days almost with pleasure. They had, she said, something the flavor of a delayed childhood, a glimpse of Eden. Spearman was for a time simply a strong and intelligent man measuring himself against nature for survival, master of a simple environment with none to question his decisions and no social complexities to warp them. ("I wished we could settle in that country, the two of us. I even begged for it. He had to go on.")

From the remembered map, Spearman knew there was an obscure pygmy settlement south of the end of the range, some fifty miles below Vestoia: merely a cluster of parallel lines that had appeared in the photographs, it might or might not be a part of the empire of Lantis. It was near the headwaters of a seventh river, which flowed, not to the coast, but eastward, into the deep, wide, violent outlet of Lake Argo. ("He never told me why he was following that river so cautiously, until we reached the villages. And history repeated itself.")

The villages were a furtive, chronically frightened community. They knew of Vestoia but believed, correctly, that the groping tentacles of empire had not yet found them. Lantis' drive was mainly to the east, where the country was easier and pygmy settlements were numerous; even her war against Pakriaa's people had been a diversion, more a matter of hurt pride than gainful conquest. Between these hidden villages and Vestoia there were meadows, dangerous with omasha, and some swampland; below the two small Vestoian lakes the current of the river Argo was too fierce for the flimsy boats of Lantis. So the villages of the seventh river, under a sly but feeble queen, waited like a rabbit in a hedge. With sharply calculated drama—but smiling this time, Ann said, like a pleased teacher at a blackboard—Ed Spearman overturned another idol and became a god.

At the end of two years, when Spearman's goddess had borne him twin sons, there was industry in the villages. There was an army of a thousand spears, bladed with iron from certain small hills in the north between Vestoia and Spearman City. These hills were dangerous with burrows, but workers of a particular kind could be made to go there. The soldiers overcame their distaste for the bow when they had watched the course of arrows properly vaned and tipped with iron or bronze. They did not need to be taught how to hate Vestoia—nevertheless they relished it when Spearman decided that political realities demanded he should tell them an epic tale, the tale of a war he and companion gods had waged against that place. Vengeance, divine or human, was a thing the pygmies had understood from the first biting and scratching of infancy.

Ann had been bewildered by that first gust of oratory against Vestoia. Spearman had neglected to prepare her for it during the long two years spent in teaching the pygmies a limited English and the beginnings of industry: it might not have been clear to himself that such a move would be necessary in order to hold his people's enthusiasm and devotion. Ann wondered. "You had thought once of going to Vestoia——" Spearman turned on her with an anger partly cynical humor: "They hurt us, didn't they? Oh, I might have toyed with the idea as a choice of evils before we found our real friends. They killed Doc, didn't they? And Paul and Sears and those milky giant friends of ours."

"But you didn't see——"

"*What?*"

Spearman believed now that he had seen the full end of that war. Ann got it through her head after a while. When he said that Vestoia must be punished for past wrongs, there was a smiling half admission of disingenuous policy. "It'll work," he said. "We can get away with it." But the death of all the others except Dorothy had become for him something like an article of faith, not to be examined. At this moment, Ann said, she had begun to think of a northward journey, but the odds were darkly against it. The twins were still nursing and sickly; the demands of mere daily living are heavy on a goddess who must also supervise housekeeping. There was, for instance, the endless squabbling treachery of the household slaves. At that time also, Ann hoped to soften or divert some changes that seemed to be taking place in Spearman himself. ("I wonder if they were really changes. . . .")

Spearman detested slavery, he said. But in a primitive economy how else could you get the work done? Even in daylight, when the kaksmas were half helpless, only the bravest soldiers would go into those hills—not to work, but only as guards for the chained lines of laborers, guards who could run fast if the kaksmas came out for a day-blind attack and leave the slaves to be consumed. Bad: Spearman was sorry such things had to be. Still, the slaves were poor or sometimes dangerous material at best; besides that, they hated responsibility and were therefore really happier in slavery and received better care than they could otherwise have had. So you had to see it as almost a eugenic, even a humanitarian measure as well as an unavoidable transitional phase, and in any case you can't make an omelette without breaking eggs. At the use of meat slaves for the palace household, Spearman had to draw the line, and he instituted laws against the custom for the rest of his little kingdom, but they were difficult to enforce without compromising matters of greater political importance. "Transitional" became a somewhat sacred word for Spearman over the years, a sustaining conception when things went badly and when his ingrained sensitivities brought from Earth were violated by the brisk egg-breaking of a Neolithic culture.

Even the first war against Vestoia, in the third year of Spearman's deification, was part of a transitional phase, although Spearman did not feel that his pygmies were advanced enough to be troubled with fine distinctions. It is better for a god to resist pressures for explanation.

That first war was well planned, with limited objective. Six hundred spearwomen and archers crossed the Argo below Vestoia and fell on the city from the east, so that there was no clue to their southern origin; they set afire a mile of the lake settlement, took three hundred captives, and vanished—again eastward, leaving a few crippled defenders to convey the message that they would come again. It had the desired effect: the armies of Lantis foamed eastward like crazed hornets, while Spearman's force slipped home across the Argo without a trace. In the following year they struck again, again from the east, but with a larger force, laying waste nearly a third of that part of the city on the eastern shores of the Vestoian lakes. The palace of Lantis, nerve center of empire, was on the west shore. Probably the queen knew nothing of what had happened until she saw the far shore buried in smoke, and by the time she crossed over, she would have learned only that Spearman's army had promised to come a third time and take Lantis herself and assume command of the empire.

They did, just six years after that lonely journey along the rocks. Ann's twin sons were five years old, five Lucifer years. In the first two campaigns, Spearman had not shown himself in person to the Vestoians. In this third battle he was at the head of his army, massive and tall; with a cold, unhappy precision, he was using a long hardwood stick with a razor-edge semicircular blade. And this time his legion had driven in out of the west, directly against the palace and the temples and sacred places of the Queen of the World.

Lantis was aging then, and sick, and bewildered; she probably never understood that it was merely a question of her own methods being used against her. Even when her city was in flames around her and her people were scattering into forest and swamp and lake, she could neither yield nor destroy herself; thus it was her misfortune to be taken alive.

A week later Ann and the children were brought by litter from Spearman City; Spearman recognized the political advantage, almost necessity, of their presence at the triumph. Lantis was ceremonially dragged through the still-smoldering and stinking streets and forced to drink an infusion of the green-flower weed that destroyed the self: this was pygmy custom, which Spearman watched in regretful disgust, anxious that his small sons should preserve the impassive dignity proper to gods. "They're far from human, you know—they don't feel things as we do. . . ." The boys were puzzled and curious.

So far as Ann knew, however, Lantis was not eaten at the festival. "He told me she was mercifully put away after the excitement died down, and another meat slave was sacrificed, made up to look like Lantis—not deception, but ritual substitution; Ed felt he'd achieved quite a step in progress there. It showed, he said, they were beginning to accept ritual for reality under the influence of ——Oh, the devil with it. . . . He moved his capital to Vestoia. The palace was restored—modernized. I lived there—two and a half years. That's where I bore him another son. I'll never know how I came to allow it—a kind of madness, hate close to love—something . . . He didn't want me any more, you know. He had some ideas about—ascetic discipline—purity—I don't know what exactly—and he didn't try to explain it to me. I'd hated him with all my mind for years—before the Vestoian wars— but I'm not a good hater. I even still imagined I could influence him a little—until the baby was born and he was in black despair because it wasn't a daughter. I had to escape. I could feel my mind, my self, rotting away—dissolving, as the Vestoian empire was dissolving, for that matter. He couldn't hold them. It began to fall apart right away. They were terrified of him and of his Spearman City bodyguards—weasels. . . . They simply drifted away into the woods and didn't come back. I doubt if they've organized anywhere else. Lantis must have had a rare sort of skill—the city was all hers: she built it out of Stone Age villagers, and it died with her. Ed tried everything to keep them—bribes, threats, endless spying and public executions by his guard. Bread and circuses, meaningless offices for favorites with fancy clothes and no duties. It didn't work. At the time I escaped, the population was down to—he'd never tell me, but my guess is under ten thousand for the while city. There was an epidemic—rather like flu. I used that as a reason to take the baby back to Spearman City, knowing Ed would need to stay and go on trying to hold things together. I thought he would let me take the twins—John—David——"

"Rest awhile," said Arek. "We're going to bring them home too." Ann could not speak. "How would you like to bathe again in our lake? I'll hold you up. Water's warm with the sun—best part of the day——"

"I'd like it. It's so pretty. What do you call it?"

"Sears Lake."

"Sears . . . What am I made of? I haven't thought or asked——"

"It was a Vestoian arrow," Wright said. "At the end he enjoyed remembering Earth."

2 "THE CITY IS A DESOLATION." MINIAAN SLIPPED OUT of shadow into the clearing, where the others waited for her without a fire; she was shaken, short of breath. No longer young, she had hurried on the ten-mile return journey from Vestoia through high-noon heat of jungle. "I could not even find the house where I was born. Oh, Pakriaa—Paul—of every ten houses, seven are empty. The streets are dirt and rubbish. No one knew me. Well, that's not strange. Those I met supposed I was a stranger, probably from the east. But the ones who were suspicious did not challenge me—they slipped into their sorry houses and stared at me through the cracks." She sat down in weariness, wiping sweat from her scarred head and shoulder. "Word of what I said will travel quickly. But not one followed me here. I made sure of that."

Arek asked, "Have you had anything to eat?"

"No, I—only walked through the streets. . . . Doc, some had English words—a few, badly spoken. No one could pronounce *d* at the beginning of a word, and they had absurd turns of speech I don't understand. One woman said to me, 'One fella goddamn skirt belong you what name?' I thought she was asking about this skirt I made in the old fashion, but then we spoke in the old tongue: I found she only wanted to know who I was and where I came from. It seems that now, under Spearman-abron-Ismar, they indicate—what word do I want?—social—social levels——"

"Castes?"

"Castes, that is it, Paul—they indicate castes by the color of a skirt. In the old days there were only two castes—soldiers and voluntary laborers, not considering the family of Lantis or the slaves at the bottom. Now there are—oh, ten, twenty, I don't know. Those who work at the dye pots must never do anything else, and they can look down on the workers in hides; this woman was a maker of arrowheads and despised both. . . . I told her (and some others) that I was a stranger from a distant village, and I said I had heard by rumor of other gods and giants, who would come one day soon to talk with Spearman-abron-Ismar—yes, they call him that, Spearman-male-issue-of-Ismar. It frightened her: she made excuses and ran away. I told it to another, an old woman, who broke out cursing and weeping. She said, 'Oh, no more of them! No more——' And sat down in the street and scattered dust on her head."

"Did you see—him?"

"No, Paul. I saw the palace—changed, with new tall doors. There were soldiers at the entrance, so I did not dare go near. They wore a headdress—it was the old bark fabric, I think, but a shape I never saw. I saw the great stockade—always the biggest thing on the shore of North Lake—still in repair; there was the same sluice, to wash away the blood of the meat slaves. There is still a ferry near it, where the crossing is narrow at the lake's inlet; I could see across—streets and tree-sheltered houses. And outside the city I saw a mound, very foul. Once the city was clean. There was a boy playing near it—ran when he saw me, but I caught him and asked him about that mound. I could hardly understand his gabble. It seems that nowadays in Vestoia children have reason to be afraid of grown women. When we could talk he told me the mound was the grave of the False Empress, the Wicked One—everyone who passes is required to defile it. A law."

Pakriaa laced her wrinkled hands at her throat, smiling at Christopher Wright, quoting a few of his own words: " 'The laws are living things: let men guard them against crippling and disease.' "

Nisana asked, "What is next to do?"

"We sleep on it," Wright said. "Long journey. We're tired. We'll go there in the morning. With our weapons of course, but . . ."

Mijok said softly, "First-light is a good time."

"I think there won't be any fighting," Miniaan said,

and she relaxed and leaned happily against Muson's plump knee and ate the meal Arek had ready for her in fastidious birdlike bites. "If they're troubled by the rumors I scattered they'll slip away and hide, not fight. They're weary, bewildered, disillusioned people—at least that is the temper of the city as I felt it."

Nisana murmured, "With Spearman's bodyguard it could be different."

"Why," said Wright, "he'd never turn them against us. Not if he's the man I used to know, or anything like that man. He came a long way with us once." But Paul had to wonder: *Was he ever with us?*

There were six giants in the party: Mijok, Arek, Muson, Elis, Sears-Danik, Dunin. Elis was the year's Governor at Adelphi, but Dorothy had held that position the year before and would assume its simple duties in his absence. Nisana's eldest twin daughters had wanted to come, but Nisana had not allowed it, requiring them to stay in school under Brodaa's temperate discipline; the only pygmies here were herself, Pakriaa, and Miniaan. The group had come 120 miles overland, after *Argo IV* set them on a beach north of the coastal range: this had seemed better than taking the sloop south, where harbor would be uncertain and the winds and currents unknown. The first twenty miles ashore had been a retracing of Abara's long-ago journey with the olifants, through swampy and treacherous jungle. After rounding the range they could follow the eastern edge of the grassland that spread on its lee side, traveling in the open only at night, to avoid omasha. For all of one day they were bedeviled by a swarm of biting flies, and since there were brown wings circling they could not escape into full sunlight, where the flies would not follow. Eventually Pakriaa found an evil-smelling plant and remembered its use from old times. The juice of the root was a protection; the smell was almost as distressing as the bites but less dangerous. Miniaan of Vestoia had never heard of the plant's use: perhaps that explained why Vestoia had never exploited the otherwise pleasant region due west of Lake Argo.

There was fitful sleep in the daylight following Miniaan's return, and then an evening meal. Arek and Muson and the two young giants seemed untroubled by tomorrow, full of speculative curiosity. Mijok was uneasy, though he would not put it in words; Elis, too, would be remembering. Wright said again, "He came a long way with us. . . . Jensen chose him—remember that: chose him from among seven hundred other physically fine youths who had the same training, the same kind of courage, who wanted the—privilege, as he did."

"I can always wonder what Jensen himself would have made of Lucifer."

Wright said, almost with reproach, "Jensen was a great engineer, Paul, but he was also a student of history. Compared with what his leadership would have been, mine has been weak, vacillating, academic—it was bound to be. I take credit for some achievements. I've said give protoplasm a chance. We have done that. We've established the climate of liberty under law (for our very small group) and proved that a human mind can bypass twenty thousand years of blundering, with no other help than a flexible language and the few basic rules of civilized action—as the so-called savages of Earth always proved it whenever they had a chance to secure a genuine education and fair treatment. But—in our material development there must have been a thousand lost opportunities—things Jensen (and probably Ed Spearman) would have seen at once."

Paul laughed. "Ed could have designed a better sloop."

Wright dismissed that with a chuckle. "Ach—she floats, boy. She sails. . . . When I get angry or impatient or discouraged—when I stick too tight to a plan of my own and fail to hear the opposing argument—then I remember that Jensen had a charity, a patience, a kindliness, almost as great as Sears had—"

"Tocwright," said Pakriaa, half amused, "why do you search yourself? Must you always be sitting in judgment on your own mind?"

"Why, yes, dear, I must." His fingers played in his white beard. "Cod-and-baked-beans origin . . . Remember my fussy little *History of the Americas,* the first book Dorothy and Nisana copied out for me when we found how to make good paper from the marsh grass . . . ? But self-searching is a vice-and-virtue not limited to the Charin tribe, Pakriaa—ask yourself. And ask Elis." The black giant smiled. "So—I'll go on with it just a little. Paul, is it weakness in me to ask that when we find Ed Spearman, you do most of the talking? I want to be—merely friendly if I can, not say much. At least until we know what sort of man he's become. Nine years ago, I don't think he ever had much resentment against you. You hear both sides —usually the surest way to make an extremist hate you bitterly, but somehow people don't. You're a—kindly listener; I only try to be, pushing down a big part of my natural temperament to do it. . . . Why, I think I never even appreciated the full nastiness of sarcasm until one time (it's not such a small matter)—one time on the space ship, when Sears reproached me for it: something that went against his own nature, by the way, because he was always too afraid of finding fault with others."

"I'll talk with him first, Doc, if you want me to. But I wonder what I can say. I keep seeing Ann. The things she told us—the things Miniaan has told us today."

"A city that never was," said Miniaan sleepily, "never was even in the old times. Maybe I dreamed it. If you are quiet, maybe I will allow us to wake up in a moment on the island of Adelphi . . ."

"Ann is not changed," Muson reflected, "even though the baby died."

Mijok said, "I'm not sure. I think she is. In what way I can't define. But she's not the same sad little thing I watched when she was sleeping in that fever. Well now, that was truly long ago. She puzzled me more than the rest of you, and you were all a great mystery—and I with a dozen words and the old terrors crawling on my skin like lice. Maybe it was her seeming weakness, her secret look of listening—which I thought I began to understand when she taught me the Earth music, but I don't suppose I ever did understand it." Mijok laughed and looked away. "Doc, it was very difficult for me to grasp that you were not begotten out of the west wind by a thunderbolt. You'll never know how difficult, because you were never a savage. You were born to be articulate. Those twenty thousand years of blundering—bad I don't doubt they were, but they gave you something. I am as if the forest had generated me, with no past."

Miniaan murmured and rolled over on her back to look

up into the leaves. "I too. I was never born. Someone with no father nor mother looked at that filthy mound they say is the grave of the Queen of the World. The mind of a white-furred Charin is my father and my mother."

Elis suggested: "Ann has come nearer to the immediate present."

"Why, Elis—" Pakriaa was surprised. "She said something like that to me herself, a short while before we came away. She said, 'My yesterdays became tomorrows before I lived them. I want to find today, Pakriaa. Where is today?'"

Miniann pursued the dark stream of her own thought, which now seemed to be giving her pleasure and not pain: "This morning I found how yesterday can bury itself with only the smallest scattering of years. There will be other cities. Never again Vestoia."

Wright asked gently, "But you can remember good and pleasant things of the old city, the way it was when you were young there?"

"Oh, I can, I can. But I'll have today, too. I think I found it first when I bore my little sons, at Adelphi." She sat up, leaning on Pakriaa's shoulder. "I've had good todays at Adelphi. I don't understand how it could have been abandoned by this Spearman I've never seen."

"In a way," Paul said, "you did see him. You were one of those who came on the canoes up Lake Argo. You saw the boat set your fleet afire."

"Yes. That was war. . . . And before I was wounded I killed, I think, seven of your people, Pakriaa. One with a blue skirt. I wounded her in the throat, and I have heard she died in the forest, looking north."

"Yes, Tamisraa. My sister Tamisraa was a bitter woman," Pakriaa said, "and quite brave. Miniaan, all that was over long ago, in a forgotten country. Now we pull weeds in the same garden."

Night came tranquilly. Elis, who kept the last quarter of the watch, waked them before first-light. There was the help of a full red moon, and they followed the sound of a swift river which flowed into North Lake through the palace district of Vestoia.

For more than a mile outside the city the jungle was like a park, undergrowth removed, vines cut away. But the vines were coming back. Greedy purple fingers curled to recapture and reclaim. . . .

In the outskirts no one halted or questioned them. They saw no armed women; here and there a man crouched in a weedy doorway with staring children half hidden behind him. Mijok, Elis, Sears-Danik and Arek walked on the outside, with shields upheld against a possible arrow or thrown spear. Rifles and pistols were now history, all ammunition spent; they lay in a closet off Wright's room at Adelphi which he called the Terrestrial Museum. Paul, Wright, and Elis had Earth-made hunting knives, still keen. Miniaan, leading them, held a spear, but there was a blue-flower garland below its blade, symbol of peace. Pakriaa and Nisana preferred to carry no weapons; Muson and young Dunin had never handled one in their lives. Miniaan said over her shoulder, "There is the old stockade. Here we turn right, toward the palace."

There was scurrying and disturbance now. Beyond Mijok's shield Paul saw a few lean women running; one of them halted at Miniaan's call and approached uneasily. There were questions, dubious replies. At the far end of the shaded avenue was a growing cluster of red bodies before a thatched building with one tall doorway. Miniaan explained: "I told her that we come peacefully and want to talk with Spearman-abron-Ismar. And she says she thinks he would be asleep at this hour."

"So?" Wright frowned and fretted. "But the word you left yesterday would certainly have reached him." The Vestoian twittered a last word or two and ran away down the street; Paul saw her elbowing through the crowd in front of the palace. "We might go forward a little. . . ."

Most of the group melted away; some forty armed women remained, in a ragged formation blocking the entrance. They made no threatening or even warning gestures, but their staring was heavy and cold. The volunteer messenger returned, pushing through them to speak again with Miniaan; once or twice a halting gabble of something like pidgin English made Miniaan wave her hand impatiently. She turned to Paul. "It seems Spearman told her to say that he is under the—the climate? The weather? Is this meaningful?"

Wright said, "Tell him his third-born son is dead and

the doorway of his palace is too narrow for our friends. Wait. . . . He asked nothing about Ann?"

"She does not say so."

"I can send him no message. You see what I meant, Paul? Paul—you—send whatever word you think best."

"Well . . . Miniaan, ask her to tell him that—Ann could not come with us. That we want to talk with him and, as Doc said, that his door is too narrow for some of us."

The soldiers seemed to catch a glimmering of it; they made way for the messenger, and it might be there was less suspicion in them, more curiosity. Sears-Danik, Tejron's dreamy eldest boy, whispered to Paul, "I am trying to remember him. Not much hair on his head—it was brown. I was only seven when he flew us to Adelphi. His voice—heavy."

"Yes. His hair may be gray now, Danny, as mine is. His face will look older—it never had a young look. His body will not have changed much."

Dunin asked, "He is older than you?"

"No, dear, a little younger."

But Spearman seemed older by far, appearing abruptly in the doorway, arms spread against its frame, face thrust intently forward and eyes squinting as if they troubled him. He wore a black loincloth of bark fabric, nothing else. His sparse hair was wholly gray with streaks of white at the temples, his cheeks, leathery, deeply grooved, and flushed. "I didn't believe her," he said. Seeing him, the guards held their spears as if they were Earth-born soldiers presenting arms, then grounded the butts; they remained rigidly at attention when Spearman paid them no heed. "I didn't suppose . . ." Spearman hiccuped; he rubbed both hands across his face.

Seeing tormented uncertainty in Christopher Wright, Paul stepped forward. "Sears died, long ago. Doc and I got through, with—some of our friends." He paused, short of the guards, and held out his hand, and Spearman stared at it, communing somehow with himself, approaching at last, clumsily, to take hold of it in the old Earth gesture. There was alcohol on his breath; his bloodshot eyes fought an open struggle with bewilderment; his handclasp was damp, unsteady, quickly withdrawn.

"Sorry," he said, "not well. Hard to get it through my head. Well—Christ, I'm a bit drunk. Not strange, is it . . . ? Mijok." His glance traveled over Pakriaa and Nisana without recognition; it lingered at Arek, but he did not speak her name. There was the beginning of a stiff smile, unreadable, as his eyes fixed on Christopher Wright.

"Ann—reached us," Wright said, hardly audible. "She—"

"Why don't you speak up, man?"

"She came along the coast," Wright said, not much more clearly. "The baby died—a little while before she reached us."

Spearman blinked, glanced at his hands, let them drop. He noticed the tight soldiers; in the antique military manner of Earth he said, "At ease. . . ." The spearwomen relaxed part way, eyes front. "Maybe," Spearman said, "maybe you came too soon."

"What do you mean?" Paul asked. "We had to come as soon as we knew you were alive. . . . Are your other children well, Ed? Are they here?"

"Oh . . . ? Yes, I see. . . . You came too soon. I still have a little town of seven or eight thousand and some very loyal followers."

Wright struck his fist into his palm. "We are not your enemies. We never were. There was a place for you at Adelphi. There is now."

"Oh . . . ? I can imagine it. So—Ann—"

"Ann came back to us. It took her a hundred days, she says. She was—is—skin and bone—"

Paul said, "She'll recover, Ed. Only needs rest and food. She wants John and David—naturally. They're her children too, Ed."

Spearman said almost absently, "Are they?"

"What!"

"I don't exactly believe your story, you know. . . . You must have been—watching—for a long time."

Behind him Paul heard Nisana's miserable whisper: "What is it? What is it?" And Wright's muffled answer: "A sickness."

"There's no truth in that, Ed," Paul said. "Five days ago we still supposed that you and Ann were lost when the lifeboat went down in the channel."

Spearman shrugged. "Yes—I think you've come too

soon. You should have worked longer in the dark. We had an epidemic here. Many died. And another trouble—mental—well, you've kept track of that, of course: the way they've fallen away from me, gone back to the forest and the old life, when I could have given them a golden age. A prophet without honor." He coughed and straightened heavy shoulders. "My God, I can't blame the poor fools—now that I know how it was done." His voice did not rise. "Without the conspiracy and interference, I could soon have started them in building a ship that—Never mind that now. I have the designs, of course. That what you came for?"

Mijok broke in, utterly bewildered: "What are you saying?"

Spearman dismissed the giant with a stare and a voice of cold politeness: "I don't blame you either. I remember you well. I suppose you had to do whatever your god ordered, without question. . . ."

The twin boys had appeared in the doorway, dressed like their father in bark fabric: slim, well-knit children, thin-faced like Ann, nine Earth years old. They halted uncertainly, perhaps driven by curiosity to violate an order of their father's. Paul tried to smile at them, and one responded but then blushed and looked worriedly away with a hand over his mouth; the other stared like a pygmy without expression. Spearman did not appear to notice them, though Paul's smile must have told him of their presence. Elis broke the silence: "Mijok and the others of my people do not create gods. We live by our own light so far as it reaches, without fear of the mysteries beyond it." His voice, so seldom loud in anything but laughter, boomed and echoed back from the thatched walls. "At Adelphi, orders derive from the laws, which are made by all of us and understood by all of us."

"Yes," Spearman nodded, upper lip drawn in, as one who saw his saddest predictions verified. "Yes, he would teach you to say that."

Arek said disgustedly, "There's no conversation here. He listens to his own mind, no other's. As it was on the beach, years ago—I remember—"

Spearman said sharply, "Wright, be careful! You've brought your bullies here, but I ought to warn you, this is the country where I still rule. There are some left who love me and understand me."

Dunin muttered to Paul, "Bullies—what word is that?" Paul squeezed her wrist, a warning to be silent.

Speaking with care and difficulty, Wright said, "Ed, your boys are about nine, Earth time. Would you say that is old enough to make certain decisions? Would you be willing, Ed, to ask them whether they want to go to Adelphi and see their mother again?"

Spearman glanced back at them. He would be seeing, Paul knew, how the boy who had smiled was staring at Wright with his mouth fallen open, how the other's blank look had cumpled into a grimace foretelling tears. "Now I really understand it!" Spearman said softly. "So it was a kidnaping—a real kidnaping. I simply would not believe it when my messengers came from Spearman City —but I should have known, I should have known. You stole Ann in order to get my children too, for your—"

There was a murmuring among the guard and in the crowd of pygmy spectators who had gathered at a safe distance. Uncomprehendingly, Paul saw a few wildly pointing arms, saw one of the guards throw away her spear and run blindly down the street. Others were doing the same. The swelling murmur was broken by thin screams. Those of the guard who remained were staring into the northeast quarter of the sky, where a break in the trees permitted a view of it, and they were transfixed— the guard and Spearman's boys and now Spearman himself, glaring at that blue patch of morning heaven with total unbelief. But then Spearman did believe it, was perhaps the first to believe it, tears starting from his gray eyes and running unregarded down the hard channels of his face. "From home! Home—oh, my God, so long a time . . . !"

The spot seemed small and slow in its descent, riding on a cushion of flame brighter than sunlight. . . .

The Vestoian pygmies were all running now. Not into their houses, nor the palace, but away down the tree-sheltered streets, a mindless stampede, weapons tossed away with an agonized crying of tiny voices.

Paul's eyes found it, held it, saw the white flame change to a vast outpouring of brilliant green like the burning of copper. "Charlesite!" Spearman cried. "They've found how to use charlesite for braking! No radioactivity."

The ship must be aiming for the open ground twenty miles away. They could hear the roaring now, almost gentle with distance.

Arek's red arm became a warmth over Paul's shoulders. She said, "I'm afraid."

3 THE GAP IN THE LEAVES WAS BLANK, THE GREEN
flame gone. Edmund Spearman gazed at the spot where
the descending ship had been, unaware of his sons, unaware that his pygmy followers had been scattered by
fear as swallows are scattered by a storm; unaware, Paul
guessed, of the two men who had been friends and now
were strangers—but these he presently saw again. His
gray eyes measured Paul and Wright, the unspeaking
giants, the small shaken figures of Pakriaa and Nisana and
Miniaan, as if they were rocks or tree stumps and his
only problem how to step around them. Addressing Wright
and Arek, whose big arm was still warm around his shoulders, Paul said carefully, "It will come down on the
meadow ground about twenty miles from here. They must
have seen Vestoia from the air; they probably made sure
there was no settlement in the open land."

Wright whispered, "It may not even have been from
Earth."

"Oh!" Mijok's black lips smiled. "It is, Doc. I forget our
eyes are better at distance. You didn't see the letters?
Black on silver, reaching halfway up the body of the ship.
J-E-N-S-E-N."

"So?" In Wright's face was a sudden blaze of belief.

Spearman stared. He said, "Quite an imagination. Glad
it was you who made it up, and not one of the men who
knew the real Jensen—a name that ought not to be taken
in vain."

"I have good eyes," said Mijok gently. "I made up
nothing."

Spearman's eyebrows lifted, a fury of mimic politeness. He stepped around the group as if they were not
rocks but dangerous animals. He passed down the street

in long strides, not looking back even for his sons. Paul stupidly watched him go, saw him reach the turning by the meat-slave stockade and break into a loping run. Stout Muson muttered, "So changed! What sickness could make such a change?"

Wright said, "It is not likely to pass. In the old days of Earth they sometimes ruled nations. Or they were put away in institutions, usually after others had been injured. Or they were fanatics of one sort and another, ridden by the devil of one idea. My profession learned a little about them—never enough. The law met them more often and learned less." He watched Paul, perhaps needing contact with a Charin mind, since the innocence of the others gave them no frame of reference. "I dare say Ed is paranoid only on the one point, technically: all his troubles are caused by me and my—what did he say?—conspiracy. A means to help him believe that only he is right and virtuous and the universe wrong. . . . It is not so much a sickness, Muson, as the sum of years of mental bad habits. Vanity and dislike of one's own kind make most of the seed, and this is the fruit."

Elis said, "We can overtake him. Six of us giants—we can carry you, overtake him in a walk, if you think best."

"Yes." Wright watched the empty street and Spearman's palace that already seemed haunted and forlorn. "I believe there's no need for haste. Twenty miles . . ." The Vestoian pygmies were not returning; the street was a desolation of rubbish and loneliness with the dull smell of neglect. One of Spearman's boys was whimpering; the other watched the place where his father had disappeared, a tension in his small face, without forgiveness. Wright said, "Who's John and who's David?"

The crying one muttered, "I'm John."

David spoke as if the words had been shaken out: "He said she wouldn't ever come back. Where is she?"

"At our island," Paul told him. "She's all right, David, and we're going to take you to her. You want that, don't you?"

"Is *he* going there?"

"We don't know, David. You want to go with us, don't you?"

"He hit her face. When she said it was his fault that

they were all giving up the city. He always had the guards. Six sat around his bed every night. John and me, we tried. We made a grass picture like the priest Kona told us to do, and did things with it and burned it. It was no good."

Arek said, "Let's forget that for now. We're going to the new ship and then the island. Shall I carry you? I've got two boys your age."

"Who're you? I never saw anybody like you."

She dropped on one knee, not too close to him. "I'm like you, David. Just big and furry, that's all."

"Your mother, David"—said Wright, and swallowed— "your mother is living in my house now. She was our friend long before you were born, you know. She came from Earth with us. . . . You're with us, aren't you?"

The boy scuffed his bare feet in the dust. John was still crying. David slapped him savagely. "You stop yakking, y'son of a bitch." The words could have no meaning for him, Paul thought, beyond the generalized stink of profanity. John stopped and rubbed his cheek without apparent anger, gulping and then nodding. When Arek reached, David let her pick him up, and he relaxed and buried his face in her fur. . . .

The giants made little of the miles. Mijok had Pakriaa and Nisana in his arms and Miniaan perched on his shoulder. They had traveled often that way on the troublesome journey to Vestoia. Elis carried Wright's trifling 140 pounds, and Muson had John, her slow voice establishing cautious friendship. Paul preferred to walk on his own feet, but before long Sears-Danik stole up behind and swept him into a living cradle. "Slow legs. Don't mind, do you, Pop?"

"Pop, huh? No, I don't mind, Danny. I was getting fifty-year-old cramps and too dumb to admit it."

Dunin chuckled. "That's Danny: knows all, sees all, says nuf'n'. I'd live with him awhile when he grows up if only he wasn't so lazy."

"What's wrong with being lazy?"

"Not a thing, rockhead. Only if you're going to explore, the way I am, you can't be lazy, the way you are." She twisted a branch into a leaf crown and walked backward before them, trying the crown on the boy's head at different angles. "Ah, wonderful! Charging asonis—whuff

whuff—and now you look just like the kink that chewed up my diary to make a nest."

"Which was your fault for leaving it on a shelf and not writing in it. Explorers have to keep diaries. Doc said so —didn't he, Paul?"

"I'm strictly neutral, to avoid bouncing."

"So anyway, Dunin, when you trip over a root and smack your fanny, I'm going to laugh."

She did. He did. . . .

It was an hour before they overtook Spearman, who glanced back without expression, without halting his powerful strides, his tanned body gleaming with sweat and effort. Dunin sobered; she caught Paul's eyes. She said, "May I carry you, Spearman? Then we can all reach the ship at the same time."

Spearman gave no sign of hearing her. He drew up at the side of the trail, staring at the ground, arms folded. David's face was hidden again at Arek's breast; John seemed to be asleep. Dunin said, "Please? Why should we leave you behind?"

Remote and desolate, Spearman watched the ground. Dunin moved on, reluctantly, no more laughter in her. "What *is* he thinking?"

Wright said, "At this moment he's probably thinking it's brutally unfair that we should go on ahead of him."

"But I asked—"

"You did. What's more he hasn't anything against you. All the same, that's about what he'll be thinking. Don't try too hard to understand it, Dunin—I'm not sure it's worth it. Let's think about the ship. Paul, is it possible, what he said about charlesite?"

"I reckon so, Doc. The flame certainly did change to green. I think I remember, long ago, hearing some engineers discuss the possibility of stepping up charlesite enough so it could be used in braking a big ship for descent, instead of keeping the atomics on all the way down. It would char everything over a wide area, but at least it wouldn't make radioactive desert. . . ."

"I can't feel it," Wright mumbled. "Mirage. . . ."

It was no mirage. The ship *Jensen* stood high above blackened ground half a mile away; even here at the edge of forest there was a lingering smell, anciently familiar. Paul felt himself grinning stupidly. "Plain carbon tet or something like it. Must have shot it out to kill any grass fires. No mirage."

Towering silver-white above a hundred-foot tripod, it flaunted the letters of a great name, and David Spearman rubbed his eyes at it, leaning against Arek's knee, accepting the protective touch of her hand. Arek said, "What— Oh Paul, what will they be like?"

Wright shook his head, plainly feeling it now—the thought, the memories, the pleasure, and something far from pleasure. Paul answered, "They will—look like us, Arek."

Pakriaa pointed up. "There! That we remember. Oh, the beautiful—"

"A boat out already?" Paul searched and found the silver flight.

Wright chattered: "Have we anything, anything white? No—you and I out in the open, Paul—rest of you keep back. They need to recognize what we are—" He was shaking, and Paul embraced his shoulders to steady him as they moved into the open ground. Wright giggled hysterically. "Damn white flag myself—my whiskers—"

The boat swooped, swelling from a dot to keen familiar lines; it circled above them twice and came to earth in a perfect landing a hundred feet away. A blank pallor in the pilot's window would be a human face; there would be a human brain shocked into new wonder. It was still necessary for Paul to help his teacher through the grass, for Wright was swaying and stumbling. Paul reminded him: "They'll be sealed up, afraid of the air."

"Ah, yes. I say they needn't be—we have good air on Lucifer. . . ."

Paul was aware of his own struggle for sanity, for clarity in the beginning of this impossible joy which was not pure joy. He heard himself shout at the top of his strong lungs: " 'Ahoy the *Jensen!*' No, they won't hear it. Yes—they did, they did."

The door slid open for a meeting of two worlds. A square little bald man, a tall gray-haired woman who fussed at her ears, troubled by the change in atmospheric pressure. Faded overalls, the human look, incredulous stares changing to belief. The bald man gulped and stumbled; he grinned and held out his hand. "Dr. Christopher Wright, I presume?"

Wright could neither speak nor let go the hand. The woman said, "You must be—well, who could forget the photographs?—you're Paul Mason."

"Yes, We never—for years we haven't even thought—"

"Mark Slade," said the bald man, "Captain Slade. This is Dr. Nora Stern . . . Sir, I—you are well? You look well—"

"We are well," said Wright.

"I'm afraid to ask—the others? Dr. Oliphant? Captain Jensen? The—the little girls? And there was a young engineer—Edmund Spearman. . . ."

Paul managed to say, "Both little girls are mothers. Dr. Oliphant and Captain Jensen died—Jensen on the ship, in the last acceleration. Spearman is—will be here before long, I think. You may find him somewhat changed—"

Wright said, "We must let Ed speak for himself, Paul."

In spite of the shock, the newness, Dr. Stern was sensitive to nuances. She said too loudly, "Beautiful country." She pressed both hands to her ears and took them away and spoke in a normal voice: "There . . . ! Oh, what strange steep hills . . . !"

"N-not like any rock of Earth," Paul stammered. "Defies erosion." *And I am speaking with the pride of a home lover.* . . . "The open ground is a little dangerous—flying carnivores. Come and meet our friends."

Captain Slade had already seen the giants and pygmies at the edge of the woods; his small monkey face was ablaze with friendly curiosity and the startled amusement that will wake at anything new, but he said, "In just a moment. Let me take this in. If I can. . . . We've done it, Nora." He filled his lungs deeply, blinking at a few tears of pleasure. "A world like ours—a new world. Oh, Nora, it'll be a long time before we can believe this, you and I. . . . High oxygen, we noticed—feels like it. Sir, your ship—"

"Lost," said Wright, tranquilly now, no longer shaking from head to foot. "Out of control in descent, fell in a lake"—he motioned over his shoulder—"a few miles over there. We call it Lake Argo. Too deep even to think of salvage. One of the lifeboats cracked up; we used the other for about a year. Our friends, Captain—you'll like our friends—"

Slade murmured, "Speculation on parallel evolution seems to have been sound—here anyway. Humanoid, I see. Two species?"

"Human," said Wright. "Their English, by the way, is better than mine. They are close to us, Captain—very dear to us."

"I—see," said Captain Slade kindly. Paul thought: *He can't see—it's too new. But maybe he will try to see.*

"How many in your party, Captain?"

Slade grinned. "Only four, Mr. Mason." *Heavens! Mister? That's me.* "A smaller crew, bigger ship. Federation thought best. We left thirteen years after you. Twelve years on the journey. Of course we've had to double in brass considerably. The other two are a young couple— Jimmy Mukerji; he's from Calcutta—Oh, and by the way, Dr. Wright, his mother was Sigrid Hoch, anthropologist, one of your students."

"Sigrid—" Wright groped in the past. "Of course. I remember." But Paul guessed that he did not.

"Jimmy's a botanist *and* engineer *and*—oh, general technician, good anywhere. Sally Marino—another good technician. Frankly I didn't want specialists—wanted kids who could turn a hand to anything, and I got 'em." Slade's friendly face saddened; he and Dr. Stern were walking clumsily to the woods, feeling the change in gravity. "Ours was to be the last interstellar ship, Dr. Wright, until either you or we came home. There'll be no building going on now. A Federation decision—matter of public opinion as well as economics. Well, the old lady over there did cost twice as much as your *Argo,* upped the Federation poll tax three per cent just to pay for her on paper. Could have got around that, maybe, but there was a beginning of public hysteria, protest—resentment at the idea of throwing lives and billions into space with nothing to show for it for many years. Fanatics on both sides, and both noisy, plus the war scare of course. Short-term thinking. Human."

"You can't blame them," said Nora Stern.

"I do blame them, Nora, now that we know it can be done. . . ."

Elis had tried to be ready with a little speech of welcome, but shyness made him stiff with dignity, and it was evident that Dunin would break loose in nervous giggling. Elis said only, "You're very welcome. We hope you'll enjoy it here." Pakriaa might have been back in the days of tribal grandeur, but her control too was only a result of shyness and wonder as she echoed the Governor's words. It was unfairly difficult for the newcomers, Paul could see —the giants' furry nakedness and majesty, the pygmies' tininess and wrinkled baldness; even the Charin-like beauty of Miniaan's features might be invisible to new Charin eyes. But Slade and Dr. Stern behaved well, with a natural friendliness. "Why," said Slade, "these boys—"

"John and David Spearman," Paul explained. "Ann's boys. Spearman—we think he'll be here shortly."

Arek asked evenly, "You've come to stay, I hope?"

"To—stay?" Slade shot a startled glance at Wright, who avoided it, giving him no help.

Paul said quickly, "Captain, we ought to have warned you, but neither Doc nor I could get our wits together until you'd opened the door. About thirteen or fourteen hours from now you'll have a fever and a period of unconsciousness. Not too much discomfort and, so far as we know, no danger—anyhow all of us recovered in fine shape and we've had excellent health ever since. We decided it's just a part of acclimation to—we call this planet Lucifer. But if you think the two others should stay in the ship till you recover—"

Dr. Stern was measuring him shrewdly. "You look very healthy, both of you, and I know we can take your word for anything. Jimmy and Sally are pretty rugged. They'll be wild to join us. Sally will be at the intercom right now, tearing her pretty hair out in handfuls. They might as well chance it with us. . . . Where do you people live? We saw a—settlement? Over there south of the lake."

Wright glanced at Paul with vague entreaty. It was Miniaan who spoke, the small silver of her voice a music

in the sun-streaked shadow: "The settlement below the
lake is a thing of the past, an empire that died. We live
on a warm island over yonder, the other side of those
mountains, the island Adelphi. We are returning there
now, after a—journey with some trouble in it."

"Adelphi," said Dr. Stern, savoring the name. "Mark
—our two boats could fly them all there with us,
couldn't they? Take out the emergency stuff to make
room."

"It would be wise," said Paul. "We could take better care
of you during the illness, at Adelphi. We have houses
there. Here it's not very safe—biting flies and some dangerous animals."

Slade was doubtful. "Anything here that could interfere with the ship if we leave it unguarded?"

Miniaan laughed. "Certainly the people of Vestoia will
not go near it."

"Nothing could harm it," said Wright. "Too big. How in
hell do you get down out of it?"

Slade chuckled and made up his mind. "Electronic lock.
Can work it from a transmitter in the lifeboat; only other
way's from inside. Lets down a ladder. Automatic derricks
in the side blisters to hoist the lifeboats if, as, and when.
They thought of—*nearly* everything." He hugged the gray-
haired woman. "Even briefing on how to get along with
each other for ten-plus years."

"Learning love can be difficult," said Pakriaa. Dr. Stern
stared at the tiny woman with new intentness. Pakriaa's
seamed face had taken on its dreamy look. "You must see
our island. Last year Mashana Dorothy was Governor of
our island. This year it is this man." She touched Elis' knee.

"A sinecure," Elis chuckled. "A sinecure, ladies'n' gentlemen."

Captain Slade laughed, standing five feet five, peering
up at the Governor's eight feet seven—half a head more
than Mijok's height. Paul thought he saw there the raw
materials of friendship. Dr. Stern said, "And you call this
planet Lucifer?"

"Light-bringer," said Nisana; there was grief in her face
not evident in any of the others. "Son of the morning,"
Paul moved toward her, wondering.

Slade had missed the overtone, and cocked a dark eyebrow. "Industries?"

Wright shrugged. "A few, sir. All we seem to need at present in such a small community."

"Oh." Slade touched the old man's jacket. "This is fine fabric. I couldn't tell it from linen. Is it?"

"Very similar." Wright took Nisana's hand on his palm. "This lady is our best weaver because her hands are so small and sure. Our loom is clumsy because, of course, our metalworking is not far advanced. But it does good work for Nisana."

"I like to weave," Nisana whispered, looking here and there and not at Paul. "I like to make new things."

Paul glimpsed the twitch of Mijok's ears, the beckoning curve of a gray finger; Mijok whispered, "He's coming, Paul. A few hundred yards away in the woods, breathing hard and limping. Is there nothing we can do for him?"

"I don't know, Mijok. I'm afraid whatever is done he must do for himself, and it's late for that, very late." He saw that Mijok was trying to understand and could not. "His mind is—living in another country. . . ."

But outwardly at least, Edmund Spearman was changed. He even searched out Dunin's worried face and apologized. "Should have accepted your offer—stupid of me." He smiled. "Wanted to show what a walker I was, I guess." John and David slipped behind Muson's back, tense and cold. Spearman shook Slade's hand, and Dr. Stern's. "My God, it doesn't seem possible. I can't take it in. Slade, you said? And Dr. Stern. We've wondered, dreamed, prayed for it. I can't tell you—I don't know what to say. . . . Good trip?"

"Excellent." Slade hugged himself. "Excellent beyond description. Ah, all the Federation needed was proof. They've got it now! Rather, they will have it in twelve years. Lordy! I'll be fifty-one." He pounded Paul on the back, and Spearman, giving way to a bubbling overflow of good nature. "There'll be a new President, whole new Council I guess—and they won't be looking for us either, man." He danced a few steps and jabbed Paul in the ribs. "Think of it! Why, it's a Tom Sawyer job. You know? You remember? When you and I walk up the middle aisle in the Federation Hall—oh, man, man . . ."

Paul had to find Nisana's face again, and the devastation of sorrow in it, before he understood. He stooped quickly to whisper, "I am not going back to Earth." The radiance in the aging red face was like a Charin girl's.

And he heard Dr. Stern remark dryly, "Mark, I believe we've got some nearer bridges to cross."

4 ONE OF THE SOFT LIZARD-OIL LAMPS GLEAMED IN Kajana's room, though it was late and the house was hushed. Paul had not been able to find sleep; Dorothy would be watching at the bedsides of the four unconscious newcomers from Earth for another hour, until Tejron relieved her. Paul tapped at Kajana's never-closed doorway. "May I come in?"

"Yes, please do." The little man smiled up from his pillows: they were filled with a stuff like dandelion down, almost as good as feathers. "Will you lift me a little?" Paul fussed over him, glad of something to do. "I was not sleepy. I finished transcribing from the shorthand, but my thought remains with it."

"Shorthand—"

"The talk of this afternoon. You didn't know I was recording it. You were all speaking somewhat beyond yourselves, in a way I wanted to preserve. I wish we had better pencils. These last are not bad, blue clay mixed with the graphite, but they still crumble too easily and the wood is big for my hand. I used the brown ink for the transcription." He shuffled the gray marsh-reed pages together. "You might like to look at it."

"Yes. Tonight, I think. Doc did say some things worth remembering."

Kajana smiled. "So did you."

"Did I . . . ? Pencils are one thing they must have had on the ship in abundance. The library too. Poor Doc, he'd have given anything for the books—so would I. . . ."

Kajana patted his hand. "Maybe it doesn't matter too much, Paul? We have our own books to make. . . . Besides—don't you think Spearman may have unloaded some things for us before he took off?"

"Not a chance. His mind wouldn't work that way."

"No? Well, you knew him better. Still, he had time, Paul. He knew we couldn't go after him: you told me he drained the fuel out of one lifeboat before he stole the other. And it was three hours, after you found he was gone, before you saw the big ship go up over the range."

"And down," Paul said, still physically shaken with the memory, the sound, the sight of it. "Down into the sea forever."

"What happened, do you think?"

"We'll never know. It was a new type of ship. His knowledge of such things was ten years old, Lucifer years. Likely the take-off was too complex for one man to handle it. After we saw it climb past the range, we stayed there—Doc and Dorothy and Miniaan and I— near the temple, just stayed there mind-sick and wondering. We saw it reappear—a dot, then a flame. He never quit trying. He had the atomics blazing all the way down. Sometimes they'd lift the ship a little, and we— I suppose we weren't breathing—we'd think yes—no, yes—no. I even thought: is he going to crash it *here?* But he was really many miles to the west, only seemed near, so bright in that darkness. A meteor—yes, call him a meteor—burned out and lost. Up to the very end, until we saw it strike the water near the western horizon, he was still trying, a mad insect heaving against the web of gravity. And we'll never know what he really wanted, either. I have an idea he may not have meant to go back to Earth. I think perhaps he wanted another star—one that never was."

And Paul wondered: *Should I tell Kajana what Doc said when it was all over? No, not now—not till I understand it myself.* ("I consider myself to blame." "What do you mean?" "Remember when Arek noticed he was gone? I saw him slip away ten minutes before she spoke. He looked at me, too. I think I may have known what he meant to do: I said nothing. Earth is a very distant place, Paul. The Federation is building no more interstellar ships, for a while—for a while." "But you—" "I may therefore be to blame. I look within and am confused, as so often. But all the same, here in our world I have helped to establish a few practical certainties." During that murmured interchange by the temple, Dorothy had been quite silent, as if she needed no question and answer, and Miniaan had ended it, saying, "Let's go back, and tell the others that something has ended.")

Kajana's old mind was roving after other matters, to him more important than Spearman or the beautiful lost ship from Earth. "Teddy," he said, "do you know, Paul, when the two silver boats came slipping down out of the sky Teddy only glanced at them once, and came running to carry me outdoors so that I could see them too. It was her first thought. Her father and mother in her, and what a new self too . . . !" Kajana was having pain, from the old hip-joint injury that would never heal. "That transcription, Paul—it's quite verbatim, even to a little hemming and hawing."

"Good." Paul studied the wizened red face, regretful that his painter's power could never record what was really Kajana—too much that must escape, even if the portrait were faithful to the small patient hands, the groove in the left fingers caused by years of effort with makeshift writing materials. Sears—and Paul could think it now without too much distress—Sears could have understood Kajana better. "Can I get you anything?"

"No, thank you, Paul. I'm very well tonight." But some other thought stirred in him, and Paul lingered, knowing what it was: a need for a particular reassurance, Kajana's only outward concession to his frailty. "Paul, what do you really think? When the time comes, will it be something like a sleep?"

"I believe so, Kajana. But not soon. We need you."

The mild face showed gratitude, then calm; it glanced beyond him. "Why, Abara—you should be snoring."

Abara followed his comfortable potbelly into the room; his fluty voice was indignant: "I never snore." He sank cross-legged by the bed, rocking lightly with a foot in each hand.

"I've heard you, old man."

"Lizard-fur!" said Abara. "Hear yourself snoring, of course."

Paul stretched. "You gentlemen settle down to a good soothing quarrel. I'll take off." Abara's left eyelid lowered and lifted gravely. "Good night."

"Good night," said the little voices. Leaving the room, Paul heard Abara murmur, "Do you remember . . ."

Paul carried a taper from the permanent fire in the common room to relight the lamp in his and Dorothy's bedroom. It was late indeed, near to the time of the rising of the red moon, seen only the night before from the jungle west of Vestoia—what had been Vestoia. Here in the long room there was still a friendly disorder from the impromptu banquet of the evening. Because of the disturbance when Spearman's flight was discovered and preoccupation with the illness of the newcomers, the common room had received only a few housekeeping flurries. Mats were still scattered in the center of the floor; earthen wine cups stood about. Carrying the taper, Paul saw by his foot a graded series of round faces drawn on the earth with a twig. Helen was apt to do that when most of her mind was elsewhere: the faces were made of neat circles, even nose and mouth. Subject to a pinch on the bottom from her halfsister, Helen called them teddies. Paul smiled sleepily and stepped around.

Kajana took pride in the sharp printlike quality of his writing; under lamplight, the brown ink shifted into gold. Kajana had not recorded the casual beginning of the banquet: the idea had evidently come to him after some remark of Kamon's. Paul could not remember it clearly, but the old giantess had been roused to it by a thing the rather sad-faced, brown-haired girl Sally Marino had mentioned: the prospect of war on the planet Earth. Kajana had taken down what followed as direct dialogue; riffling through the gray pages, Paul noticed that Kajana had inserted no comment of his own at all. The phonetic shorthand, Paul knew, was Kajana's invention—ideal for his own use, but he had not been able to teach it even to Nisana. Too intricate, she said, needing the hyperacute ear which was a gift Kajana could not share.

SLADE: There seems never to be a single cause of war, only a group of causes coming to a particular focus in time. Our world, madam—

WRIGHT: Just Kamon. Somehow we've never formed the habit of courtesy titles, Captain. Names, nicknames, and a few titles of function—as for instance, if Elis were conducting one of our meetings, we'd address him as Governor.

SLADE: Oh. Pleasant, I should think. Our world, Kamon, is still divided in two parts. An ideological division. There is the Asian Empire of Jenga. Let me show you—the map—

DUNIN: Here. I grabbed it. And what a map! If only we could make such things!

DOROTHY: In time, sugar. Takes mighty complex machinery to make such a map.

SLADE: One of the things that must come on the next trip from Earth. Well—here is the Asian Empire. You can see the vastness of it, one land mass, almost all of a continent—

MUKERJI: Except my country.

NORA STERN: Well, naturally, Jimmy—

MUKERJI: I tend to be sensitive on the point, since we joined the Federation somewhat belatedly.

SLADE: That's the Asian Empire. And there they believe, and have long believed, that individual man is nothing—an ant in a colony—the state is everything, a sole reason for existence. The state—

WRIGHT: Which exists only in the minds of individual men.

SLADE: Ye-es. . . . For them the state takes the place of God, of reason, of ethics, of—Oh, it's be-all and end-all, so far as an individualist like myself can understand their doctrine. A hundred years ago this empire was two great states; they had the same doctrine then but called it by a less honest name, communism, derived from certain naïve social theories of about a hundred years earlier—

SPEARMAN: Naïve?

SLADE: Before I went in for engineering, sir, I majored in history at McGill. With the help of a great deal of coffee, I even read *Das Kapital*. It is not logical even from its own dogmatic premises. Incidentally I think it can still be found in secondhand bookstores.

SPEARMAN: As a matter of fact, when I left Earth, it was quite readily available in up-to-date editions from the Collectivist Press.

SLADE: Oh. Yes, I dare say it was. . . . Well, Kamon,

about a hundred years ago those two Asian states, still
paying lip service to the—debatable doctrine of communism (satisfactory, Mr. Spearman?)—attacked each
other in a long war, making use of recently discovered
atomic weapons as well as man-made pestilence and other
devices. It was not actually a doctrinal war, but simply
a power struggle between two tyrannies. It was hideous,
incredibly destructive, and the only saving thing about it
was that it prevented them from visiting the same disaster
on the rest of the world. Neither side won, of course; a
few decades later a new dictator—a little one-eyed zea-
lot from Mongolia—inherited the desolation and built on
the ruins a new monolithic state, which still exists.

AREK: But what actually was this theory—this communism?

SLADE: Oh, the theory. Originally an appeal to the
dispossessed. In the nineteenth century and earlier there
were masses of poor, widespread suffering and injustice,
too much economic and political power in the hands of a
few, who abused their power with stupidity and cruelty.
Marx and other theorists imagined, or said they imagined,
that the situation could be remedied by reversal—give
power to the dispossessed (the proletariat, as they called
them) and injustice would right itself. Why they imagined
that the proletariat was any more fitted to rule than its
oppressors—why they supposed it would not abuse
power quite as viciously—they never bothered to explain.
Naturally the realists among them weren't concerned
with any utopian outcome: they simply saw the doctrine
as a means to personal power for themselves and used it
accordingly. The first important one of these was a
furious little man named Lenin. He may have believed
his own theories for a while—there seems to have been
some short-lived experimentation with the contradictions
of actual communism when he first won power in Russia
—but absolute power corrupts absolutely, as somebody
said. The foundations of an old-new despotism were well
established before he died—and was unofficially deified
and kept in a glass case for the consolation of the
atheist faithful. Matter of fact, Arek, a good many things
in Earth history would make a cat laugh. . . . The actual
cure for the ugly situation that existed turned out to be

a gradual economic leveling combined with the (very slow and difficult) growth of representative government —so that there would be no swollen fortunes, no severe poverty, and no heavy concentrations of unchecked political power. But that was most undramatic procedure: it needed the work of centuries. No bloody revolution could ever achieve such an end, nor could any other evil means ever bring it any nearer. In the Federation we begin to have—an approximation of it. The Asian Empire is merely despotism, old and stale, old as the Pharaohs, committed to the policy of violence and carrying the burden of slavery under modern names: the natural product of fanatic doctrine after the power-hungry have taken it over and made use of it.

SPEARMAN: Jenga's empire is not collectivism. It is a perversion of it.

ANN: If you'll excuse me—

DOROTHY: Honey, of course! I think you got up too soon. The boys are in bed. Come on—let me tuck you in and fuss at you. . . .

STERN: She's been ill?

WRIGHT: Yes. For a long time. But now I think she—

SPEARMAN: What—

AREK: Captain, tell us about the other part of Earth, the part you come from.

SLADE: Canada? Oh, you mean the Federation itself. It's very great, miss—I mean, Arek. Let's have the map again, my dear. All of North America—here—parts of South America, the United States of Europe, Union of Islam, Japan, India, parts of Africa outside of Islam—then over here there's Australia and New Zealand, and here's the Republic of Oceania. Almost all the rest of the world, you see. Here's Federal City. Find it? Follow my finger east of Winnipeg—lake country, and very lovely: I was born near there. The city was planned and built new in 1985; seems long ago, isn't really. And then, Arek, there are some small countries which have preferred to keep their national unity outside of the Federation instead of inside it, although they're affiliated with us and there aren't any barriers to travel and other intercourse. A somewhat technical distinction, since local sovereignties are well enough preserved within the Federation.

WRIGHT: Not entirely a technicality. At the time we left Earth, there were some tendencies in the Federation that could lead to overcentralization, even with the recognition of limited powers. And too much emphasis on the admitted glories of machine civilization. I think it's an excellent thing that some parts of the world should be a little insulated from the enthusiasms of material progress. The Federation itself will be the better for it.

SLADE: Perhaps. I think I know what you mean, Doctor. I was always a small-government man, myself. Still, under the threat of Jenga—

STERN: I can't see it as much of a threat.

SALLY MARINO: I don't know. . . .

STERN: The empire will break down sooner or later, of its own rigidity.

SLADE: But while we wait for that, the Federation has to be strong, in the military as well as other senses.

MUKERJI: If we do just wait for it.

STERN: Preventive war is an absurdity, Jimmy.

MUKERJI: Yes, but—

STERN: Gradualist methods. The Federation can afford to wait. The same gradualist methods that made the Union of Islam possible, so long ago.

PAUL: I don't think the leadership of Turkey was gradualist exactly, Dr. Stern. It took thirty years after 1960, but considering the problem, that was great speed. Only a people with immense moral courage and good sense would have dared to undertake it at all. They weren't fanatics; they weren't ridden by the devil of one idea; they had to work with intelligent compromise, temperate adjustments, yielding here and sternness there and patience all the time—but once they took up the task they didn't rest or let go, and by 1990 there was a healthy union ready for full membership in the Federation.

SLADE: Yes, that was speed. I expect you've given your friends here a pretty good account of Earth history?

PAUL: We've tried. I don't know if we can allow ourselves more than a B-plus. The subject is too enormous, and all we had were imperfect memories. In the midst of our own work for Lucifer, which is—paramount.

WRIGHT: Not even books. Captain, when you showed us over the ship, it was very difficult for my fingers not to steal a lens and a pocketful of those microtexts. . . .

SLADE: My dear friend! Why didn't you say so? All you want. That's for your friends here, entirely. No need to take any of our library back to Earth if they can use it.

WRIGHT: I—excuse me—I don't know what to say.

SLADE: And by the way, Doctor, before I forget again to mention it: after you left—I think it was in 2060 —they perfected a new drug which actually makes the accelerations quite bearable. I don't know too much about it. Muscular relaxation is a factor, and Nora can tell you more about it. But I understand that even for persons past the—optimum age—

WRIGHT: A moment, please. . . . I cannot go back to Earth, Captain Slade. You mean it with the greatest kindness but it is impossible.

SLADE: Why, forgive me, I supposed—I took it for granted—

WRIGHT: My place is here. This is my work. These are my people.

TEJRON: I knew—I knew—

WRIGHT: What, my dear? I don't understand.

TEJRON: Oh, I should keep silent: this is for you to decide. But you've said it. You won't leave us.

WRIGHT: No. No, I won't ever leave you. This is my home.

SLADE: But—

SPEARMAN: Can't argue with the passion of an expatriate. The grass is always greener—

PAUL: It could be no other way, Captain, at least for Dr. Wright and me, and I'm certain my wife will say the same when she comes back.

WRIGHT: In some ways, Captain, the distance between Earth and Lucifer is greater than the simple light years between our two stars.

SLADE: I'm—sorry. Wasn't expecting it, that's all. Let me get used to the idea a little.

SPEARMAN: You can consider me neutral, Captain Slade. I have no place on Lucifer. One more utopia. Idealism running contrary to obvious facts. It will break up—fine-spun intellectual quarrels—no central control.

PAUL: Until, sometime, a strong man takes over and makes an empire out of it . . . ?

WRIGHT: Please—

SPEARMAN: No comment. . . .

STERN: If I might differ with you, Mr. Spearman, it seems to me—after being shown over this lovely island —the domesticated cattle and those wonderful white beasts—the plantations and the houses—the perfect English and adult thinking of our new friends—above all, the school—it seems to me that Dr. Wright and his colleagues are realists of the first water. Of course I'm strongly prejudiced in their favor, because—well, during the twelve years of our journey I dreamed constantly of some such achievement as this myself. So it's like coming home. I'm a doctor, Mr. Spearman; before I was chosen for the journey, I ran a clinic. As an intern, I had a lot of ambulance and emergency service at one of the big hospitals in Melbourne; I saw a superabundance of— let's call them obvious facts. Now I think the sunny quiet here, the good health and intelligence of the children, the gardens, the devotion of these people to each other and to their work, the searching thought they've given to their laws and their future—I fancy those are obvious facts too . . . ?

WRIGHT: Man is neither good nor bad, but both. But he can swing the balance.

STERN: Too right. I think I understand you, Doctor — why you want to stay here. I think I understand it very well.

SLADE: I wouldn't urge you. It's only that I—took something else for granted. Foolishly. Let me be just a listener.

ELIS: And let me fill your cup. You're behind us, Captain.

MINIAAN: The big jug is empty. How'd'at happen?

MUSON: Portrait of a fat woman going away with another big jug.

PAUL: Bless you, lady.

MUSON: It was you that finished emptying it. I think.

NISANA: Couldn't have been me. . . .

STERN: Are there any important physiological differences?

WRIGHT: Nothing of first importance. Minor differences in blood chemistry, shape of hands and feet. Our friends have the hind brain in the spinal column, which may be

the reason for their better muscular co-ordination and
—you know, Doctor, I have often wished that the human
race of Earth, which we call Charin, had more room in its
head for the expansion of the frontal lobes.

ELIS: I have a very high opinion of your frontal lobes,
Christopher Wright. I have noticed that sometimes a large
skull merely rattles.

STERN: Just the same the point is well taken.

PAUL: Might call it the miracle of the lobes and wishes.

PAKRIAA: Why don't you wait till Muson comes
back . . . ?

SALLY MARINO: Don't you—now, maybe this is a
foolish question—don't you have to work awfully hard—
I mean, with so few technical aids? The—oh, oil lamps,
the necessarily primitive—of course, you've done miracles to have as much as you do have, starting from almost nothing. What I'm trying to say, doesn't mere survival take up so much time and effort that it—well, wears
you down?

PAUL: We have shelter, clothing, enough to eat—

MINIAAN: And drink.

PAUL: What we call a family, Sally, is made up of
members of all three races. Such a unit may have seven or
eight adults or more. Shelter, food—the basic needs are
supplied by each family working for itself; the large family unit distributes the labor pretty well; and, if any
family was stricken with misfortune (none has been so
far) the others would all help as a matter of course. Now,
we do have the germs of beginning industries in textiles,
sugar—

MINIAAN: Wine making.

ABARA: The lady is pied.

MINIAAN: The lady is not pied. Only very happy, and
Vestoia is a dead city, and the little illuama will be mak-
ing their nests where—Oh, Abara, you venerable ruin,
I love you, I love you. . . .

ABARA: Well, not right here in front of all these nice
people. . . .

MUKERJI: Beautiful way of life. Oh, here's Muson.
Have we drunk to everybody? Seems as though we must
have overlooked somebody, earlier.

NISANA: I don't think so. Yes, we have. Let's drink to the olifants.

WRIGHT: And their seven calves. . . .

PAUL: In textiles, for instance—Nisana does no housework because her worktime is at the loom; each household sends somebody over to work in the fiber and sugar plantations across the lake. The system works, Sally, in this very tiny community where everyone knows and respects everyone else, where all the laws and customs encourage the ironing out of differences before they become serious. And so far, work has never become oppressive. Most of it we enjoy; the boring, unpleasing jobs are shared because we know they have to be done and we don't want anyone to have to carry too much of their weight. And so far, we don't hunger for the complex and fascinating possessions we knew on Earth. Such hungers will come. Communities will grow. The best laws will fail sometimes; there will be disputes, mistakes, injustices. But we are forewarned by memories of Earth. Doc, I'm trying to say things you could say better—

WRIGHT: No. Go on.

PAUL: Well . . . We plan, tentatively, a hundred family units here at Jensen City, a population of maybe a thousand adults, no larger. When that point is reached (several years away) then we must plan and build another town, probably here on the island. At that point we add new problems and perplexities. We may not need a monetary system until there are several towns; when we do, it will not develop haphazardly, but with the aid of all past knowledge we possess, for safeguard and guidance.

SLADE: And when there are fifteen or twenty such communities?

PAUL: They will want an over-all government; a miniature of a federal system, we suppose. A republic, with fully functional representative procedures, checked and safeguarded against every abuse of power. Because in all our study and memories of history, we've found no other type of government that can operate with fairness to majorities and minorities alike and leave men as free as any social animal can ever be free. For that matter, Captain, we sometimes glance ahead to a time when there will be hundreds or thousands of towns: a time when our great-grandchildren of all three races may want to experiment with large cities, elaborate industries. Such things will bring their own heavy difficulties, but we have reason to hope that our great-grandchildren will have the patience and courage to solve them as they arise. Brodaa, tell them about the school.

BRODAA: I am not good in exposition, Paul. . . . We are—strict, Captain, that the children should learn all the tested factual knowledge we can give them. They must read, speak, write—clearly, precisely, honestly. We do not allow them to leave a method half learned, a task half done. If there is a question, they must search for an answer; if there is no sufficient answer known, they must learn to test the insufficient answers and wait judgment. My own language has flaws—I am an old woman—I still go to school, to Paul, Mashana Dorothy, Dr. Wright, to learn more for my own sake and for the little ones I teach. They must learn the fundamental methods and facts as soon as they can start to think at all. We are never afraid of teaching any child too much or too soon —we respect them. Oh, Mashana, I was wishing you would return.

DOROTHY: Need has arisen for the Dope? What goes on more or less?

ELIS: Education.

PAUL: How is—

SPEARMAN: How is she?

DOROTHY: She is asleep, Ed. Nothing to worry about.

PAKRIAA: She will be healed.

MIJOK: Education on Lucifer. Pakriaa and I have the pleasantest part of the teaching, I think. We show them the ways of the forest and the open ground, the plants and other living things, how to hunt without cruelty or waste, how to be safe and happy alone in the woods at night, when to fear and not to fear. As Samis shows them the care of the tame beasts, and the work in the plantations. . . .

WRIGHT: I'll add a little too, though Brodaa could do it better—

MUKERJI: Come here, kink.

DOROTHY: Why, he loves you! That one won't usually

go to anybody but Muson. His wife is due to have kittens and he's blue about it.

MUKERJI: Kittens—kinkens—

DOROTHY: Just kittens. Seven at one whack. Oof—shet ma mouf.

HELEN: Mother, if you looked at seven kittens now they'd be fourteen.

DOROTHY: Such comment, from a lady allowed to sit up late. Such, I might add, perfectly accurate comment. Sleepy, baby?

HELEN: Not a bit.

DOROTHY: You are too. You snuggle like a kitten half full of milk. Half an hour, huh?

HELEN: Mm.

WRIGHT: We see to it, Captain, that our children are not stuffed with inflated words, equivocal words. When you talk with them, they won't be chattering to you about freedom, democracy, truth, justice. They learn these words closely; we see to it that they learn them with caution. When they use them we say—define, define. Democracy by what means, within what limits, toward what end? Freedom from what, for what? For what's the profit if I rattle on about freedom in a semantic vacuum? I am free to speak, not free to kill and wound; I must be free from slavery to the whims of others. I can never be free from the bonds of a hundred duties, responsibilities, loyalties to persons I love and principles I cherish. Words without definition are sheer noise, and noise never drummed any race into Paradise. Oh, the thing's obvious as a child's building blocks—but I recall how on Earth men tended to forget it twenty-four hours a day, and here on Lucifer we forget it often enough—myself included. But we do not forget it when we teach our children. . . . One other thing—before this wine takes me back to second childhood—as soon, Captain, as their minds are old enough—

AREK: Where did Spearman go?

WRIGHT: Oh, he—he just stepped out, I think. Stretch his legs or something. As soon as their minds are old enough to think with some independence and explore, we insist that they start the lifetime struggle with man's primary dilemma—

ELIS: I hoped you would speak of that, my brother.

WRIGHT: That he is an individual, his selfhood precious and inviolate, yet he must live in harmony with other individuals whose right to life and welfare is as certain as his own. Approach the study of society from any direction you will, that problem is at the heart of it, and must be a thousand generations from now, because it must be met anew with every infant born. We think, here, that the most rewarding answer is in the old virtues of self-knowledge, charity, honesty, forbearance, patience. Now, those are all words that demand definition and multiple definition; on that basis we have our children study them, search the depth and height of them, in the not so simple problems of childhood through the tougher ones of adolescence and maturity. We make them understand that lip service will not do: if one is to make himself honest he must eat honesty with breakfast, sweat with it in the sun, laugh and play and suffer with it and lie down with it at night until it's near as the oxygen in his blood. Yes, we aim high. Cruelly high, would you say? We don't think so. Perfection is a cold spot on top of a mountain, and nobody ever climbed there. We have trouble and fun and arguments; sometimes the garden weeds grow until tomorrow or the day after, but we sleep well.

DOROTHY: Speaking of perfection and goodness and things and stuff—I know it was Paul who put those violin strings by Nan's bed, but which one of you supplied them?

SLADE: Well, he told me—

DOROTHY: Will it be all right if I reach over this daughter of mine and kiss you?

SLADE: They did brief us, back on Earth, that we must respect local customs—

MIJOK: And perhaps even another drink could do him no harm.

PAKRIAA: He's pied.

ELIS: I would not say that. Speaking as Governor, I say that the local wine industry deserves every encouragement it can get—and has, ever since Samis' favorite kink had kittens in the bottom of the vest bat.

SAMIS: Correction.

MIJOK: Best vat. Speaking as Lieutenant Governor. Just elected—did it myself.

MUSON: The toastmistress has been quiet lately.

NISANA: Who, me?

PAUL: By acclamation, yes.

NISANA: Le'me think. We did drink to the children—those in bed and those who ought to be—

HELEN: 'Ception.

DOROTHY: Great big woman. You weigh a ton, sweet stuff, 'n' so do your eyelids, they do.

NISANA: And we drank to the olifants. No no—I am too happy—my mind is a lake without a breeze. You propose the toast, Pakriaa.

SALLY: Matter of fact I'm already sort of whooliol-licky—I think—

DOROTHY: Hey—maybe it's not just the wine. Paul—Doc—it must be almost thirteen hours—

PAUL: Yes—yes, almost. Maybe you'd better—

SALLY: No, let's have one more toast. At least one more, Pakriaa?

WRIGHT: I'll drink with you, Pakriaa.

PAKRIAA: Oh—let us be happy. Friends, I give you the wine itself and the earth that made it. I give you birth and death and the journey of our days and nights between them, the shining of green fields, the patience of the forest, the little stars, the great stars, the love and the thought, the labor and the laughter, the good morning sky.

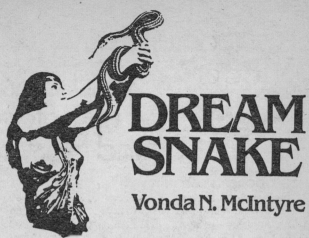

DREAM SNAKE

Vonda N. McIntyre

"Rich in character, background and incident—
unusually absorbing and moving."

Publishers Weekly

"This is an exciting future-dream with real
characters, a believable mythos and, what's
more important, an excellent readable story."

Frank Herbert

The *"haunting, rich and tender novel"** of a
unique healer and her strange ordeal.

** Robert Silverberg*

A Dell Book $2.25   (11729-1)

World Class SF & Fantasy by the Masters

THEODORE STURGEON
- [ ] The Dreaming Jewels $1.75 (11803-4)
- [ ] Visions and Venturers $1.75 (12648-7)
- [ ] The Stars Are the Styx $2.25 (18006-6)

PHILIP K. DICK
- [ ] The Zap Gun $1.75 (19907-7)
- [ ] Time Out of Joint $2.25 (18860-1)

**L. SPRAGUE DE CAMP &
FLETCHER PRATT**
- [ ] Land of Unreason $1.75 (14736-0)

JACK WILLIAMSON
- [ ] Darker Than You Think $1.75 (11746-1)

EDGAR PANGBORN
- [ ] Still I Persist in Wondering $1.75 (18277-8)

L. RON HUBBARD
- [ ] Slaves of Sleep $1.75 (17646-8)